# The Wizard of TV

### ★★★

Merlin made a slight gesture with his hands and Martens's ears began to grow. For a few more moments, the audience didn't notice, and Martens himself apparently felt nothing. He was in full rave, pointing at Merlin and calling him a fraud and demanding that he confess his real name, suggesting that if he refused, it was probably because he had a police record. Meanwhile, his ears continued to grow steadily.

The studio audience noticed, and there were gasps of astonishment. Martens's ears were becoming long, more pointed, reaching above his head, sprouting fur. Still holding the microphone, Martens raised his hands to his ears.

*"My ears! What the hell's happening?"*

And then Martens's nose began to grow. His teeth looked larger now and his hands, still clapped to the sides of his head, were growing dark and misshapen.

*"Help me! Helllp mee-hawww, hee-hawww! Hee-haw!"*

"Stay on him!" The director shouted into his headset. Camera Three, give me a wide shot!"

"Silence!" Merlin said. Turning directly to the camera, he continued, "Let what happened here stand as proof of my assertions. I *am* Merlin Ambrosius.

*"And I have come to bring back magic to the world..."*

Then all hell brok

D0188347

## ALSO BY SIMON HAWKE

The Wizard of 4th Street
The Wizard of Whitechapel
The Wizard of Sunset Strip
The Wizard of Rue Morgue
Samurai Wizard
The Reluctant Sorcerer
The Nine Lives of Catseye Gomez

# THE WIZARD OF CAMELOT

# SIMON HAWKE

WARNER BOOKS

A Time Warner Company

WARNER BOOKS EDITION

Copyright © 1993 by Simon Hawke
All rights reserved.

Questar® is a registered trademark of Warner Books, Inc.

Cover design by Don Puckey
Cover illustration by David Mattingly
Hand lettering by Ron Zinn

Warner Books, Inc.
1271 Avenue of the Americas
New York, NY 10020

W A Time Warner Company

Printed in the United States of America

First Printing: July, 1993

10 9 8 7 6 5 4 3 2 1

*For Natasha*

# ABOUT THE AUTHOR

Thomas Malory was born and educated in London, served as a decorated career soldier in the army, participating in most of the Internal Pacification Campaigns during the Collapse, and retired with the rank of sergeant-major. Upon retirement, he joined New Scotland Yard's elite London Urban Assault Division, since disbanded. He left the police force to work with Merlin Ambrosius in founding the International Center for Thaumaturgical Studies, which eventually grew into the International Thaumaturgical Commission, and he still holds an honorary seat on its board.

Though he never became an adept himself, he is widely regarded as the co-founder of the Second Thaumaturgic Age, and played a key role in developing the administrative programs of the I.T.C., chairing its first regulatory committee and presiding over its first adept certification programs. Best known as Merlin's closest friend and trusted advisor, Malory is regarded as the leading authority on Professor Ambrosius, and is currently engaged in writing the definitive work on his life, *Merlin, The Man Behind The Myth*. He lives with his wife, Jenny, and his thaumagene familiar, Victor, in Geneva, Switzerland.

# CHAPTER
# 1

My name is Thomas Malory, and I was there when magic came back into the world. I was there right from the very start, when the Second Thaumaturgic Age began. It began with one, single, desperate act born of fury and frustration. It began with one blow of an axe. And that axe was mine.

For most of my adult life up to that time, I had served in the armed forces of His Majesty, and I had retired with the rank of sergeant-major in the infantry. I had lived the simple life of a soldier. It was often a hard life, but these days I find myself wishing I could return, if not to the type of life I led then, at least to the obscurity that I enjoyed. I've gained the status of celebrity in my advanced years, however reluctantly, and fame is truly something I could easily have done without.

There was once another Malory, Sir Thomas Malory, who wrote *Le Morte d'Arthur*. However, he was no relation and, in those days, I was unaware of the fateful irony involved in my bearing the same name as his. I was unaware of a great many things back in those days, those dark, terrible days. I was unaware of the influence fate wields in people's lives. I never really thought about such things back then. There were more immediate, far more pressing matters to occupy all my attention, matters pertaining to survival.

In the army, I had served with the L.U.A.D., which stood for London Urban Assault Division. It was a rather dramatic name, but quite appropriate, all things considered. I saw a great deal of action in my time with the Loo, as we called it, during the International Pacification Campaigns. The word "loo" is British slang for toilet or, as the Americans might say, the "crapper." And that, too, was appropriate, in its own way.

I'd put in over twenty years with the service and I was approaching my fortieth birthday. I had a wife, Jenny, and two small children; Christine, aged eleven, and Michelle, aged nine, and I wanted nothing quite so much as to find a safe and reasonably peaceful haven for them. In those dark days of the Collapse, "reasonably peaceful" was about as much as anyone could hope for. And, for many people, it was a hope never to be realized.

London was a war zone that erupted into full-scale mass street riots on the average of several times a year. The army was frequently called in to quell them. These domestic police actions, taking place in various large British cities, became known as the Internal Pacification Campaigns. They occurred with such frequency that the major ones were simply referred to by number, in a rather Yank-like military shorthand, such as In-Pac 9, which erupted in London, In-Pac 10, which broke out in Coventry, and so forth. The minor campaigns occurred so often that no one even bothered counting them.

I had seen a good number of my mates go down in those campaigns and I'd had about enough.

I wanted out.

I moved my family to Loughborough, in the Midlands, approximately one hundred miles north of London, near Nottingham. It was not exactly a small town, but it was a fair distance from London, which was the point of the whole thing. The level of crime and violence in London had become intolerable and I feared for my family's safety.

I purchased a house, a small cottage, really, on the outskirts of the town, but nevertheless, it came quite dearly and wiped out all my savings. There was, of course, no possibility of financing the purchase with a mortgage. No one was taking any flyers on such things back then. Businesses were failing left and right, banks and underwriting firms among them, and credit was a non-existent thing. One paid with cash or one simply didn't buy at all, and with the economy collapsing, prices fluctuated wildly, not only from day to day, but from hour to hour.

Things grew worse with each passing week, nor was the madness confined to British soil. The Collapse was a world-wide phenomenon, as everyone knows now, though few people living today have any firsthand knowledge of what it was really like. That period has since been greatly romanticized in films, novels, and on television, but it's one thing to see the Collapse fancifully depicted in a film or television series and quite another to have actually lived through it. Modern generations seem to have a great feeling of nostalgia for the past, somehow perceiving that period as a time of great adventure and derring-do, but at the risk of sounding like an old cur-mudgeon, I must say frankly that young people today have absolutely no idea what those days were really like. They simply haven't got a clue.

The Collapse was a bloody nightmare. The most densely populated urban areas were hit the hardest, and those were the places where the violence was the most pronounced. I had wanted to remove my family from the environs of the city at all costs, and so I bought the house in Loughborough, spending all the money I had carefully saved over the years. In retrospect, I still don't think it was a bad decision, considering the circumstances. Cash was at a premium and everyone was liquidating everything they owned in the way of long-term investments, fighting for the short-term gain.

The Collapse had changed people's ways of thinking. Money was steadily losing value, and so such things as homes, savings, and investments were losing their value, as well. Sellers were anxious to get as much as they possibly could, but with no one offering any financing, cash had to be the bottom line, and so prices fell dramatically. Unfortunately, the value of what I'd saved had fallen dramatically, as well. With financial institutions failing left and right, I was lucky to have pulled out my money when I had and to have spent it while it was still worth something. At least we had a home. We had precious little else.

The problem, once I had my family settled in our new home, was how to afford its upkeep. On the plus side of the ledger, we owned it, free and clear, and we didn't have to worry about such things as taxes and insurance. No one was writing any policies, because the insurance industry had collapsed, and no one was paying any taxes, because the beleaguered government had lost practically all ability to enforce collection, save for such built-in revenues as sales taxes, which had risen alarmingly as a consequence. In short, the government was quickly going broke. In the meantime, what budget there was went to support essential services such as hospitals and fire departments, the military and the police, and so forth. Since the most densely populated urban centers were the greatest drain on these limited resources, the outlying areas had to go begging and were largely left to fend for themselves.

This meant that if our house burned down, or was vandalized or burgled, neither it nor our few possessions could be replaced. Food was becoming more and more expensive, and with constant power outages, rapidly diminishing supplies of heating oil, and the scarcity of gas, we were forced to rely on wood or coal for fuel. The price of coal had skyrocketed, and the price of cordwood was rising rapidly, as well. The petroleum reserves had been almost entirely depleted, and what petrol was available was rationed among essential government, medical, police, and military personnel.

It seemed pointless to bemoan the policies that had brought

about such a disastrous state of affairs, because environmentalists and scientists had been predicting it for years and we had no one but ourselves to blame. Toward the end, people had started to wake up at last, and serious attempts were made to practice conservation and responsible resource management, but it was simply too little, too late. The time had come to pay the piper. Everything was going to hell in a handbasket in a hurry.

I had managed to remove my family from London, but to support them, I had to return to the city myself. There were damn few jobs around for anyone, and what work was available paid very little and was often done for barter. Thanks to my military background, I was fortunate to find employment with the Metropolitan Police Department or, as it was and is more commonly known, New Scotland Yard. They were woefully understaffed considering the job they had to do, and the pay wasn't much, but it was still a great deal more than what most other people had.

Given the distance between Loughborough and London, as well as the price and rationing of what little petrol reserves were left, there was no possibility of commuting every day. While the rail lines still ran somewhat sporadically, half the time the trains were stalled, or else the tracks were torn up by angry citizens, wanting to strike back at the government in any way they could, all of which meant I couldn't spend much time with Jenny and the girls. During the week, I lived in London, in a grimy, bug-infested, little flat, the cheapest I could find, and weekends, as often as I could, I went to see my family. The strain of separation was severe on all of us, but there was simply nothing else to do. Somehow, I told them, I would eventually find a way to work it out. Surely, things couldn't keep on growing worse. Yet, day by day, they did.

Most people never realize how fragile a thing a city truly was in those days, how little it took to disrupt its equilibrium. A sanitation strike would have the refuse piling up in mountains within only a few days, bringing out the rats and giving them a place to breed, and creating an eye-watering miasma of decay that hung over the city like a poison cloud. A power blackout would bring a city to a standstill, turning people into feral, looting beasts that preyed on one another in the darkness. A labor action disrupting the delivery of food and supplies would cause shortages and price gouging, and an oil crisis, whether genuine or artificially induced by profiteers, would result in a shortage of petrol at the pumps, traffic tied up by cars waiting in long lines, and tempers flaring dangerously. All these things and more had happened in the past, and yet each time such an event occurred, people had simply settled back into their usual routines as soon as it had passed and continued to take everything for granted, as before. And that was how we got into the mess now known as the Collapse.

It wasn't something that happened overnight, of course. Like a snowball rolling down a mountain slope, it had started slowly, growing and gathering momentum as it went, until it turned into an avalanche that swept over everything in its path. The warning signs had been present for years, only they had been largely ignored. Even when things began to fall apart, people chose not to believe it. One is tempted to lay the blame on governments and multinational corporations, but the fact is that the people, all the people, ultimately shared responsibility, because we should have been the ones to stop it.

There were those who saw it coming, to be sure, who had seen it coming for decades, and their numbers had grown considerably in the years immediately prior to the Collapse, but unfortunately, they were still not numerous enough to make a difference. They had tried to do something and had failed, and their failure had led to anger and frustration, which in turn had led to desperation, which had led to eco-terrorism. That had been merely the first hint of the violence that would come. My generation had grown up with it, and by the time I'd reached my teens, the avalanche was well and truly underway and no one could do anything to stop it.

It is with some amusement that I regard the London bobbies these days, with their return to the traditions of the pre-Collapse period, and their rather quaint, nostalgically styled uniforms, for in my days with New Scotland Yard, we looked less like policemen than like SAS commandos in full battle dress. We carried not billy clubs and whistles, but fully automatic weapons, and our uniforms were not blue serge, but mottled gray fatigues that were known as "urban camo." Our riot helmets made us resemble some outlandish cross between motorcyclists and astronauts and they were the only way to differentiate us from the military troops, aside from the word "POLICE" stenciled across our backs in large, black letters.

And, oh, how I despised those bloody helmets! The army knew better than to be saddled with such a worthless piece of junk. I longed for the simple metal helmet I had worn when I was in the army, but some idiot bureaucrat had apparently decided that the riot helmets were not only highly functional, which was debatable, but that their polarized visors had some sort of intimidating, psychological effect, which was a joke. In any event, only the greenest rookies used the visors, and not for very long, at that. Most of us simply tore them off, and many of the hardcore, swaggering, old veterans simply dispensed with the helmets altogether. Having seen as much, if not more, action as any of the veteran police officers, I kept my helmet, hot and sweaty as it was, because I'd seen more than my share of head wounds and I had a family to think of. I did hack off my visor, however, because I couldn't see well enough to shoot worth a damn with the bloody thing in place. And, sad to say, police officers expended a great many bullets in those days.

There is a popular program on television presently called *Collapse Cops*, depicting a team of police officers (a male and female, of course) "fighting crime during the dark days of the Collapse." There is a great deal of gunplay and camaraderie, coupled with sexual innuendo (the beauteous Officer Storm somehow contrives to be caught in her bra and panties at least

once every episode), the villainous perpetrators are all uni-
formly malevolent, and each program ends with our heroes
managing to touch the lives of several citizens and make their
burdens easier to bear. I only wish it had been so.

There were, naturally, women on the police force and in the
military, but I never encountered any who were even remotely
like the leggy, pouty-lipped Ms. Storm. The women with
whom I served were all serious professionals and there was not
a tube of lipstick or an eyebrow pencil to be found among
them. Glamor was the very least of their concerns and
romance between fellow officers was rare. Given the situation
in the streets, I did not know of a single officer, either male or
female, who would risk the complications of a romantic entan-
glement on the job. As to the malevolent perpetrators and the
citizens whose lives we touched, I only wish that, in reality,
the lines had been so clearly drawn. I can best illustrate with
an example, one that stands out in my mind as vividly as if it
had happened only yesterday, for it was the proverbial straw
that finally broke the camel's back.

We were called upon to suppress a sniper. The term "suppress" was a euphemism for killing the poor bastard, because
with the high level of violence in the streets, there was neither
the time nor the manpower to engage in the luxury of negotia-
tion, even if hostages were being held, which was quite often
the case. Possession of firearms of any sort was strictly illegal,
of course, but it was a law that had become completely unen-
forceable. The demand for firearms had become so great
among the general populace that a thriving black market existed to supply them and no sooner would we shut down one
basement machine-shop operation than a dozen others would
spring up. If a citizen were apprehended using a firearm in a
situation that was clearly self-defense, the usual procedure
was simply to confiscate the weapon and let the poor devil go
and seek to buy himself another at a ludicrously inflated price.
However, a sniper was something else again.

By the time we arrived on the scene, a large number of shots had already been fired. Fortunately, no one had been killed or injured yet, which seemed only a matter of either dumb luck or lousy marksmanship. In fact, it turned out to be superior marksmanship, something of which I have no doubt, for the fire that was subsequently directed at us came uncomfortably close, but avoided hitting anyone. No one can come so consistently close while still avoiding a direct hit without being a very good shot, indeed. However, when we first arrived, we did not know that, nor would it have made a difference if we had. Our orders for suppression were specific.

The streets in the vicinity were empty. Everyone had prudently fled the scene the moment the sniper opened up, but we followed procedure and cordoned off the area, as well as making announcements over the bullhorn that everyone should stay inside and avoid coming near the windows. As per procedure, the sniper was given one chance and one chance only to give up his weapon and surrender, and when his answer came in a burst of automatic fire, we proceeded to deploy for suppression.

It was an old and all too well-practiced drill. The sniper had stationed himself in a front flat on the fourth floor of a building in a residential section of the East Side. We stationed marksmen on the rooftops of the opposing buildings, and on the ground as well, taking cover behind our vehicles. Our main concern was to make certain no innocent lives were lost, but situations of this sort had become so commonplace that the building's residents had all evacuated the premises within moments after the sniper opened up, exiting at the rear of the building through the basement corridors without incident. After checking to make certain none of the flats in the immediate vicinity of the sniper were still occupied, we proceeded with the drill to take him out.

We moved cautiously, but quickly. Within moments, we had a squad inside the building. My partner and I were with that squad. My partner, Sergeant Royceton, was a hard-nosed veteran with twenty years experience on the force. A tough old bird, Ian Royceton could chew ten-penny nails and spit them out as tacks. We moved up the stairwell to the fourth floor and carefully proceeded down the corridor, toward the sniper's flat, moving from doorway to doorway and providing cover for each other as we went. Outside, our fellow officers were laying down some covering fire to occupy the sniper's attention and, hopefully, divert him from our approach.

We had fully expected to find that he had barricaded himself inside, and as a result, we had brought along a battering ram and some tear gas bombs. To our surprise, we discovered the door was not only unlocked, but open. It actually stood ajar. We stood so close, outside in the corridor, that from within, we could hear the sniper firing his weapon and the periodic dropping of empty magazines to the floor. Royceton and I glanced at one another and no words needed to be said. We knew exactly what to do. We would wait until the next empty magazine dropped and burst in on him while he was in the process of reloading.

It went off like clockwork. The next time we heard the metallic clatter of an empty magazine falling to the floor, I kicked the door fully open and both Royceton and I went in shooting. The poor devil never had a chance. Our bullets stitched into him and he jerked convulsively, then fell back through the shattered window glass and down four floors into the street, where his broken, lifeless body lay bleeding on the sidewalk. A quick and efficient operation, and I breathed a sigh of relief that it was over and that we'd escaped unscathed. Then I heard Royceton's sharp intake of breath and he said, "Oh, my God." I turned quickly, my weapon ready, but it was not a threat he was reacting to.

I followed his gaze and, through the open bedroom doorway, I saw the bodies lying on the bed, upon the blood-soaked sheets. On the night-stand beside the bed, we found the heartbreaking note that he had left. I have since tried to forget that note, and though the years have blurred the memory, so that I can no longer recall his exact words, the substance of his last message to the world is with me still, and there is no forgetting it.

He was not, apparently, a well-educated man, and that was reflected in the poor syntax of his suicide note, for in effect, it was exactly that. His tone was simple and despondent, deeply woeful, and in a mad sort of way, it even sounded reasonable. He began by addressing us, the police, his executioners. He started off with an apology. He stated that it was not his intention to hurt anyone, a remark that was diabolically incongruous with the corpses on the bed, and that he hoped no policemen or innocent bystanders had been harmed by any of his bullets.

"I will try my level best," he wrote—or words to that effect—"to avoid hitting anyone," and he went on to say that if, by accident, someone was killed or wounded, that he did not mean it and was truly, deeply sorry.

I listened as Royceton read the words out loud to me and I recall how stunned and mystified I felt at the crippled logic the sniper's twisted mind displayed. Here, he had murdered his entire family, and as he had written the note, possibly with their freshly slain bodies on the bed behind him, he stated his sincere intention to avoid hurting anyone and apologized profusely in the event he had. It seemed, however, that he did not consider what he'd done to them to be an act of murder, but an act of mercy, of release from a life that had become unbearable.

I stared at their bodies as Royceton continued to read from the note, and even tough-as-nails Royceton, hardened, seasoned veteran of two decades of street combat, could not stop his voice from breaking. There lay the sniper's wife and his two young daughters, about the same age as my own. He gave their names. I still recall them. Suzanne, his wife, and daughters Barbara and Irene. He wrote about their desperate plight, so similar to that of all too many others. They were cold and hungry, and he could find no work that would allow him to provide for them.

His wife was ill and bedridden, though the illness was not

specified, and his eldest daughter, Barbara, had begun to pros-
titute herself for food. She was thirteen. He had been out,
searching unsuccessfully for work, having been given notice
of eviction if he could not come up with the delinquent rent by
morning, and he had returned to find his wife and children
arguing. Irene wanted to do her part to help and join her sister
on the streets. Irene was nine.

What occurred afterward was something we would never
know, for he began to relate what happened, then broke off,
ending with one more apology, this time to God, and then he
signed his name, James Whitby, in large and bold, flourishing
script, as if with his final signature, he had tried to impart
some importance and dignity to his name.

His actions were not, of course, those of a sane man. The
poor devil's mind had snapped. It was possible he was unsta-
ble to begin with, but there was also the haunting possibility
that he had been as sane as any one of us and that, in his last
extremity, his reason simply had fled. The most curious thing
was that he had told us virtually nothing of himself. He was,
and would remain, a cipher.

He had signed his name, in big, bold letters, and yet he had
said nothing about who and what he was. He had made no
personal statement. He had died as he had lived, merely
another average, insignificant little man whom one would
never notice on the street, a man who, one might infer, held no
pretensions, but cared about his family and did whatever he
was able to get by. And when all his best efforts came to
nought, and he saw his family suffering in result, his wife sick,
one daughter degraded and the baby of the family wanting to
degrade herself as well to make up for Daddy's shortcom-
ings . . . Well, he apparently broke down and decided death
was preferable for all of them, a release from a life that was no
longer worth living.

I remember Royceton dropped the note down on the bed,
not intentionally, he had simply let go of it, and it fluttered onto

the bloody chest of little Irene. Royceton shut his eyes and turned away, then murmured, ''You know, I can almost understand the poor sod.''

It was at that moment that I reached the turning point. Complete and total burnout. I went numb. I had absolutely nothing left. My memory won't serve as to what, exactly, happened at that point. I seem to recall taking off my helmet and dropping it to the floor. I may have given my assault rifle to one of the others, I simply don't remember, but I know that I no longer had it several hours later, when I was on the train to Loughborough. I recall only one thing clearly, and that was a driving urge to get back to my family and be with them. I felt an urgency mere words cannot convey. I simply wanted to get back and hold my wife and daughters in my arms and never let them go.

The train broke down a short way out from Loughborough and I got out with the rest of the passengers and walked the remainder of the way. I do not recall how long it took. It seemed like hours, plodding along the tracks, and it was raining. Not a hard, driving rain, but a steady drizzle, yet by the time I reached our home, I was soaked through to the skin and shivering. Jenny heard the front door open and came running out to greet me. Our daughters were asleep, and she had been in bed with them, yet she was all bundled up, as were they, tucked beneath the blankets in their warmest clothes. They'd been burning wood for heat. It was all we could afford, and Jenny had run out. There was no money for getting any more. They had already burned some of the furniture and I, simple fool that I was, had left behind what little money I had left in London.

Jenny saw the look on my face and tried to tell me that it didn't matter. She was glad to have me home, and wouldn't the girls be happy when they woke up to see their daddy had returned, but all I could see as I looked down at their sleeping forms, huddled close together, were the bullet-riddled corpses of Barbara and Irene. It was as if an ice-cold fist had grabbed my guts and started squeezing. I left the bedroom and went out to get my axe.

Jenny grew alarmed when she saw what I intended. Chopping wood without a permit was a criminal offense. She tried to stop me, but I ignored her protests and went out, determined that come what may, my girls would never share the fate of poor James Whitby's daughters.

Not far from where we lived was a protected natural preserve, all that remained of Sherwood Forest, once a sprawling woodland, now a fenced-in acreage that was mined and patrolled by guards armed with automatic weapons. The surrounding countryside had been virtually denuded of trees as cordwood continued to go up in price and what was not chopped down by individuals for their own use was razed by opportunistic profiteers who sought to gain from other people's hardship. There was a thriving market in illegally cut cordwood and the authorities had been forced to take up drastic measures to protect the few remaining acres of woodland that were left.

I was not in a reasonable state of mind, but if I knew what I risked, I didn't give a damn. I was in such a state that I never gave any consideration to how I would manage to carry enough wood back to serve our needs, even assuming I would not be caught. One thought, and one thought only, was foremost in my mind. *Wood*. Wood, Goddamn it! At that point, the thinnest, hair's-breadth of a line separated me from poor James Whitby. I was on the razor's edge.

The rain was falling much harder as I cut my way through the concertina wire and breeched the fence without encountering any of the guards, who doubtless believed no one in their right mind would venture out on such a night. And, indeed, no one in their right mind had. I used my knife to probe for mines as I made my way farther back into the trees, thinking I would need some cover for my work, and should probably go some distance in to make certain any noise I made would not attract attention. I passed any number of small trees I could have chopped down easily, thinking, "Just a little farther, better safe than sorry," and other such nonsense. I have no idea how far I went, but before long, I realized I had lost all sense of direction. And, in that one moment, however briefly, my presence of mind returned and I thought, "Dear God, what am I doing?" My family had need of me, and there I was, probably catching my death of cold, breaking the law and committing a felony, endangering my life and, in consequence, theirs by my foolishness. What if I was blown up by a mine? What if I was shot in the act of chopping down a tree, or caught and arrested as I was bringing out . . . what? A measly armload of wood?

I felt despair overwhelm me and I put my head down in my arms as I lay upon the muddy ground and wept, the rain commingling with my tears. "Fool! Fool!" I cried to myself. "You're risking everything! You've walked off the job, left all your money behind in London, you've ruined everything!" And then, as I looked up, I saw a sight that banished all reason from my mind.

Before me, scarcely twenty yards away, was the largest oak tree I had ever seen, the grandfather of all English oaks. Its spreading upper branches were as thick as my thigh, its aged, gnarled trunk so wide that several men with their hands linked together could not encompass it. There it stood, an ancient leviathan, enough wood to keep my family warm for *years* to come. I stared at it, my gaze traveling up its trunk to its lofty canopy of branches, and I went absolutely mad.

I stood and gripped my axe in both hands, raising it high overhead, and I screamed as I charged the tree like some battle-maddened, Hun barbarian running at a Roman phalanx. In that moment of absolute insanity, I had become one with the slain James Whitby. The tree became the focal point for all my fury and frustration, my grief and helplessness, my anger at the whole damned world. I could have chopped away at its gargantuan trunk until the crack of doom and never have had a hope of felling it, but that thought never occurred to me. It couldn't have occurred to me. I wasn't thinking, I was just reacting, like a wounded beast that had been brought to bay.

I struck the tree a blow with all the power I could muster. The force of that blow ran up through the axe handle, through my hands, up my arms into my shoulders, and in the next instant, I was flying. I landed on my back some distance away, momentarily stunned and on the verge of losing consciousness. I felt a throbbing, tingling sensation all over my body, not unlike that which I had once experienced as a child when I had stuck my finger into an electric socket.

At the precise moment that I struck the giant oak tree with my axe, a bolt of lightning had come lancing down from the clouds and hit the tree. As least, that was my first impression, because it seemed there could have been no other explanation. Certainly, it never would have occurred to me that the lightning could have come not from the sky, but *from within the tree itself.*

As I recovered from my shock, I raised myself up slightly and stared at the smoking remnants of the tree. My vision was still somewhat blurred, but I could see that as large as it was, the oak had been split completely in two, right down the middle, from its uppermost branches straight down to where its trunk rose from the ground. Smoke swirled and eddied all around it, and as it slowly dissipated, I saw what appeared to be a figure standing in the cleft.

I blinked, and shook my head, and blinked again. My first quick impression was that I had been illuminated briefly in that flash of lightning and now some guard stood over me, but the man I saw was dressed nothing like a guard, and he carried no weapons, save for a long, slender wooden staff.

He wore some sort of robe, emblazoned with curious symbols, and he wore a high, conical hat. He had a long white beard and snowy hair that fell well past his shoulders. And as I stared at him with disbelief, he looked down at me and said, "Greetings, good sir. My name is Merlin."

# CHAPTER
# 2

It seems impossible to imagine these days that the name of Merlin would not instantly be recognized, even without Ambrosius appended to it, but back then, Merlin was, at best, part of an obscure legend, a piece of folklore, a onetime curiosity to academics who had occasionally debated whether or not he and King Arthur had ever actually existed. And those debates had ceased with the coming of the Collapse.

The legend of King Arthur and his Knights of the Round Table had once fascinated schoolchildren all over the world. Scores of books had been written on the subject, both novels and scholarly studies, and the story had also been the basis for films, television programs, comedies, dramatic plays, and musicals. Graduate students had written papers on the subject, and historians had searched for the authentic British king on whom Arthur had supposedly been based, as they had searched for Merlin, the legendary wizard who had been his mentor and advisor. That time had passed, however.

Universities had closed during the Collapse, for there had been no one to attend them. Schools had become little more than poorly operated day-care centers over which a pall of gloom had hung, for teachers had left the profession in droves, driven out of it by the sheer necessity for survival, and those who watched over the largely empty classrooms, save for a few diehard idealists, were often barely more educated than their students. Anyone capable of finding work of *any* kind, regardless of how young or old, was either working, out looking for work, or preying upon those who had it. Faced with the disaster of the Collapse, people had ceased regarding education as a priority. Mere survival had become challenging enough.

I had grown up during the Collapse, and though I'd had some schooling, I had joined the service as soon as I was old enough and my real education had been shaped by the events I lived through. I had always loved to read, however, and in my childhood, I had been exposed to the story of King Arthur, but that had been over three decades earlier and a lot of water had flowed under the bridge since then. In any event, the memory was hardly foremost in my mind at that particular time, which was not surprising, considering the circumstances. I did not connect the name of Merlin with King Arthur, and consequently, it meant nothing to me.

I had, after all, been suffering from an emotional trauma, and I wasn't even thinking clearly. The shock had, to some extent, restored me to my senses, but I was still not quite myself. I gazed at the strangely garbed old man standing there before me in the rain, in the cleft of that bifurcated tree, which had been peeled back as if it were a huge banana skin, and all I could do was simply stare at him. He looked away, and for a moment, he seemed to have eliminated me from his consideration. He took a deep breath, filling his lungs, then exhaled heavily, stretching and rolling his shoulders, as a man might upon awakening from a long and restful sleep. He craned his neck back and looked up at the sky, allowing the rain to fall upon his face, and then he sighed, wearily, or perhaps contentedly. He looked around, then focused his gaze on me once more.

He stepped down out of the center of the ruined tree, his movements stiff and awkward as he labored to walk toward me. He seemed extremely old and frail, but when he spoke, the strength and deep resonance of his voice belied appearances.

"Are you injured?" he asked.

I shook my head, still somewhat dazed and unable to think of anything to say.

"Well, then what are you doing stretched out there in the mud? Get up."

He extended his wooden staff toward me. I reached out and took hold of it, and he pulled me to my feet with surprising ease for a man of his advanced years.

"What is your name?" he asked.

"Tom," I said. "Tom Malory."

His eyes widened slightly with surprise, as if my name sounded familiar to him. "Thomas Malory?" he said, as if uncertain he had heard correctly.

"Yes, sir." I do not know if I appended the "sir" out of politeness to a senior gentleman, or out of habit born of years of service in the military, but in any case, he seemed to warrant it, for there was a firmness and authority about him that impressed itself upon me instantly.

Standing close to him, I could now make out his features clearly. His face was lined with age beneath the beard, and there were crow's-feet around his eyes, which were deeply set and a startling, periwinkle blue. His nose was sharp and prominent, with a slight hook to it, giving him something of the aspect of an eagle. He had pronounced cheekbones and a high forehead. His eyes, however, were his most striking feature. Aside from their startling, bright blue color, they were very direct and penetrating in their gaze, and they looked wise. How one deduces or infers such a thing I cannot imagine, save perhaps from experience of having seen other men possessed of wisdom with such eyes, but the impression was quite clear and forceful. After all these years, I can still remember that first meeting with complete and utter clarity, despite the fact that my thinking at the time was anything but clear.

"Thomas Malory," he said again, and smiled. "An ironic twist of fate. An omen. And, I think, a good one."

I simply stared at him. I had absolutely no idea what he was talking about.

"My name means nothing to you?" he asked, and then he gave it again, this time more fully. "Merlin? Merlin Ambrosius?"

I felt as if there were a slight tug at my memory, for there did seem to be a vague familiarity about the name, but I couldn't put my finger on it. "No, sir," I replied, "I don't think so. Have we met before?"

"No," he said with a slight shake of his head. "No matter. Do you live nearby?"

I stammered something about how I lived not too far away, within walking distance. I wanted to ask him for directions, for I'd lost my way. However, I couldn't seem to form the words. I could not stop staring at him. It was not so much that he looked so damned outlandish, but there was a compelling presence about him that commanded my attention. In later years, many writers were to remark upon that, and expend considerable verbiage attempting to define exactly what it was about him that produced such an effect, but the long and short of it was simply that the man exuded power. He was of slightly less than average height, and he was quite slim then, though he began to put on weight in later years, and became rather stout and stocky. However, he was by no means physically imposing, though one somehow received the impression that he was.

"I don't suppose I could impose upon you for something to eat?" he said. "It has been a long time since I have tasted any food."

It was not the sort of query I hadn't heard at least a thousand times before. The streets were teeming with beggars and pathetic, homeless wretches who had been reduced to sleeping in the alleys and digging through the refuse for their sustenance, and though I did not think of myself as either insensitive or heartless, I had, like most people, become inured to them out of necessity. To comply with such requests was not only to invite trouble, but even a saint would have been forced to learn how to reject them, because they were so numerous. Even Christ, deluged with innumerable demands to heal the sick, had responded with exasperation. And yet, despite all that, with the shadow of James Whitby still upon me, I found that I could not deny him.

"We haven't very much," I said, more by way of an apology than as an excuse, "but I'm sure we can come up with something. However, we haven't any wood and I . . ."

My voice trailed off as I recalled why I'd come there in the first place, and what a foolish risk I'd taken, and for a moment, I felt at odds with myself. I was already there, the risk had already been taken, and it seemed pointless not to complete my mission. I bent down to pick up the axe I'd dropped, only to see that it was broken. The handle had splintered and the head had snapped clean off.

"Never fear," said Merlin. "Do not concern yourself. It is late, the weather is beastly, and your family must be worried. Come."

He started walking purposefully in the direction I had come from. I suddenly recalled the mines, and shouted out a warning. Then I saw that he was not walking in a straight line, but in a serpentine manner, holding his staff out in front of him as if it were some sort of metal detector. Astonished, I followed in his wake and we reached the fence without incident. I stopped for a moment and looked back the way we'd come, scarcely believing that any of this was happening. Where had he come from? That lightning bolt must have narrowly missed him. What had he been doing there? And why on earth was he dressed in such a peculiar fashion?

The rain had slackened considerably. It fell as a fine mist as we headed home together. I noticed, as we walked, that bit by bit, his frailty and stiffness seemed to disappear, and the dampness did not seem to bother his old bones at all. In fact, I soon had to quick march to keep up with him. Jenny was frantic with worry by the time we came in through the door, though the girls were still asleep.

"Oh, thank God!" she said, throwing her arms around me. "Thank God you're safe!"

"It's all right," I said, holding her tightly. "I'm sorry. I didn't mean to frighten you. But I'm afraid I brought no wood and—"

"There is no need for concern," Merlin said, standing at the rear of the kitchen, by the door to the enclosed back entryway. "You seem to have an adequate supply."

Jenny turned toward him, puzzled, and shook her head. "But we have no wood," she said. "We'd run out, you see, and we had to break up some of the furniture to—"

"Nonsense," Merlin interrupted her. "There is plenty here. See for yourself."

With a confused expression on her face, Jenny went toward him and looked. I heard her gasp. "My God! But . . . how can that be? It's impossible!" She turned toward me with a look of complete mystification. "*Tom . . .*"

I frowned and went to look for myself. The entire back entryway was stacked with split cordwood right up to the ceiling.

"Tom, there wasn't any wood at all!" said Jenny with disbelief. "I swear to you . . . none of this was here before!"

"Ah, we seem to have all the makings of a proper feast here," I heard Merlin say, and I turned around to see him standing at the open pantry.

"Now, see here, old chap," I said, moving toward him, and then I stopped and stared with slack-jawed astonishment at the contents of the pantry. There were smoked hams and partridges, sausages, loaves of fresh-baked bread, a turkey, salted venison, sacks of flour and salt and sugar, jars of comb honey, dried fruits, a veritable cornucopia of food taking up every square inch of space.

"*What the devil . . .*" I said.

I heard Jenny gasp behind me and I turned to see her staring over my shoulder at the contents of the pantry, her eyes wide with disbelief.

"Tom . . . I . . . I don't understand . . ." she said, shaking her head. "*None* of this was here before! I know it seems impossible, but you simply *must* believe me!"

"I believe you, Jenny," I said slowly, turning to look toward the strange old man. He had gone back into the living room and was now seated on the couch, removing a pouch from his robe and packing a large, curved briar with tobacco.

"Tom . . . who *is* that old man?" asked Jenny.

I stared at him as he puffed his pipe alight. Was it merely my overwrought imagination, or had he not struck a match? For a moment, I could have sworn he'd simply snapped his fingers and the flame came from his thumb. But, clearly, that was absurd.

"I met him in the woods," I replied uncertainly. "He . . . uh . . . he said his name was . . . Merlin, I think."

"Merlin?" said Jenny. "Like the wizard in the legend of King Arthur?"

All of a sudden, it came back to me. I remembered the story of how he helped Arthur become king, and how he had advised him at his castle, known as Camelot, and how in the end, the sorceress Morgan le Fay had tricked him and betrayed him, placing him under a spell and immuring his body in the cleft of a giant oak . . . *a giant oak*!

"No," I said, "it can't be! That's ridiculous. It's more than ridiculous, it's insane."

"What's insane?" asked Jenny. "Tom, who *is* he? Why have you brought him here? What's *happening*?"

"I don't know," I said, entering the living room. Merlin looked up at me and smiled, puffing on his pipe contentedly. The burning tobacco gave off the odor of vanilla cookies. No, I thought, it smelled more like fresh-baked apples . . . No, not apples, raspberries. No, not raspberries either, but . . . and then I realized that the scent of his tobacco somehow seemed to change with each and every puff he took. He sat there, happily blowing perfect smoke rings.

"So . . . when do we eat?" he asked.

He ate with the appetite of an entire platoon. Jenny had wanted to wake up the girls, for they had gone to bed cold and hungry, but I told her to let them sleep. There was plenty of food for them to fill their bellies in the morning and the house had warmed up nicely with a roaring fire in the hearth. Both Jenny and I were famished, but even after we'd filled ourselves to bursting, Merlin was still eating, putting food away like a bulimic gone berserk. I had never seen anyone eat like that. It was incredible. He ate enough for at least half a dozen ravenous lumberjacks.

As if he were reading my mind, he said, "I do not wish to seem a glutton, but wizards need to eat a great deal more than most other people do. It has to do with the principles that govern the universe, you see. You cannot expend energy without having to replenish it. Magic has a cost. It drains your life force of energy, and you must recover that energy or risk consuming yourself."

Throughout the meal, he had spoken at length about himself, and we listened with fascinated incredulity as he told us his story. And what a story it was! I didn't believe a word of it, of course, though I had to admit that his delusion, for I was convinced it was that, had a remarkable consistency. Yet, there was still the matter of the food mysteriously appearing out of nowhere, and the cordwood, which had not been there before. If there was any truth to his assertions, which clearly seemed impossible, then it was difficult to argue with the apparent fact that he had somehow produced it, which also seemed impossible. I was certain there had to be another explanation.

"I see," I replied. "But there's one thing I don't quite understand. If it is your own energy you are using in, uh . . . magically creating all the food we're eating, and the wood we're burning in the fireplace, then a certain amount of energy must be expended in the act, which means there is that much less energy inherent in the product. You cannot keep creating your own energy out of nothing. It violates the laws of thermodynamics. There must soon come a point of diminishing returns, if you see what I mean."

"Quite correct," said Merlin with a smile. "I thought you were a bright fellow. Obviously, I cannot simply create my own sustenance, not only for the reason you just mentioned, but because you cannot create matter, you can only alter its form, which is a well-known principle of alchemy."

"We call it physics," Jenny said.

"Physics? Physics . . . interesting. I shall have to remember that. In any event, I did not create this fine food we are enjoying, nor the wood that is heating this home even as we speak. I merely borrowed it, in a manner of speaking."

"Borrowed it?" I asked with a puzzled frown. "From *where*?"

"Oh, here and there," he replied with a shrug. "The wood was taken from the very tree in which I was confined. I merely altered its form somewhat and transported it here. And it certainly does my heart good to see that damnable tree burn after being imprisoned within it for so long. As for the food, some of it was wild, such as the partridges and the turkey, and some of it had been stored elsewhere, such as the hams and sausages and the like."

"You mean you *stole* it?" I said, caught up in what he was saying and forgetting for the moment that I did not believe a word of it.

"Well, I cannot say for certain where it came from, you understand," he said, "but I had assumed that there were storehouses of food nearby, so I simply directed my spell in such a manner that it would seek out the greatest source of supply and divert some of it. Robbing from the rich to give to the poor, as my old friend Robin Hood might have put it."

"You *knew* Robin Hood?" asked Jenny, fascinated. I stared at her. She saw the look I gave her and shrugged, as if to say she couldn't help it.

"Oh, most certainly," Merlin replied. "His proper name was Locksley, you understand, and he was always something of a scoundrel, even before he was forced to turn outlaw. His legend has far eclipsed his true stature, however, as has been the case with the story of Arthur. In truth, Locksley was as far removed from the romantic image of the noble outlaw as can be. He was a coarse and stocky fellow, a profane brawler given to drinking himself senseless. If not for Marian, those so-called 'Merry Men' of his would have had no effective leadership whatever."

"You mean Maid Marian?" asked Jenny. I glanced at her again, but she ignored me.

"Oh, she was no maid, I can tell you that," said Merlin with a chuckle. "She was a fine and strapping lass who could bend a bow and swing a broadsword with the best of them. Large-framed and rather plain to look upon, she was nothing at all like the fine and delicate young maid she is portrayed as in the legend. She was the sheriff's wife, you see, but the old sheriff could never quite satisfy her, uh, voracious appetites, and she had quite a taste for younger men. It led her into trouble, so she ran off to take up with Locksley and his boys, and never ceased to bedevil her husband ever after. But then I've gone on long enough. It is late and, doubtless, you have grown weary of listening to me. We can discuss things further in the morning."

"In the morning?" I said, concerned that he had apparently invited himself to spend the night.

"Yes, there will be plenty of time for us to talk, and I am looking forward to meeting your fine young daughters."

"Uh . . . well, I suppose I should clear the table and get the dishes done," Jenny said. "Tom . . . could you help me in the kitchen?"

Before I could reply to Jenny's obvious invitation to a discreet conference in the kitchen, Merlin said, "Nonsense, I won't hear of it. You two go off to bed. I will take care of everything."

"We wouldn't want you to go to any trouble," Jenny said. "Besides, you're our guest and—"

"I insist," said Merlin. "Besides, it won't be any trouble at all. Now go, off with you, else your two young girls will run you ragged in the morning. And don't concern yourselves about me. I shall manage excellently. Go on now, and good night to you."

"Uh . . . good night," said Jenny, taking me by the arm and pulling me into our bedroom. No sooner had she shut the door behind us than she turned to face me with an expression of alarm. "*Tom* . . ."

"Yes, yes, I know," I said, "I'm a bit concerned about him, too."

"A *bit* concerned?" she said.

"Well, he's quite mad, obviously, but he seems harmless. He's actually rather charming in his own eccentric sort of way. I don't really think there's any cause to worry. I still have my pistol, and there's the revolver in the night stand, and the shotgun in the closet. Besides, we can't really turn him out, can we? He's an old man, and it's beastly out."

"Tom . . . what if he's truly . . . I mean, what if he really is who he says he is?" she asked.

"Oh, come on, you can't be serious!"

"What about the *wood*?" she asked, her eyes wide. "And what about all that food? Where on earth could it have come from? Unless you believe that I've been hiding something from you and—"

I interrupted quickly. "No, no, of course not, darling, don't be silly."

"Tom, you *do* believe me, don't you, when I say that none of it was there before?"

"Of course I believe you," I replied. "There simply must be some other, more rational explanation."

"Like what?" she asked, raising her eyebrows.

I shook my head, at a complete loss to explain it. "I'll be damned if I know," I said. "Perhaps some secret benefactor snuck in somehow and put all that stuff there while you and the girls were sleeping. It sounds improbable, perhaps, but I can't think of any other logical explanation."

"But why?" she asked. "And how? Tom, it would have taken *hours* to stack all that wood, much less to bring in all that food. And how could anyone possibly have done it without waking me? It seems impossible."

"And his being Merlin, the court wizard to King Arthur, seems possible to you?" I said.

"What about his pipe?" she asked. "Did you notice that the scent of his tobacco kept on changing? And I never saw him use a lighter or a match. Did you notice that, as well? "

"Yes, I noticed," I admitted. "But perhaps he really is a magician, you know, a stage magician, and he was using sleight of hand. Perhaps his delusion stems from that, I don't know, but he cannot possibly be who he says he is. Magic simply doesn't *exist,* for God's sake! There's no such thing. Besides, if he really *were* King Arthur's Merlin, that would make him several thousand years old, and frankly, he doesn't look a day over seventy."

"Very funny," Jenny said wryly. "But even if all that is true, it still doesn't change the fact that you've brought a crazy old man into our home and now it seems we're stuck with him."

"Yes, I know," I said, frowning. "Well, we'll simply have to keep an eye on him. For tonight, at least. In the morning, I'm sure he'll be on his way."

Jenny opened the door a crack and peered out, then gasped and shut it again quickly. "Tom . . ." she said, in a voice scarcely above a whisper, "*look*!"

I went to the door and opened it. We'd been in the bedroom only a few minutes, and yet already the table was clear and set for breakfast in the morning. I carefully tiptoed out and, with Jenny right behind me, checked the kitchen. The dishes had not only been washed, but they were dry and stacked in their proper places in the cupboard, and the food had all been put away.

The old man sat in the darkened living room, illuminated only by the flickering firelight, with his back to us. He was watching the telly with rapt fascination, smoke curling up from his pipe. Not only had the table been cleared, the dishes washed and dried, and the food put away, but the entire house was absolutely spotless.

"Wonderful thing, this box," said Merlin, speaking with his back to us, though we'd made hardly a sound coming out of the bedroom. "I have quite a bit of catching up to do, it seems. This should prove quite helpful."

"Uh . . . yes," I replied uneasily. "I, uh, see you've tidied up some. Thank you."

"No need to mention it," he said. "It was no trouble at all."

"Yes . . . well . . . good night."

"Good night. Sleep well."

We went back into the bedroom and shut the door. For a long moment, we simply stared at one another, unable to think of a single thing to say. Jenny moistened her lips and finally broke the silence.

"Tom . . . I think he really *is* Merlin!"

"Well, there's one way to be certain," I said. "In the morning, you can ask him to turn into an owl and if he does, I suppose that'll clinch it. The girls will get quite a kick out of that."

"How can you joke at a time like this?" she asked.

"How can you not?" I countered. "This is crazy! I keep

thinking there has to be some rational explanation for all this, but I can't dismiss the evidence of my own senses. Unless I've gone completely mad, as well.''

"Then I must be mad, too," said Jenny. "You *saw* him come out of that tree, didn't you?"

"I saw him standing where the lightning struck," I said. "That's not quite the same thing."

"Where else could he have come from? And why else does he look the way he does?"

"Jenny, I have absolutely no idea. I was not exactly in a rational state of mind. I don't *know* what's happening! I can't explain it, but there has to be some explanation that makes sense!"

"I'd love to hear it," she replied.

"God, so would I!"

"I won't be able to sleep a wink," she said.

"Neither will I," I said, and then I yawned, suddenly.

Jenny yawned as well. "How could anyone possibly sleep at a time like this?"

"Damned if I know," I replied, but my eyelids unaccountably felt extremely heavy.

"I *do* feel tired, though," said Jenny wearily. "It's been quite a day. I think perhaps I'll just lay down for a little while."

"Yes, good idea," I said, yawning again. "We don't have to sleep. We can talk and try to make some sense of all this."

We both lay down on the bed, but we did not do any talking. Intense exhaustion seemed to overwhelm us and, within moments, Jenny was fast asleep. As I drifted off myself, I seemed to hear the bedroom door open softly, and then someone covered us up with a blanket. I thought I heard a voice say, "Problems are best solved in the morning," and then I remember nothing more.

In the morning, I awoke to the high-pitched sound of girlish laughter and the pleasant smell of coffee brewing. I could also smell eggs and bacon frying.

"Mmmm," Jenny murmured as she stirred beside me. "That smells absolutely marvelous!"

"*Oh, do it again! Do it again!*"

It was little Michelle's voice, and we both came completely awake instantly. For a moment, Jenny looked confused, then she remembered our house guest and bolted out of bed. Neither of us had undressed the previous night, and we both hurried to the kitchen, where the sight that greeted us brought us both up short and rendered us absolutely speechless.

Breakfast was cooking itself. *Literally*, cooking itself. Merlin sat on a chair, which he had pulled back from the table, and Michelle was sitting on his knee, in a rapture of delight, clapping her hands with glee. Christine stood by the stove, staring with a mixture of awe and fascination as the eggs in the frying pan obligingly turned themselves over and the bacon rose up as it was done, levitating out of the pan on the adjoining burner to float gracefully over onto a plate set on the counter top.

A mixing bowl stirred by a wooden spurtle was suspended in midair, then it tipped over to pour dollops of pancake batter into a frying pan. The pancakes flipped themselves as they became done on one side, and Michelle clapped with delight and cried, "Oh, higher! *Higher*!" Complying with her demands, the pancakes flipped once more, describing elaborate parabolas in the air, flying up to just below the ceiling before they landed back in the pan again.

"It's a trick," Christine insisted, frowning as she seemed to scan for wires or some other hidden agency that might have performed the feat.

"Yes, but you must admit it is a neat trick," Merlin said.

"How is it done?" Christine asked, framing with childish innocence the one question that raced through both mine and Jenny's minds, only we could not bring ourselves to ask it. We were both absolutely stupefied with disbelief.

"It's magic," Merlin said, glancing at us and acknowledging our presence with a smile and a nod.

"There's no such thing as magic!" Christine said.

"There is *so*!" argued her sister.

"Is *not*!" Christine insisted.

"How do you know?" asked Merlin.

"Because there simply isn't, that's all," replied Christine.

"What makes you so certain?" asked Merlin.

"Magic only happens in fairy tales," said Christine.

"Who told you so?" asked Merlin, raising his bushy eyebrows.

"Everyone knows *that*," Christine replied with scorn. How could a grownup possibly be so stupid? Breakfast, meanwhile, continued to prepare itself during the discussion.

"Well, *I* didn't know it," Merlin said. "And since I am *someone*, then I suppose that means that *everyone* didn't know it."

"Well, it's true," Christine said.

"But how do you *know* it's true?" persisted Merlin. "Because someone told you it was true?"

"Yes," Christine said confidently.

"Do you believe everything that people tell you?" Merlin asked. "Suppose I said that you could fly. Would you believe that?"

"No, that's silly," Christine said. "Everyone knows people can't fly. Only birds can fly."

"Well, I suppose you must be a bird then," Merlin said. Christine suddenly floated up into the air. She cried out with alarm and I felt Jenny's grip tighten on my arm, but I merely looked at her and shook my head.

"*Help! Put me down!*" Christine cried, making bicycling motions with her legs.

"Put you down?" said Merlin. "Don't be silly. Everyone knows people can't fly."

Michelle was squealing with mirth as she bounced on Merlin's knee. "Don't! Don't put her down! Keep her up there! Make her go *higher*!"

"Yes, you cannot possibly be a person," Merlin said. "You must be a bird. And the birds fly by flapping their wings. So . . . flap your wings."

"*Mommy*!"

"Flap your wings, I said!"

Christine began to flap her arms, as if she were a bird, and slowly gently, she took off, floating gracefully around the room.

"Mommy! Daddy! *Look*! Christine's *flying*!" cried Michelle.

"I'm flying!" said Christine as she slowly circled the room, apparently in full control of her flight. Her alarm turned to astonishment and joy. "I'm really *flying*!"

She circled the kitchen, then floated out into the living room and made several circles around it as we watched, slack-jawed.

"*Wheeee! I'm flying! I'm flying!*"

" Uncle Merlin, *I* want to fly, too!" Michelle demanded.

"You do?" said Merlin.

"Yes, please? *Please*, can't I fly, like Christine?"

"You want to be a bird, as well?"

"Oh, yes, please! I want to be a *bird*!"

"Then flap your wings," said Merlin.

Michelle began to flap her arms enthusiastically and she, too, rose up into the air and floated off to join Christine in flying laps around the living room.

"*I'm a bird! I'm a bird!*" she cried.

"*Tom*," said Jenny, "*for God's sake, pinch me so I know I'm not dreaming!*"

"If you are, then I'm having the same dream," I said. "*Ouch*!"

"Now pinch me back!"

I pinched her and she gave out a small cry, for she had pinched me hard and I'd been none too gentle myself.

"It's *true*," she whispered. "My God, Tom, it's all true! He really *is* Merlin!"

"Did you have any doubt?" asked Merlin, his eyes crinkling with amusement. "All right, little birds, time to come home to roost! Breakfast is ready!"

"No, not yet! " Michelle protested.

"Now none of that," said Merlin. "Do what your uncle Merlin tells you."

They both settled gently to the floor, despite Michelle flapping her arms furiously in a futile effort to remain airborne. "Oh, no! Please, Uncle Merlin, can't we fly a little longer?"

"Yes, please!" Christine said. "Just a few more minutes! Can't we fly a few more minutes? "

"*Fly*?" said Merlin, feigning astonishment. "Don't be silly. *Everyone* knows people can't fly."

They both fell silent and simply stared at him.

"Just as everyone knows there's no such thing as magic," he added. "Magic only happens in fairy tales. Everyone knows *that*. Now sit down and eat your breakfast."

"Oh, *pooh!*" Michelle said, stamping her foot and pouting as she sat down at the table.

"One does not say 'pooh' to one's elders," Merlin admonished her. Then, turning to Christine, he added, "And one should not believe everything that people say, even if a lot of people say it's true. You should always think for yourself. I'm certain your father and mother would agree. That does not mean you shouldn't listen to them, mind you, but you should always think about the things you hear, and not simply accept them because it's what you were told. People who don't think for themselves often get into a lot of trouble that way. Remember that."

Christine nodded solemnly, her eyes wide as she hung on his every word. "I will," she said.

"Good." Merlin turned toward us and raised his eyebrows. "How do you like your eggs?"

# CHAPTER
## 3

Under ordinary circumstances, a hearty, robust breakfast such as Merlin had provided would have been quite an unaccustomed treat for us in those lean days, yet no repast, however sumptuous, could compete with what the girls had just experienced. They were so excited, they could hardly eat a bite. I was somewhat disappointed that my unexpected return home had passed completely without comment from my daughters, but then I could hardly hold a candle to the newly adopted "Uncle Merlin." What's a visit from Daddy, after all, when you've just been flown around the living room?

I was concerned they would discuss their "Uncle Merlin" with their friends among the local children, describing how he had made the kitchen come alive, then turned them into birds. Given such assertions, proof would certainly be required, and I could not imagine how our neighbors would respond to their children being levitated. "Uncle Merlin," on the other hand, did not seem at all concerned. Quite the opposite, in fact.

"No, no, let them talk about it, by all means," he insisted, after Jenny had dragged our reluctant girls away from him. "I don't see how you could prevent them, in any event. Besides, I have no intention of keeping my presence here a secret. I *want* people to know about me. And the sooner, the better. We have much to do.''

"*We*?" I said. "And what, precisely, is it that 'we' are going to do?"

"Why, announce my presence to the world, of course," he replied, as if it were the most natural thing to do. "I suppose that will take some time, though, and that is only the beginning. Oh, yes, only the beginning. We have quite a task ahead of us, Thomas. Quite a task, indeed."

"Just a moment," I said. "I'm not quite certain what you're getting at, but before you start making any plans, I think we need to talk about this. I do have a full-time job, you know. I'm a police officer. Or at least I was, until yesterday. I'll need to report in as soon as possible and make some effort to explain my absence, otherwise I'll be left with no means to provide for my family."

"You need have no concerns for your family's welfare," Merlin said. "Never fear, I shall see to that. As for your job, it is of no consequence. We have far more important work to do. I know what must be done, you see, but I'm not certain how best to go about it. And that is where I need your help."

"*You* need *my* help?" I said.

"Most assuredly. I spent the night watching your television, and listening to your radio. What marvelous devices! Highly informative, indeed. They have shown me that there is much to do. It seems the world once again has need of me."

"I have no idea what the world will make of you," I replied dubiously. "But what is it that you have in mind, exactly?"

"You know, Thomas, during my long sleep within the great oak, I was not entirely ignorant of events that took place in the world outside," he said. "I saw the years roll by in dreams. And the years turned into decades, and the decades into centuries. Thaumaturgy, the discipline of magic, became forgotten

as the years went by, and as mankind began to seek enlightenment in other ways. I dreamed about the wars, the leaps of
knowledge resulting in miraculous inventions, the growth of
industry and what you call technology, humanity's astonishing
ventures beyond the confines of this world, the promise of
peace and prosperity, and now this . . . the Collapse, as you
call it.''

He sighed and stroked his long, gray beard. There was a
troubled expression on his face. I merely listened, saying
nothing, caught up in his spell. And it *was* a spell, which he
cast merely by his presence.

I kept thinking how surreal it all seemed. There we were,
sitting at the breakfast table, the dishes not yet cleared away,
me drinking my tea and Merlin smoking his curved pipe with
its ever-changing odors, and it seemed for all the world as if an
elderly, avuncular neighbor had dropped by for a friendly
morning chat. Old Mr. Ambrosius, from next door. A bit
eccentric, perhaps, but a pleasant, harmless, and altogether
rather charming bloke. One who had stepped out of a tree he
happened to have slept in for about two thousand years.

''So many things have changed,'' he said. ''And yet, in
essence, much has remained the same. There is still ambition,
greed and lust for power. There is still poverty and hunger.
There are still those who have much, and those who have
nothing. In its driven quest for progress, humanity has over-
reached itself. You have achieved progress at the expense of
enlightenment. And see what has resulted. You have poisoned
the very air you breathe, befouled the water that you drink,
and stripped the Earth of her resources. Humanity has pissed
in its own well, Thomas. Your miraculous machines are wind-
ing down, and your marvelous technology is now of little use
to you. It shall not replace that which was lost . . . or that
which was forgotten.''

He sat silent for a moment, pensive, shaking his head as if
with paternal disapproval.

"Well, I can hardly disagree," I said, "but you still haven't told me what it is you plan to do."

"My plan," he said, "is to bring back the forgotten knowledge. There is great need of it."

"What, you mean *magic*?" I said.

"Yes. The discipline of thaumaturgy, or magic, if you prefer. My greatest strength, indeed, my greatest satisfaction, has always been derived from teaching. Therefore, I shall instruct others in the Craft, so that the age of magic may return."

I could only gape at him. "But . . . how on Earth do you propose to teach a supernatural ability?"

"There is nothing supernatural about it," he replied. "Magic has always been a fact of nature, governed by its laws. Granted, it does take a certain talent not all people possess in equal measure, but everyone possesses the latent faculty, at least to some degree."

"I wouldn't know," I said. "In all my life, I've never met anyone like that. That is, not till I met you."

"Haven't you?" he said. "Chances are you have experienced your own latent magical potential without even realizing it. Consider, have you ever had a sense or an impression for which you had no rational explanation, such as seeing a place for the very first time, yet somehow feeling as if you had been there before?"

"Well, yes," I admitted, "but that's not at all uncommon. It's known as *déjà vu*, and there's a perfectly logical explanation for it."

Merlin raised his eyebrows. "Is there, indeed? I would very much like to hear it."

"Frankly, I'm not really an expert at this sort of thing," I said, "but the accepted scientific theory is that it's actually a sort of cerebral short circuit. What happens is that you perceive or experience something in the instant that it actually occurs, and your mind registers the event as your senses supply the information to your brain, only a sort of sensory loop occurs, an error in data input, and the perception is registered

not once, but twice. As a result, you experience the sense of
*déjà vu*, of having already seen something before, and in a
manner of speaking, you have. Your mind has actually perceived the same thing twice in the same instant.''

"Fascinating," Merlin said. "And you *believe* this?"

"It seems a logical explanation," I replied.

"Ah. I see. And any explanation that does *not* seem logical
is not to be considered, I suppose."

"Well, why should it be, if it's illogical?"

"Because it might very well be true," Merlin replied, "as I
believe I demonstrated to your daughters' satisfaction."

"Well . . . I certainly can't argue with that," I was forced to
admit. "I actually saw them floating in midair, though I can
still scarcely believe it. Either it was magic, or you're some
sort of master hypnotist.''

"Hypnotist?" said Merlin, frowning.

"Someone who can put people in a trance and induce them
to believe things, or do things they otherwise might not do. It's
called hypnotism, or the power of suggestion."

"Indeed?" said Merlin. "And how is this accomplished?"

I shrugged. "I don't know exactly how it's done, and I've
never experienced it myself, but there are different methods,
depending on the hypnotist. There are those who perform it as
an entertainment, and have the subject follow some sort of
bright and shiny object with their eyes while they tell them that
their eyelids are growing very heavy, and they're feeling very
tired and sleepy and so on, until the trance state is induced.
Then they use the power of suggestion to make the subject
cluck like a chicken, or something equally amusing. Hypnotism has also been used by therapists to help people overcome
emotional problems, or perhaps bad habits. Sometimes it's
used to perform regressions, in which the subject is induced to
recall some event in the past, such as a traumatic experience
the subject has blocked out due to inability to cope with it.
Some people have even remembered so-called 'past lives'

under hypnosis, which encourages those who believe in rein-
carnation, but has otherwise been greeted with skepticism, the
theory being that the relaxed subconscious was merely being
imaginative during the trance.''

"Fascinating. And is that what you believe I did?'' asked
Merlin. "You think I induced you to believe you saw your
daughters fly? And that I also induced your wife and daughters to believe it happened, when it did not really occur at
all?''

I cleared my throat uneasily. "Well, no, I didn't say that,
exactly . . . I mean . . . that is . . .''

Merlin smiled. "Let us look at it another way," he said.
"You find it difficult to believe you really saw your daughters
floating in midair, but you have no difficulty believing in this
hypnotism?''

"Well . . . no, of course not. But then hypnotism isn't
magic.''

"Really?'' Merlin said. "In my time, it was known as a
spell of compulsion.''

"Somehow, I don't think that's quite the same thing," I
replied, unable to repress a smile.

"I see," he said. "You mean if I were to claim that I could
place you under a spell and compel you to act in a certain way,
you would disbelieve it. Yet, if I claimed to be a hypnotist who
could use this power of suggestion to accomplish the very
same thing, you would have no difficulty in believing that?''

I suddenly felt uncertain of my ground. "Uh . . . well, no, if
you put it that way, I suppose I wouldn't. But then everyone
knows that hypnotism isn't magic. It's merely a technique, a
skill that almost anyone can learn.''

"One could say the same thing about magic," Merlin said.
"In fact, I just did, mere moments ago.''

I felt confused. "I don't understand. Are you suggesting
that hypnotism *is* magic?''

"Forget about hypnotism," Merlin said with a dismissive

wave of his hand. "The word 'magic' is what seems to be troubling you. So tell me, what do you understand magic to be?"

I took a deep breath and exhaled heavily. "Well, I'm not sure I understand magic to *be* anything," I replied. "What I mean is, I'd always believed that there was no such thing, except in fairy tales."

"What is it in these fairy tales, then?" asked Merlin.

I shrugged. "As I said before, it's a supernatural ability."

"To do what?"

"To . . ." I shook my head, searching for the right way to put it. "To, uh, influence your environment in some fantastic way. To conjure up demons, I suppose, or turn people into toadstools or something."

"Stop there," said Merlin. "Never mind the conjuring of demons and turning people into toadstools. Those are fairly difficult spells, only for advanced and highly skilled adepts."

"You mean it's actually *possible* to conjure up a demon? Or turn someone into a toadstool?"

"Certainly," Merlin replied. "But never mind that for now. If I tried to explain it, you would only become even more confused. We need to take things slowly. What you first said, that magic is a way of influencing one's environment, is exactly correct. That is all magic is, in essence. And I have already told you that there is nothing supernatural about it. It's a skill that may be learned, albeit not easily, just as this hypnotism you described. I'm quite certain that, in time, I could teach you to perform a few fairly simple and undemanding spells yourself. It's no different from any other form of knowledge. Consider your television. I have no idea how it works, exactly, but I believe I understand the principle involved. Within it are some sort of devices for storing and receiving energy, which is transmitted through the ether and then transformed into the sounds and images you see. It is nothing less than sorcery, Thomas, only you do not *choose* to call it sorcery. On the television, I heard a number of references to something called BBC, the British Broadcasting Company. Interesting word, *broadcasting*. One may infer that it entails casting a spell over a broad area, so that anyone who owns one of these television boxes may receive it."

"But broadcasting has nothing to do with casting *spells*." I protested, restraining a silly urge to giggle. "It's merely the science of electronics."

"Electronics, broadcasting, science, magic . . . call it what you will," replied Merlin with a shrug. "Take away the name and what do you have? Knowledge of certain natural principles and the application of those principles. That's all magic is. Knowledge and application. And a certain degree of skill, of course. You understand the television, so it is no great mystery to you. It does not seem supernatural. It would only seem so if you didn't understand it. Magic is no different. Once you understand the principles involved, you shall accept it as easily as you accept the television."

"You make it sound almost simple," I said.

"I did not *say* it was simple," Merlin replied. "Do you possess the skill to craft a television?"

"You mean could I actually build one from scratch? Well, no, but . . ."

"But if you had the knowledge, and the skill to apply that knowledge, and the proper materials and tools, then you could do it, could you not?"

I shrugged. "I suppose so."

"So it is with magic," Merlin said. "To cast a spell, you merely need a knowledge of thaumaturgy, the skill to apply that knowledge, and the proper materials and tools. There is nothing impossible about magic. Unless, of course, you insist that your entire family has experienced a common delusion for which I was somehow responsible. I cannot convince you if you refuse to be convinced, Thomas. I could easily fly you around the room, as well, but if you chose to remain stubborn in your disbelief, you would maintain that I had tricked you somehow and that it never really happened. Perhaps if I turned you into a toadstool . . .''

"No need to go that far," I said hastily. "You've convinced me."

"Are you certain?"

"Absolutely. I think."

Merlin chuckled. "You remind me a bit of Modred," he said. "He never took anything on faith, either. It took Arthur an army to convince him, and he lost his life in the process. I hope I won't need to go to such lengths on your behalf."

"Well, it's all rather hard to take, you know," I said with classic understatement.

"I understand," said Merlin sympathetically. "A challenge to one's beliefs is always difficult to deal with. And if your reaction is typical of what I can expect, then I shall have my work cut out for me. You can see why I will need your help."

"I still don't understand exactly what it is you want me to do," I said. "I mean, why *me*? I'm no one special. I should think you'd want someone more important, more influential . . . someone in authority."

"Such a person would undoubtedly find me a threat to his authority," Merlin replied. "Important and influential individuals have their own vested interests at heart. No, you are the man for me, Thomas. You are the first one I saw when I awoke, and I believe it was an omen. Fate brought us together. You and I shall bring magic back into the world."

"But *how*?" I asked. "What do you propose to do, start some sort of school where people can take classes in Elementary Sorcery? Practice levitation and turn lead into gold for their homework assignments?"

"An excellent idea," Merlin said. "A school would enable apprentices to come to me, rather than my needing to seek them out. You see, Thomas, you are already proving your worth. Yes, a school, like your universities, where I can train sorcerers who can then go out and train others. I believe that is just the way to do it.''

"I was only joking," I said.

"Well, it's an excellent idea, just the same. We shall start a school. We must begin at once."

"Hold on," I said. "It isn't quite that simple, you know."

"Why not?"

"Well, for one thing, you would need a place to do it. I don't mean to sound inhospitable, but after all, this is my home. I can't have you bringing strangers in here to practice spells in my own living room."

"Quite so, quite so," said Merlin, nodding. "That would be an altogether unreasonable imposition and I would never think of asking it. I had thought we might obtain a building of some sort, something suitable with living quarters for the students, and for the serving staff, as well as kitchens, an alchemical laboratory, and perhaps a meeting hall . . .''

I laughed. "What about a swimming pool and a Jacuzzi? You have no idea what you're asking. Assuming you'd be lucky enough to find such a building, where would you find the money to pay for it? It would cost a fortune merely to pay for its upkeep, and you would still need to purchase supplies, and budget for the necessary funds to publicize the school, and pass various health and zoning inspections for the kitchens and the dormitories, and obtain certification and . . . oh, good Lord, I can't even believe I'm seriously having this conversation!"

"You seem somewhat less than enthusiastic about our prospects," Merlin said with a frown.

"Oh, it isn't that," I said with a sigh. "Quite the contrary. Half the time I'm convinced I'm dreaming all this, and the other half I'm having the most thrilling experience of my entire life. But things are nowhere near as simple as you seem to think they are. Everything's falling apart, for God's sake.

There's rioting in the streets. Society is breaking down. The whole bloody world is being plunged into a state of anarchy and suddenly you come along to announce that you're a two-thousand-year-old wizard who just woke up from a nap inside a tree to save the human race by opening a school for sorcerers. People will think you're absolutely cracked!''

"You don't seem to think so," he replied.

"I wouldn't be so sure. Perhaps I'm absolutely cracked, as well," I said. "For all I know, I've gone completely potty and I'm hallucinating all of this.''

"I think you know better than that," said Merlin.

"Well, perhaps I do, but I'm still only one person. You'll have to convince the entire world! Even if you do manage to pull it off somehow, we haven't even *begun* to consider the effect it would have!''

"You think it would be helpful to discuss it?" Merlin asked.

I snorted. "I wouldn't even know where to start!''

"I never claimed that it would be an easy task," said Merlin. "Clearly, the first thing we have to do is make my presence known, and convince people that I am precisely who I claim to be. We shall need to bring our message to as many people as we can, and as quickly as we can. Tell me, what do you think of my appearing on the television?''

"Television?" I said. "You want to go on *television?*''

"Why not?" he asked.

"Why *not?*" I said.

And then I thought, indeed, why not? It would be perfect. Once convinced that he was genuine, the media people would be tripping all over themselves to have a crack at him. He would be an absolute sensation. But would he be able to weather the resulting storm?

"How is it done?" he asked. "Would it be difficult to arrange?''

"Oh, it could be arranged easily enough, I suppose," I

replied, "but you have no idea what you'd be letting yourself in for."

"Will it not allow me to bring my message to many people at one time?"

"It'll do that, all right," I said. "It should be quite a memorable broadcast. But aren't you rushing things a bit? I mean, you *have* been asleep for about two thousand years." I shook my head. "Merely saying it sounds fantastic. Things have changed a great deal more than you may think. People have changed. You've got an awful lot of catching up to do."

"Perhaps," said Merlin, nodding in agreement. "I sensed how the world was changing while I remained imprisoned in the oak, and while I marveled at the visions that unfolded in my dreams, there is still much about this day and age I do not know or understand. However, I shall have you for my guide in that regard. Each of us shall teach the other."

"I don't think you have any idea what you're asking me to do," I said. "Lord knows, it's hard enough for me to accept who and what you are without trying to catch you up about two thousand years! It would be a massive undertaking, and one for which I'm hopelessly ill qualified."

"I am confident that you will do your best," said Merlin. "And you will find me a quick and eager student. Besides, as I have said, I do have some idea of what the modern world is like. What I require is advice and more detailed instruction. As we go out into the world, I shall be your apprentice, Thomas, and you shall be mine. It will be a partnership from which we both shall benefit."

"But what about my family?" I said. "Who will look after them while we're doing all this?"

"I told you, you need have no concern about your family. I shall see to it that they are well protected and provided for, I promise you."

"Not that I doubt your word, you understand," I said, "but would you mind telling me *how*?"

"A perfectly fair and reasonable question," he replied. "First, I shall devise a powerful warding spell that will protect this dwelling, and prevent anyone from entering with malicious intent. Next, I shall prepare protective charms for Jenny and both your daughters, to ward off harm when they venture from this dwelling. I shall also create a familiar to watch over them and see to their every need. For the present, I think that should suffice."

"A familiar?" I said, once again feeling a vague tug at some old memory from childhood. "What is that?"

Merlin shrugged. "It could be almost anything. Well perhaps not. We should give some thought to that. It should be the sort of familiar your family would feel comfortable with. Have you a dog?"

"No, we have no pets," I said, having no idea what he meant. Surely, he didn't think some sort of guard dog would answer to the need?

"No, dog, eh?" Merlin said, stroking his beard thoughtfully.

"The girls always wanted one, but we never could afford it," I said. "Even a stray dog would need to be fed, and things being as they are . . . Well, it would only be an added burden. Besides a dog would hardly provide adequate protection these days."

"Well, put it out of your mind for the present," he replied. "I shall give some thought to the matter while I work on the protective charms. As for the warding spell, we can see to that at once."

"*We*?" I said, somewhat hesitantly.

"A warding spell is a relatively simple thing," said Merlin, "and it would make as good a point as any to begin your education. Why not call Jenny and the girls? They can assist us and lend their energies to the task."

"Is . . . uh . . . is it safe?" I asked uncertainly.

"I would never expose your family to any danger," Merlin

reassured me. "I think they will find the process both fascinating and enjoyable."

I went to fetch Jenny and the girls, who hardly needed any encouragement to drop their lessons and play with Uncle Merlin. They came bounding in like kittens, anxious to fly around the room once more. However, much to their disappointment, Merlin refused to oblige them. When their faces fell and they began to whine petulantly, he held up an admonishing finger and they fell silent instantly, an act of obedience they'd never given quite so readily to either Jenny or myself. I had no idea how he did it.

"Now let us understand one thing," their Uncle Merlin told them. "Magic is not to be employed for the purposes of play or amusement. It is not something to be taken lightly. I know that you enjoyed your brief experience as birds, but beyond that enjoyment, what was it you learned?"

Our daughters screwed their faces up in concentration. Then, finally, Christine hit upon the answer. "To always think for ourselves, and not to think a thing is true merely because someone said it was."

"Very good," said Merlin, patting her on the head. "That was the purpose of the lesson. Now in this case, the lesson happened to have been enjoyable. But remember that not all lessons are enjoyable. Some are learned with difficulty and great hardship. And once a lesson has been learned, there should be no need to repeat it. Now, we are about to have our second lesson. Are your prepared to learn it?"

They both nodded expectantly while Jenny glanced at me nervously. I merely nodded, as if I knew what in bloody hell was going on, though I felt no such security.

"Your father and I have a great deal of work to do," said Merlin, "important work that may take us from you for some periods of time. Therefore, what we are going to do is weave a spell that will protect this home while your father and I are away. We shall all do it together. Would you like to help me weave a magic spell?"

They responded eagerly, and Merlin proceeded to tell them what to do.

"We shall require certain things to weave the spell," he said. He turned to Jenny. "Have you any candles?"

Jenny said we did, and started to get them, but Merlin stopped her and suggested that Michelle bring the candles. Each of us would take part in assembling the ingredients of the spell and, in this way, we would all bring a part of ourselves to the process, thereby imbuing it with our energies, whatever in hell that meant. Michelle complied eagerly, pleased to be given the responsibility. In this manner, each of us was given a part to play.

Jenny brought a mirror from our bedroom. Christine brought a small saucepan from the kitchen, and a cup which would be used to keep some salt in. After fetching the candles, Michelle was directed to bring Merlin a goblet. The closest thing we possessed to a goblet was a simple drinking glass, but Merlin pronounced that it would do. My task was to prepare some herbs, which were readily available from our pantry, as Jenny grew and dried them for use in seasoning our food. I ground up the herbs and mixed them together under Merlin's direction, preparing an incense into which he mixed some of his tobacco, to help it burn.

At his request, Jenny brought him a curved steel knife with a plain, unfinished, wooden handle, which she used in the garden, and I was directed to fetch a knife with a black handle, preferably a double-edged one. This proved to be an easy task, as I had a number of such knives, combat blades I carried either in my boot or in a sheath clipped to my belt. I brought Merlin my entire collection, and he chose a dagger with an eight-inch blade that tapered to a sharp point. It had a knobbed steel pommel, the better to crush skulls with, and a serrated, steel crossguard. Altogether, it was a rather nasty and serious piece of work, and I wondered, with some anxiety, what role it was meant to play in what we were about to do. My curiosity did not long go unabated.

With the help of Jenny and the girls, Merlin cleared the table and covered it with a fresh cloth, a red one, as it happened, though he claimed the color made no difference. Then, he had each of us arrange the items we had brought upon the table top, in a certain order. He had us specifically arrange these things so that, as he sat facing them, he sat facing to the north. Farthest from him, he had Jenny place one candle in a brass holder to his left, and another he had me place to his right. Christine was directed to place the saucepan in the center, slightly ahead of the candles. In front of the candle to his left, Merlin had Christine place the "goblet," the drinking glass which she had filled with water. Across from it, to his right, and in front of the second candle, he placed a cup, into which he poured some salt.

The center of the table was to remain bare, but before him, where his plate would be if he were sitting down to dine, he placed the two knives, points facing away from him and angled inward, so that they formed a triangle with no base. That done, he nodded, apparently satisfied with the arrangement, and bid us all to take our seats around the table.

"Now," he said, "so that no one will feel apprehensive, I will explain what we have done, and what we are about to do. And I do mean *we*, for we are going to do it all together. First of all, there is no need to feel frightened or apprehensive. I know that many tales have been told over the years about how magic is derived from unholy rites, and pacts with demons, and all that sort of nonsense. However, nonsense is exactly what it is."

He turned to the girls and smiled. "Have you girls ever wished for something very hard, and then had it come true?"

They both nodded.

"Well, think of magic the same way. Now, perhaps the thing you wished for came true merely because it just happened to turn out that way. But perhaps it came true because you wished for it so very hard. Who can say for certain? Making magic work is just like wishing for something very hard. You may think of a wizard as someone who is very good at wishing. But, of course, it is not really quite that simple. You have to know just how to wish, and you have to do it in a special way, depending on what you are wishing for. That is what we are going to do right now. We are going to wish for something in a special way and, by doing so, make magic. You understand?''

I realized that his comments, while phrased for the benefit of our young daughters, were equally meant for Jenny and myself. Jenny realized it also, for we all nodded together. We said nothing, because despite Merlin's bantering, paternal tone, we were still somehow impressed with the solemnity of the occasion. We are going to do magic, I thought, and ridiculously—or perhaps, not so ridiculously—I felt an anticipatory thrill not unlike that which I had experienced as a child on Christmas morning.

''Now in order to wish for something in a special way, the way we're going to do in order to make magic,'' Merlin continued, ''it helps to have certain things that will serve to focus our attention and our energies on what we have to do. That is what we have done here. What we have constructed here,'' he indicated the table before us, ''is called an altar.''

''You mean, like in church?'' asked Michelle.

''No, not really, this one is different,'' Merlin said.

''Is it holy?'' asked Michelle again.

''That depends on what you mean, Michelle,'' he said. ''It's not the same as the altar in a Christian church, you understand, but we will use it in a ritual, just as there are rituals in church. You see, long before there was a Christian church, some people worshipped in this way, with an altar much like this.''

''But this isn't a *real* altar,'' Christine said, emboldened by her little sister's questions. ''These are just things we had around the house. It's like a play altar.'' She frowned. ''Isn't that wrong?''

Jenny glanced at me uneasily, then looked to Merlin. It

seemed that we could be treading on delicate ground here. However, Merlin took the question in stride.

"It would be wrong if we were making fun of an altar in a Christian church," he said, "or perhaps pretending this was an altar in a Christian church, but that is not what we are doing. Do you have any friends who are not Christian?"

"Yes," said Michelle, "there's Michael. He's Jewish. And he doesn't go to church. He goes to temple."

"Well, a temple is a little like a church, is it not?" said Merlin. "Only it's a different faith, a different religion, is that not so?"

The girls both nodded. It was, I think, the first time we had ever discussed comparative theology in our home, and I was following the discussion with interest, while at the same time feeling somewhat guilty that we had never really talked about such things before. The girls had questions, but I'd had little in the way of answers. I felt envious of how easily and naturally Merlin seemed to be going about it. Not bad for someone who'd slept through most of human history, I thought.

"Well, this is like a different religion," Merlin said. "In fact, once it was a very important religion."

"What was it called?" asked Michelle.

"It was called many different things," said Merlin. "Some people called it the Craft, some people called it Wicca, while others called it witchcraft."

"Witchcraft!" said Christine. "You mean like the witches in stories who fly about on brooms and cast evil spells?"

"No, not at all like that," said Merlin. "Those stories were made up by people who thought witches were bad. Sometimes people make up stories about other people whom they do not like. Some people respect what others believe and some do not. Some people think the way they believe is the only right way, and that everyone who does not believe the way they do is wrong. You mentioned your friend, who is Jewish."

"Michael," said Michelle.

"Yes, Michael," Merlin said, nodding. "You don't think Michael is wrong in being Jewish, do you? It is as right for him to be Jewish as it is for you to be Christian, is it not? We could say that you are all right, only in different ways. What is right for each person is what matters."

"What were witches really like?" Christine asked. "What was right for them?"

"Probably much the same things that are right for you," said Merlin, "only they went about the way they did things in slightly different ways. You see, the word 'witch' comes from the word 'Wicca,' which is a very old word that means 'to bend.' And witches were said to have the ability to bend the ways of nature, though that wasn't quite correct. The truth is they were wise in the ways of nature, and able to bend *with* it. They loved nature, and respected it. They knew how to make medicines from plants, and how to foretell what the weather was going to be from watching how animals behaved, and how to help babies be born. People often came to them for advice."

"What about magic?" asked Michelle.

"Yes, they knew about magic, too," said Merlin, "and what we are about to do is just the sort of thing that witches did once, many years ago. Now, each of these things before us has a purpose. Think of this candle to my left as being a symbol of all in nature that is female, and think of this candle on my right as being a symbol of all in nature that is male. In this way, we achieve an harmonious balance, you see, and balance is everything in magic."

"What's the saucepan for?" Christine asked.

"The saucepan is our cauldron," Merlin said. "Granted, it does not look much like a cauldron, but for our purposes, it will serve. In it, we will burn our incense, which shall symbolize the sweetness of the air we breathe."

"What about the cup with the salt in it?" Michelle asked.

"The salt shall symbolize the earth," said Merlin, "and the drinking glass, our goblet, contains the water, which, of course, shall represent the life-giving element of water in the lakes and oceans of the world, and in the rain that falls to make things grow. Therefore, as you can see, we have the four elements of nature, earth, air, fire, and water."

"What are the knives for?" asked Christine.

"Ah, the knives are most important," Merlin said. "They are our tools, you see. This knife, with the plain wood handle, is our bolline, which is used for the cutting of herbs, and inscribing symbols, and so forth. A purely practical tool, in other words, used for the same sort of things that any ordinary knife is used for. This black-handled knife, however, is our athame, and it is very different. From the moment we consecrate it to its purpose, it shall be used *only* for that purpose, and never again for any other thing."

"What *is* its purpose?" asked Michelle

"I was just about to tell you," Merlin said. "Be patient. All shall be made clear. This knife shall be our magic wand. Sometimes an actual wand is used, cut from willow, oak, or cherry wood, and sometimes wizards have made very fancy wands indeed, but a plain one will do just as well. You will notice that I carry a plain, knotty, wooden staff, which I use as both my wand and as my walking stick. Sometimes, instead of a wand, a sword is used, because a blade has always been considered an object of great power, and it looks impressive, too. However, a knife is much more convenient to hold than a sword, and it will serve as well."

"Why must the handle be black?" Jenny asked.

"An excellent question," Merlin said. "It is because white is a color that reflects, while black is a color that absorbs, and the athame is meant to absorb and store the power of whomever wields it. We shall use it to absorb our power, then release it as we direct. Now, it is best for us to work our spell in darkness, or dim light, so that our thoughts and energies may be better focused. So, Thomas, if you will be so kind as to pull the drapes, we shall begin."

# CHAPTER

**"Y**ou mean that's all there is to it?" asked Christine.
"Yes," said Merlin. "Why, you did not think it
was sufficient?"

"Well, no, but . . . I just thought there would be something
more," she said, sounding a little disappointed.

To be honest, I was a bit disappointed myself, though at the
same time, I felt somewhat relieved. I hadn't really known
what to expect, but it certainly wasn't the simple sort of ceremony we'd just taken part in.

After I had pulled the drapes, Merlin asked Jenny to light the
candles, then he himself ignited the incense. As we all stood
around the table, Merlin picked up the saucepan containing the
incense and walked around us, in a clockwise circle around the
table, explaining that this was done to purify the space where we
had gathered in our circle. That done, he returned to his place,
put down the saucepan with the burning incense, and picked up
the black-handled knife, or the athame, as he called it. As he
explained what he was doing, he asked us all to think about it, to
concentrate our thoughts upon the task that was being performed, and to think of that task as being accomplished when it

was done. He consecrated the knife by simply placing it in the center of the table and sprinkling it first with a pinch of salt, and then with a few drops of water from the "goblet."

He then passed the blade through the smoke rising from the incense and held it up ceremoniously, resting across both his palms. This accomplished, he then used the knife to consecrate the other objects on our altar, touching each item lightly with its blade, and asking us to think of the object touched as being purified. When this was done, he took the mirror Jenny had brought from our bedroom and placed it in the center of the table.

He then picked up the athame in his right hand and held it before him, blade pointing upwards, asking us to concentrate upon the blade, and think about sending our energies into it. Then he "drew" the circle with the blade, walking around the table with it, once again in a clockwise direction, pointing the blade at the floor and drawing an imaginary circle all around us. While he did so, he asked us to think about the circle being drawn, and to visualize it in our minds as if we could actually see it. Inside the circle, he explained, we were now protected, and in a place of peace.

Taking his place once more, he said that we would now invoke the energies of earth, air, fire, and water, and in order to do so, all that was necessary was to invite their symbolic spirits to attend us in our circle. He faced to the north, and said, "Spirit of the North, Spirit of Earth, we ask that you attend our circle." Then he had Christine face to the east and invoke the Spirit of Air, and when she had done so, he asked Michelle to face to the south and invoke the Spirit of Fire. Jenny was then requested to face the west and invoke the Spirit of Water, which she did, quite solemnly, getting into the spirit of the thing, no pun intended.

Merlin then pronounced that the circle was complete, and we all joined hands and closed our eyes as he asked us to think about our energies flowing from one to the other of us, going around in a clockwise circle.

"As you feel the energy enter into you," he said, "send it on, giving it a little nudge of your own, and imagine it going round and round, growing stronger and stronger as it continues to flow around the circle."

Under any other circumstances, I suppose I would have felt a little foolish engaged in such an exercise, which seemed like no more than a child's game, but I had seen my daughters levitated, the kitchen come to life, and the pantry miraculously stocked with enough supplies to last us for weeks. Had Merlin claimed we could invoke the shade of Father Christmas by singing, "Ring Around the Roses," I would have been tempted to believe him. However, nothing quite so terribly dramatic occurred.

As we stood there with our hands joined, and I visualized our energies flowing around us, it did seem to me as if I felt *something* passing through me, something warm and pleasant and indefinable, though of course that could be rationalized away as wishful thinking. But then, according to Merlin, that's just what magic was—wishful thinking. After a few moments of this silent energy transference, Merlin pronounced that we were ready to proceed.

He took the mirror and held it before him at about chest level, with the mirror facing away from him, toward the candle flames. As he slowly walked around the circle, he asked us to watch the mirror and see the candle flames reflected there, and to imagine that as the mirror reflected the light of the candle flames, so all evil would be reflected from our home. And he had us chant together:

"Candle flames in mirror bright,
banish evil from our sight.
Earth and Water, Fire and Air,
Free this dwelling of despair.
Let not evil's slightest trace
enter on this peaceful place.
Grant the wish that we desire,
Air and Water, Earth and Fire."

As we chanted, we made several circuits of the circle with our hands joined, except for Merlin, of course, who was holding the mirror, and thus had to hook elbows with us. It was exactly like "Ring Around The Roses," in fact. We moved faster and faster, and I lost count of how many times we went around, but when we were through, Merlin replaced the mirror in the center of the table, then had us all join hands once more and imagine a feeling of warmth, security, and happiness flowing through us and throughout every corner of our home.

The spirits of the four quarters were then thanked for their presence in our circle and bid to depart in peace, then Merlin took the athame and cleared the circle, "cutting" it with the knife as he walked around the table once again, and the simple ritual was done. There had been no pyrotechnics, or levitations, or disembodied voices, nothing, in fact, that seemed very magical at all.

"You expected something more spectacular, is that it?" Merlin asked Christine. "Something wondrous?"

"Well . . . I suppose so," she replied, trying unsuccessfully to hide her disappointment.

"You know what is the most wondrous thing in all the universe, Christine?" he asked.

"No, what?"

"Your life. The power that makes you live and breathe, the power that makes you wonder, and ask questions, and think for yourself. That is the greatest power in all the universe, Christine, and it is within *you*. And you have just used that power to help weave a spell that will keep this home and all within it safe from harm. It is now a secure and peaceful place, and all who enter it shall feel warm, happy, and contented. And, with a little help from your mother, your father, and your sister, and of course, with a little help from me, *you* have done it. Now what could be more wondrous than that?"

"*I* thought it was wondrous," said Michelle. "And it was fun, too! Especially the chanting part. Could we do it again?"

"No, once was sufficient," Merlin said. "And now that we are finished, you can help put everything away in its proper place, then run along and play so that your parents and I may discuss some matters of importance."

After we had settled down in the living room and Merlin had his pipe going once again, I ventured a reaction to our little ceremony. "I must admit feeling somewhat like Christine," I said. "It wasn't quite what I expected."

"Umm. You would have felt better if I'd conjured up a demon, or flashed a few lightning bolts about?"

"No, I don't think I would have cared for that particularly, but . . . well, it's rather hard to believe that what we just did will actually accomplish anything. Not that I'm questioning your word, you understand," I added hastily, "but . . . well, no offense, but it did seem a bit childish."

"I thought it was rather poignant," Jenny said, "simple and touching, and quite spiritual in its own way."

"Very nicely put," said Merlin. "You see, Thomas, you are missing the point. The point of the whole thing was to perform a ritual that your entire family could become involved in, thereby imbuing the spell with their personal energies. I could certainly have done something much more dramatic, such as making the energy aura visible or having the circle glow or burn with flame. However, I did not think the girls would have responded well to that, and the simple truth is that magic does not need to be visibly dramatic. It only needs to be effective."

"Perhaps," I said, "but if you expect to convince a television audience, then I'd suggest you consider something more dramatic than a simple pagan ritual. People have seen that sort of thing before, you know. Some years ago, there was quite a revival in pagan spirituality, and though it's not quite as common today, we still have so-called 'witches' who gather in covens, take off all their clothes and prance about while chanting various bits of doggerel. Of course, it's all a load of non-sense and no one takes it very seriously."

"In every load of nonsense, there is always at least one grain of truth," said Merlin. "And who are you to say what is nonsense? Magic does not require nakedness, but if some people find it helps them, then I see no harm in it. As for the chanting, the chants themselves are not important. They are merely a means of helping focus one's energy, which is the purpose of the ritual, as well. In itself, a ritual accomplishes nothing, and if one merely goes through the motions, it is absolutely useless. An advanced adept can easily do without rituals or chants, though such things can be comforting. Mor-ganna was quite fond of chants, for instance, but she had no need of them. She was powerful enough to cast a spell with a mere glance or gesture."

"Morganna?" I said. "You mean Morgan le Fay?" It still seemed fantastic that these legendary characters had actually existed, and that two thousand some odd years after they had lived, I was speaking with a man who'd known them all.

Merlin grunted. "Yes, Morgan le Fay, as she so styled her-self, the ungrateful, manipulative, little vixen. Lacked the spine to confront me herself, so she employed guile, deceit, and trickery, the traditional weapons of a woman."

"I think you may find that women have changed a great deal, along with the times," Jenny said.

"Have they? For the better or for the worse?"

"I suppose that depends on your perspective," she replied.

"A most feminine reply," Merlin said, "which is to say, an elusive one. Might I ask you to elaborate upon it?"

"Well, if you believe that women are secondary in status and importance to men," said Jenny, "and that their proper place is in subservience to males, then you will find that things have changed considerably for the worse."

"I see," said Merlin. "Well, in truth, I have never believed that a woman's place was merely to serve man, else I would never have taken on Morganna as a pupil. And anyone who believes that women of my time were subservient should have met Guinevere. Nevertheless, I must apologize for my remark, for I did not mean to give offense. I confess to a certain bitterness in that regard.''

"Apology accepted," my wife said with a smile.

Merlin grunted. "Most gracious of you. Now what was I speaking of?"

"The purposes of chants and rituals," I said.

"Ah, yes, quite so. They might seem foolish or nonsensical, or even childish, and yet that is their very virtue. Children follow rituals in their play, and they often employ some form of chanting. It is often spontaneous, and what arises from it is a sort of power, which can either result in heightened feelings of joy or, as in the case where chanting is employed to tease someone, an energy directed against the object of their scorn.''

"Well, no one likes being teased," I said. "I don't know that I'd consider that a projection of power."

"No?" said Merlin. "Then consider what would make you feel worse, if one person heaped scorn upon you, or if a dozen people did it all at once?"

"Having a dozen people do it would be worse, of course," I said, "but that's merely a matter of degree."

"Precisely," Merlin said. "A dozen people together can project more energy than one person by himself. Unless, of course, that one person is a powerful adept.''

I shrugged. "It sounds like a mere matter of semantics to me.''

"Semantics?"

"Playing with words."

"You fool," said Merlin.

He said it simply, in a perfectly calm and ordinary tone of voice, and yet suddenly I felt as stung as if he'd slapped me. My initial response was shock that he should say that, and then I felt myself flush deeply, and a profound feeling of pain and humiliation overwhelmed me such as I hadn't felt since I was scolded by my father as a child. I heard Jenny draw her breath in sharply, and I found I could not look at her, nor look Merlin in the face. I did not feel anger, I just felt extremely hurt.

"Forgive me, Thomas," Merlin said soothingly. "I did not really mean that. You are not a fool, of course, but you were being obstinate again and I thought a small demonstration might be instructive. I do not play with words, for I know that words can be powerful things, especially when used by an adept."

I simply stared at him, "You mean . . ."

"Consider the words I used," said Merlin. "Two very simple words. 'You fool.' By themselves, they may produce differing results. They might induce anger, or mere irritation, or embarrassment . . . it depends on who says them and how they are said, of course, but also on the directed energy behind them. I made a point of saying them in a very calm and offhand manner, but I directed enough energy behind them to produce the effect that you experienced. Forgive me, I know it was unpleasant, but I needed to make my point."

"You made it, all right," I said. "A policeman, of necessity, learns to be thick-skinned, yet for a moment, I felt on the verge of tears." I shook my head. "I wouldn't have thought mere words could do that to me."

"Mere *words* did not," said Merlin. "You are still missing the point. Why is it that one person may say something to another and produce little or no reaction, while another person might say the very same thing and reduce someone to tears? Why is it that one person giving a speech might fail to move a crowd, while another giving the same speech can incite that same crowd to riot? Is it simply that the second person is a better speaker, or is it that there is a force of personality behind the speech? And, if so, what is the *nature* of that force if not directed energy?"

"I concede your point," I said, still smarting from his demonstrative rebuke, even though I knew he didn't really mean it. The effect had been unsettling, to say the least.

"The Wiccan ritual, or faith, or philosophy, call it what you will," said Merlin, "bears the same relationship to magic as learning how to crawl does to walking and then running, which is not to say that it possesses no validity, merely that it is only a beginning. The many cultures of the world have all had their different systems of belief, but in essence, they might all be considered as paths leading to a common destination."

"Who would have guessed that Merlin the Magician was a Unitarian?" I said with a grin.

"Unitarian?" said Merlin.

"Never mind," I said. "It was just a joke."

"How would you define that common destination?" Jenny asked, with a sour glance at me.

"As the ultimate realization of the Craft," he said, "a union of the rationally developed mind with the full capacity latent in the spirit."

"It sounds as if you're speaking of Zen," said Jenny.

"Ah, yes, indeed," Merlin said, nodding.

"You know about Zen Buddhism?" I asked, with some surprise.

"I am aware of the teachings of Gautama Buddha," Merlin said, "though perhaps, in this case, I should say those of his disciple, Bodhidharma, who founded the Zen philosophy. They came before my time, after all, and I have always sought to study the ideas of prophets and philosophers. Knowledge of other lands was difficult to come by in my day, but there were ways to seek it out if you took the trouble. In the teachings of the Buddha, I found much of value, yet I disagreed with the principle of rejecting the material world as a place of pain and suffering, meant only to be transcended for some higher realm. It is not the material world that must be transcended, but our own material limitations. Most of the religious prophets of the world have taught that the ultimate realization of the soul's potential is to be found in some other world that exists on a spiritual plane, when in fact, it can be found in this one, if we but learn to tap the undeveloped powers of our minds.''

"I take it back," I said to Jenny. "He's not a unitarian, he's a parapsychologist."

Merlin raised his eyebrows. "Explain, please."

"The study of what is called the paranormal," she replied, giving me a dirty look. "Mind over matter, telepathy . . . that is, communication by thought . . . telekinesis, which is the power to move objects with one's mind, extrasensory perception, which includes things such as the ability to see into the future, and having prophetic dreams, and deducing things about a person you've never met from an object that had been in that person's possession. . . . Parapsychology is the study of such phenomena."

"Indeed?" said Merlin with surprise. "And these things are seriously studied in this day and age?"

"Well, to say that they are studied seriously might be somewhat misleading," I said. "That is, they've been studied in the past, but given the present state of things, I doubt much research is going on today. As to how seriously they were studied, it would be difficult to say. There were supposedly some serious scientific studies, but I don't believe any of them produced anything conclusive. And there were all sorts of groups devoted to such research, only I'm not sure how seriously they were regarded. They were not generally regarded very seriously by the scientific establishment, which dismissed such things as being either fraudulent or the results of coincidence."

"Still, a lot of people believe in the paranormal," said Jenny. "And not, it would appear, without some justification," she added, with a significant glance at me. I knew that I was misbehaving, but I couldn't seem to help myself. The situation was so bizarre and fantastic, it was almost comical. How often does one sit down to discuss such things as Zen and ESP with an honest-to-God sorcerer?

"So then the interest exists," said Merlin. "I find that highly encouraging."

"You may find it less encouraging after you've had contact with some of those people," I said, "as you undoubtedly will, if you go on television. They'll come crawling out of the woodwork by the dozens."

"And this is not a thing to be desired?" Merlin asked.

"I'll leave you to judge that for yourself," I said. "But the main thing I think you need to realize is that what you'll be saying will fly in the face of everything that is commonly accepted as reality. The very fact that you are who you are will be difficult enough for most people to accept, without your contradicting the entire scientific establishment and most of the world's faiths. People will probably sit still for your telling them that scientists haven't got a clue as to how the world really works, because most people neither like nor understand scientists to begin with, but when you go contradicting their religion, they'll want to burn you at the stake."

"They still do such things?" asked Merlin with concern.

"Not literally," said Jenny.

"No, they simply ostracize you, or dismiss you as a crackpot, or perhaps, in an extreme case, they shoot you," I said. "I don't suppose you're impervious to bullets?"

"Ah, yes, these projectile weapons I saw in my dreams," said Merlin. He shrugged. "Merely a more efficient way of throwing rocks."

"You can dodge a rock," I pointed out, "but I doubt even you are fast enough to dodge a bullet." I hesitated. "I assume you *can* be killed?"

"Of course," said Merlin. "I am a wizard, Thomas, not a god. I am flesh and blood, just as you are. And I realize there may be those who would consider me a threat and would wish to eliminate that threat. It was so in the past, and I expect it will be so in the present.''

''Well, just remember that bullets aren't broadswords,'' I said.

''I shall remember that,'' he said. ''However, while I may indeed contradict the teachings of your scientists, I have no intention of attacking anyone's faith. It is not salvation in the next world that I am seeking, but a more practical salvation in this one.''

''I don't think I'd put it quite that way, if I were you,'' I said. ''That's liable to be misconstrued.''

''Perhaps,'' said Merlin. ''I shall choose my words more carefully, and try them out on you before I say them on the television. Then you can advise me if you see any flaw in them.''

I sighed and glanced at Jenny. ''He really thinks it's that simple,'' I said, shaking my head.

''Is there some flaw in my reasoning?'' he asked.

''It isn't that,'' I said. ''It's just that . . . well, how shall I put it? Media people, that is to say, television interviewers and reporters, are quite good at making people say things they don't really mean to say, and making them look foolish. They thrive on controversy and sensationalism. They'll say something like, 'Is it true you cheated on your wife?' No matter how you answer that, they can make you look bad. If you say no, then they'll report that you've denied cheating on your wife, which is factually true, but still creates an impression of guilt, if you see what I mean.''

''I see,'' said Merlin. ''We had such people in my day, as well. They usually became royal ministers. Never fear, Thomas, I shall not allow them to put words into my mouth. I will trust the people to judge the truth of my assertions for themselves.''

There was simply no dissuading him. He was determined to appear on television, which had absolutely fascinated him, and nothing I could say would convince him he should put it off until he'd had more time to acclimate himself to the tumultuous world of the late twenty-second century. It would remain for that world to acclimate itself to him.

Arranging a television booking for a two-thousand-year-old sorcerer turned out to be a bit more difficult than I had thought. Naturally, I called the BBC first, but didn't get very far before they hung up on me. I then tried several of the news programs directly, including CNN, and they all hung up on me, as well. Obviously, they thought I was some sort of crackpot or someone trying to play a silly joke. That left me with my court of last resort, the chat shows.

I should probably explain that television programming was very different during the time of the Collapse then it is now. Today, there is a great deal of programming to choose from, both from the government-supported and the independent stations, as well as the various cable networks. There are variety shows, and situation comedies, musical programs, anthology shows, drama, cop shows, daytime serials, films, and sports, you name it. There's something for every taste. Not so during the Collapse.

Novelists and screenwriters these days are fond of portraying the period as something similar to a post-holocaust scenario, and while there is some truth in these fanciful depictions, the fact is that everything did not come abruptly grinding to a halt, leaving a world of perpetual darkness in which street gangs and commando forces battled, and everyone walked about in rags, or castoff bits of clothing assembled to appear like some sort of piratical ensemble. True, there were many homeless, often living in rusted and abandoned vehicles, and there was much rioting and looting. Street gangs and police did frequently battle in the streets, and the crime rate was higher than at any other time in living memory. However, there was electrical power available, although with frequent blackouts, and newspapers struggled to put out if not daily, then at least weekly editions, and the radio and television stations continued their broadcasts, though much of the time they were either blacked out due to power failures or the broadcast consisted of the legend "Technical Difficulties" appearing on the screen.

Society was breaking down, yet like a punch-drunk heavy-weight, it continued stumbling along, often held up by nothing more than diminishing inertia. Life during that time was much like tending to some vast and ancient machine, held together by little more than spit and baling wire. Something would let go, and there would be a rush to mend it, and while one breakdown was being tended to, a dozen other malfunctions would occur. Yet, despite the seeming hopelessness of it all, the tenders of this aging and broken-down machine kept to their task like relentless worker ants, for there was simply nothing else to do. The pressure was too great for many of them. The suicide rate had risen exponentially and breakdowns, such as that suffered by poor James Whitby, were endemic. And for all too many people, there was little or no hope at all.

For a large segment of the population, those who still had homes or were not reduced to living in burned-out or aban-doned buildings without power, television became a vital life-line to whatever fragile fabric of reality they still possessed. It was like a drug, both a painkiller and an aphrodisiac, a cheap hallucinogen that granted blissful, merciful escape from the dreary hopelessness of their lives. People became very stressed during the frequent blackouts, terrified the set wouldn't come back on, and they would part with almost any-thing before they gave up their precious telly. Even those who had no power in their homes, and did without such luxuries as telephones and heat and working plumbing, often went hun-gry to purchase batteries for their small, portable TV's at incredibly inflated prices. And the programming they had to choose from was dictated by the times.

Gone were the elaborate productions, save for reruns of old programs and films. Only those shows cheapest to produce were aired, and this meant newscasts, the ubiquitous game shows, which had gained more allure than ever in such trying times, and, of course, the chat shows. They had become the dominant form of programming, from "electronic ministries" featuring fire and brimstone preachers to various interview programs. The basest of these were sensationalistic, prurient, muck-raking purveyors of sleaze, and they were, of course, the most popular. And among the hosts of these so-called "issue-oriented" programs, no one was more popular than Billy Martens.

The program was always opened with stimulating, staccato music and a flashing video montage of Martens, sartorially elegant, darkly handsome and whipcord slim, interviewing guests, alternately showcasing his many moods. Here he was, being charming, now here's a shot of him being confrontational, followed by one of Martens expressing outrage, then mirth, then a salacious leer, then anger, and finally a pose reminiscent of an old American recruiting poster, with Martens looking stern and pointing at the camera with his forefinger. Over this, a stentorian announcer would intone, "It's the *Billy Martens Show*! And now, ladies and gentlemen, it's time once again to meet the host of our program . . ." (cue applause from the studio audience) "*Billy Martens!*"

Martens would saunter out from backstage, nodding to the crew and shaking hands with members of the audience, one of whom, sitting in the front row, would hand him his microphone, and the camera would zoom in for a tight close-up of Martens looking earnest as he announced what the theme of that day's program would be. Child prostitutes. Vigilante squads. Housewives who traded illicit sex for food and clothing. Apocalyptic prophets who proclaimed that the Collapse was merely the first stage of the Second Coming. Some hapless, lower-echelon, government bureaucrat delivered up as a scapegoat for whatever new disaster had befallen the city. Satan worshippers . . . and a two-thousand-year-old sorcerer who had once been the court wizard to King Arthur.

Oh, yes, the Martens show would be only too happy to have Merlin on. What was his last name, you say? Ambrosia? Well, whatever. And he claims to be what? Marvelous! And you say he levitates things? Casts spells? Really? Stupendous! When can he come in for a pre-interview with our staff? Will he be able to levitate something in the office? Does he wear a robe and a pointy hat and all? Oh, good, wonderful, wonderful! How soon can he come in?

I made the appointment and hung up the phone with a weary sigh of resignation. Merlin seemed quite pleased.

"Excellent," he said. "We seem to be making progress."

"I wouldn't exactly call the *Billy Martens Show* progress," I replied.

"You think we could have made a better choice? " he said.

"There *was* no other choice. No one else was even remotely interested. Not that I can blame them. When I listened to myself trying to tell them about you, I realized I sounded like a complete lunatic. Fortunately, or unfortunately, as the case may be, that doesn't seem to bother Mr. Martens."

"It is but a beginning, Thomas," Merlin said. "We must start somewhere."

"Have you ever *seen* the *Billy Martens Show*?"

"No, it was not one of those I watched," he said. "When is it on?"

I glanced at my watch. "In about two hours, assuming there's no blackout."

"Then I shall make a point of watching it," he said.

"Good idea. There's still time to back out."

"I have no intention of backing out, Thomas," he said. "You say that many people watch this Billy Martens?"

"Thousands," I replied. "Hundreds of thousands. Millions. There's no accounting for taste."

"Well, then it is the very thing we need," he said.

Somehow, I wasn't getting through to him. I liked the old chap, and I had come to believe in him, and in what he was trying to accomplish. I had been skeptical at first, but my skepticism had disappeared completely. I had seen him do astonishing things, miraculous things, and my natural, human tendency to rationalize these things away had never really manifested itself, except in the most superficial way. Perhaps I was prepared to believe because I'd been through an emotional wringer and was ready to grasp at straws, to accept anything that seemed to offer the hope of a better world. However, I think it was more than that. My wife was an intelligent, sophisticated woman, and she believed in him, as well. That same effect would later be experienced by everyone who was exposed to him for any length of time. However, I was yet to discover this phenomenon. It was all so new, and it had all happened so quickly, that I hadn't much time to question my own responses.

I saw his determination to go through with it, and I felt the need to warn him about what was almost certainly going to happen. Billy Martens would try to make a fool of him for the amusement of his audience, and I was concerned about what the consequences might be.

"Look," I said, "I don't think you fully comprehend what it is I'm trying to say. You've never seen the *Billy Martens Show*. We're going to watch it in a little while, and perhaps then you'll understand. He's not a very pleasant man. In fact, he's slime. His only concern is entertaining the audience, most of whom are not much better, and he'll do it at your expense."

"I see," said Merlin. "Much like a court jester."

"Not a bad analogy," I said, "except he's probably far worse. What I mean is, he's almost certainly going to make fun of you, and you'll be on his home ground. Now, I don't really know how you react to such things, but . . . well, how shall I put it?"

"You are concerned that I may lose my temper?" Merlin said.

"Uh . . . well . . . yes, frankly. I mean, if you were to harm him in any way, it would be, uh . . . counterproductive."

He smiled. "You may rest easy, Thomas. I can promise you that I shall not lose my temper, and I shall not cause him any harm. I appreciate your concern on my behalf. We will watch the Billy Martens Show together, and I will form my own assessment of him, keeping your remarks in mind, and then I shall listen to any suggestions you may have as to how we should proceed."

I still did not feel very reassured, but there was not much else to say. We watched the show together when it came on, and though I no longer remember what his "theme" was that day, I do recall Merlin's reaction to the program. He sat through the whole thing silently, merely pursing his lips and nodding every now and then, and when it was over, he cleared his throat, turned to me, and said, "I now see what you meant. He is an obnoxious, loathsome person. Utterly vile. He deserves to be strung up by his thumbs."

"Now remember, you promised . . ." I said.

"And I shall keep my word," Merlin replied. "Never fear, Thomas. Billy Martens is not nearly as formidable as you imagine. I know just how to handle him."

"Yes," I said. "That's just what I'm afraid of."

# CHAPTER
# 5

**B**illy Martens was much too shrewd to air his programs live. The shows were all taped in advance, which gave him the control of editing and allowed him to rebroadcast programs later if there was a blackout. If Martens had his way, the tape of Merlin's appearance on his program would probably have been burned. However, Martens was dealing with a sorcerer, and Merlin was not someone to be bullied.

In later years, after he had become a well-known and influential broadcasting executive, Martens told a very different version of the story, in which he took credit for bringing Merlin out of obscurity and breaking "the hottest news story of the millennium." He told this story so often and so earnestly that it eventually came to be accepted as the truth, and he went to great lengths to make certain all existing copies of the original, unedited tape were destroyed. Having accomplished what he had set out to do, Merlin never bothered to contest his version of events, but I still possess an unedited copy of that tape, and I can prove what really happened.

The pre-interview, as they called it, took place in the offices of the *Billy Martens Show*, though we did not meet the man himself, and would not until the actual show was being taped. I wasn't sure what to expect from this meeting, but Merlin seemed to know exactly what he was about, and as events proceeded to follow their course, he demonstrated an uncommon degree of media savvy. He had, apparently, learned much more from watching television than I had assumed.

He arrived for the interview dressed in his dark blue robe, emblazoned with its multitude of mystical symbols, and wearing his tall, conical hat and carrying his staff. Jenny had washed the robe for him, and he'd washed and combed his long hair and beard, so that he looked the very image of the legendary wizard, which in fact, he was. In other words, he looked like someone Martens could have a field day with.

During the pre-interview, which was conducted by an attractive and very personable young woman, he sat calmly in his chair and told the story of who he was, and what he was, and how he had returned. The young woman smiled and nodded, asked a question here and there, and took notes.

When asked to "demonstrate his powers," Merlin levitated a coffee cup and then a stapler on the young woman's desk. She clapped her hands and beamed and said that it was "wonderful," and seemed generally quite amazed, though it was perfectly clear to me she thought it was merely a stage magician's trick. She then booked Merlin for a taping the following week and we stayed long enough for her to explain how everything would work. The entire pre-interview lasted no longer than twenty minutes or so and, after we had left, I could no longer contain myself.

"I can't believe it," I said. "I said you'd need to do something dramatic to impress them, so what do you do? You levitate a stapler!"

"You don't think that was sufficiently dramatic?" he replied with a perfectly straight face.

"She thought it was a simple trick," I said, "something any amateur magician can do!"

"Amateur?" said Merlin, raising his bushy eyebrows.

"Oh, you know what I mean," I said, feeling exasperated. "An illusion, stage magic."

He smiled. "Yes, I knew what you meant. You are disappointed that I did not overwhelm that young woman with my magical abilities. However, it was never my intent to overwhelm her, merely to arrange an appearance on the show. That has now been done. They expected a foolish old man, dressed in robes and with a long white beard, and that is precisely what they got."

"Ah, I see," I said. "So now you're going to get a haircut and some new clothes, perhaps a sport coat, a nice shirt and necktie and some flannel trousers, so that you'll appear quite normal, and—"

He stopped me. "No, I do not think so, Thomas. I had given that some thought, and have decided to remain exactly as I am, at least for the present. If people expect a wizard to look a certain way, then perhaps I shouldn't disappoint them. I have become a legendary figure, so why not take advantage of it? Appearance seems to play an important role on television, and if people see me as I am now, as outlandish as my garb may seem in this day and age, they will remember it. I must create a significant impression. If I appear no different from anyone else, then the effect will be diminished."

I had to concede his point, but I still felt uneasy about the whole thing. Personally, I thought it would be better if he were to get a haircut and trim his beard, at least, and wear a nice tweed jacket, so that he would appear more dignified, more professional, which only goes to show how little I knew. In any event, the program was still a week away, and I imagined that in that week, we could at least enjoy a little peace and quiet. I would have an opportunity to spend more time with him, and at least begin to give him some idea of what the modern world was like. However, that was not to be.

The first crisis came the day after the pre-interview while we were sitting down to supper. Earlier in the day, our daughters had brought home some of their friends to meet their "Uncle Merlin," and of course, it was obligatory for them to have a demonstration. I sat, biting my lip, as I watched children float around my living room like giant hummingbirds, flapping their arms and squealing with delight, knocking over lamps and bumping into walls, and later, in the evening, the other shoe dropped.

A delegation of concerned parents came to visit, several of them with their children in tow, presumably so they could confront our "Uncle Merlin" with the wild stories they'd been telling and recant before them. Imagine their reaction when "Uncle Merlin" cheerfully corroborated what the kids had said.

"Now see, here, Mr. . . . uh . . ."

"Ambrosius," said Merlin, helpfully.

"Yes, well, Mr. Ambrosius, I can certainly appreciate your sense of fun," one of the fathers, Allan Stewart, said, "but in these difficult times, we try to raise our children to know the difference between reality and games of pretend."

"Who said we were pretending?" Merlin asked.

Stewart cleared his throat in irritation. "I'm afraid I do. not have a sense of humor about this sort of thing, sir."

"How unfortunate," said Merlin. "Life must be very trying when you do not have a sense of humor."

"You may joke, Mr. Ambrosius, but we are not amused," said Stewart, sounding very monarchial. He had apparently been appointed spokesman for the group. "Now my son insists you made him fly, and he would not change his tune even after I warmed his bottom for him, for which he has you to thank."

"I beg to disagree," said Merlin. "He has only his father to thank for that, and it is a sad thing when a child is punished for telling the truth. Even if it were not the truth, there is little to be gained in beating children. It only produces resentment and rebellion, and teaches them that violence is the answer to the slightest problem. I think you should apologize to your son, Mr. Stewart, for you punished him unjustly."

Stewart's face flushed beet red and he turned on me angrily. "See here, Malory, this is all your fault. I will not presume to tell you whom you can or cannot take into your own home, but I think my neighbors here will all agree that we do not wish to have our children exposed to your addlepated relatives. Lord knows, it's hard enough to raise children these days without having some senile, old fool go filling their heads with all sorts of nonsense!"

"*Addlepated?* Senile, old fool?" said Merlin.

I closed my eyes. I was afraid to see what was going to happen next.

"If you want to have your uncle making your own daughters neurotic, unable to distinguish fact from fantasy, well, I can't say I approve, but that's entirely your business," Stewart said. "However, the rest of us are not going to have *our* children—"

At this point, Stewart was interrupted by a screech from his wife, and startled gasps from their other neighbors, and to his surprise, Stewart abruptly realized that he was delivering his diatribe from about one foot off the floor.

"What the devil!"

He broke off suddenly, staring down with astonishment, then began sputtering incoherently as he kicked his legs, trying to regain a footing on the floor beneath him.

"Why, whatever is the matter, Mr. Stewart?" Merlin asked.

Elizabeth Stewart's eyes were wide as saucers and her hand went to her mouth. The others all backed away a step or two, an involuntary, shocked reaction. There were expressions of "Oh, my God!" and "I don't believe it!" and other such things, while Stewart vainly tried to get his feet back on the floor.

"What . . . how . . . Great Heavens, it's impossible! Put me down! *Put me down, I tell you!*"

"Put you *down*, Mr. Stewart?" Merlin said, with feigned

surprise. "Why, whatever do you mean? What seems to be the trouble?"

"*I'm floating a foot above the bloody ground, damn you!* You know perfectly well what the trouble is! *Now put me down!*"

"Floating a foot above the ground?" said Merlin. He frowned. "Dear me. Perhaps it is you who cannot distinguish fact from fantasy, Mr. Stewart. I clearly heard you say it was impossible."

"It's a trick!" said Stewart to the others. "It's a bloody, cheap, stage magician's trick! Now *put me down this instant!*"

"A cheap, stage magician's trick?" said Merlin. "Oh, now, really, Mr. Stewart, I fear that you have gone too far. You shall have to be taught a lesson."

As we all watched, Stewart rose another foot above the floor, and then another, until his head finally bumped the ceiling. And he *still* continued to rise, so that he had to hunch over, and finally was pressed up against the ceiling, suspended over our heads on his hands and knees, like a fly crawling upside down.

Mrs. Stewart's neck was craned way back as she stared up at her husband with the others, open-mouthed, unable to speak.

"*Get me down from here!*" yelled Stewart, panicking. "*Get me down off this bloody ceiling!*"

"Oh, yes, indeed," said Merlin. "We do seem to have a problem here. The man claims he's on the ceiling, when everyone knows such a thing is quite impossible. People cannot crawl upon the ceiling, every idiot knows that. See, here, Stewart, if you do not cease this nonsense immediately, you are going to be punished."

"*Malory! Malory, for God's sake, tell him to put me down!*"

Merlin shook his head. "Well, I see he insists on being stubborn. We shall have to warm his bottom for him. After all, it's the sort of discipline he apparently believes in."

And with a gesture from Merlin, the flat iron spade rose up from the rack of fireplace tools. It floated across the room toward Stewart, and proceeded to administer a sound spanking.

"*Helllp!*" cried Stewart.

Elizabeth Stewart's eyes rolled back and she fainted dead away. Unfortunately, everyone else was so raptly watching her husband being spanked by a floating fireplace spade that no one moved to catch her.

"Look out!" I cried, leaping from my chair, but Merlin was quicker than I and, with a gesture, he stopped her fall, so that she was left heeled over at a forty-five degree angle, unconsciously defying gravity. Jenny could not restrain herself from giggling.

"I, uh . . . think you've made your point," I said to Merlin.

The fireplace spade ceased to belabor Stewart's buttocks and returned to its place. As gently as a feather, Stewart floated down from the ceiling and was set down on his feet once more, with both his pride and his bum smarting. He stared at Merlin with white showing all around his irises, too stunned to speak.

"See to your wife, Mr. Stewart," Merlin said.

Stewart approached his wife, who was leaning over like the Tower of Pisa, and gingerly reached out for her, but then hesitated, pulling his hands back.

"What's . . . holding her there?" he asked.

"I am," Merlin said. "And if you will be so kind as to steady her, I shall let go. I believe she's only swooned."

Stewart took hold of his wife and, released, she slumped into his arms. Her eyelids flickered as she came to. "Allan," she said, "I . . . must have fainted. I've had the *strangest* dream. . . ."

Then she became fully aware of her surroundings and gave a little gasp, realizing that it hadn't been a dream, after all.

"*Allan* . . ."

"It's all right, darling," he said, though he didn't sound at all sure of himself. The others merely stood there, gaping, too shocked to say anything. "How . . ." Stewart's voice cracked and he cleared his throat, then swallowed hard. "How on Earth did you *do* that? Malory . . . who is he? *What* is he? And don't tell me he's your bloody uncle!"

"I think we'd all better sit down," I said. "This may take awhile . . ."

Stewart did apologize to his son for spanking him, and he later became one of Merlin's most ardent friends and supporters. He was an unemployed solicitor, reduced to working occasional odd jobs, as were many of his neighbors. His legal skills, however, turned out to be quite useful as things progressed, not only for Merlin and myself, but for Stewart himself, for he prospered as a result and founded what is now one of the most respected and prestigious firms in London. His wife, Elizabeth, retained the curious ability to lean over at an improbable angle while still remaining on her feet, which tickled her no end. It was a stunt she often pulled at parties.

The news of what had happened, and who "Uncle Merlin" really was, spread throughout the neighborhood like wildfire and during the next week, we were inundated with visitors, all wanting to float around the room or crawl upon the ceiling. Yet, it was nothing compared to what happened after Merlin appeared on the *Billy Martens Show*.

Martens, not surprisingly, had stacked the deck. Merlin was to be part of a panel, which Martens had filled out with a bunch of looney eccentrics, all of whom had one thing in common—a dramatic solution that would lift the world out of the Collapse. The theme of the show was "Saving the Human Race."

One panel member was a doddering old codger who spoke in brief little gasps and wheezes, and claimed, rather charmingly, to have "invented a brand-new fossil fuel." This miraculous substance turned out to be human excrement, which he subjected to a process he claimed would produce enough methane gas to power not only vehicles, but entire cities. Apparently, all we had to do was defecate with a vengeance and, well, it seems unnecessary to expound further on the idea.

Another panelist was a middle-aged matron from Luton who claimed to have been visited by beings from outer space. In exchange for her sexual favors, they promised to deliver up a powerful crystal from their home world, an energy crystal that emitted "stellar rays." These rays were apparently the solution to all our problems. When asked if she could produce this wondrous crystal, she replied that she'd be happy to, only she hadn't quite finished paying for it yet. Martens gave the audience a broad wink and a leer and thanked her for the sacrifice she was making on behalf of humankind, then followed up with pointed questions about the exact nature of this "payment" and the manner in which it was rendered. The audience enjoyed it mightily, and I sat backstage in the green room, watching the monitor and groaning.

Next up was Princess Isis, a.k.a. Mary Margaret Atherton, though she bristled at the use of her birthname and claimed it was no longer valid, as that was "another incarnation." The present incarnation was a child of the old Egyptian gods, who had given the secrets of "pyramid power" to the ancient high priests of the Pharaohs, and who might be induced to part with them again if we all converted to her cult and worshipped them by constructing an entire city of pyramids. Martens declared it a splendid idea and had her lead the audience in a chant to the old gods, which raised a lot of mirth, even if it did fail to raise the ancient spirits.

Then there was Lucretia, no last name given, who was there apparently to provide relief from all the comedy and give the audience something at which to vent their spleens. An avowed Satanist, she took great umbrage at all this levity, and excoriated the audience and Martens. She condemned them all for not taking seriously what was happening in the world, which was clearly signaling the coming of the Antichrist. She was a shapely ash-blonde and very lovely, and wore a sheer, clinging black gown that left scarcely anything to the imagination. Every statement she made was roundly jeered, and those members of the audience who were not shouting her down were busy undressing her with their eyes. Martens played the Grand Inquisitor to her witch, and after a while, I could watch no more. I simply put my head down in my hands and mumbled, "God, I told him so, I told him so."

Merlin sat through all this in silence till his turn came, and Martens was saving him for last, so that having mocked, censured, and chastised, he could go out on a note of ridicule.

"And, finally," he said, "we go from Satan to black magic, which seems only logical, I suppose. Our last guest, as you might well guess from his attire, is none other than Mr. Merlin Ambrosius, or as he is better known to the world at large, Merlin the Magician, legendary court wizard to King Arthur and his Knights of the Round Table!"

After all that had already happened, I had been certain that Merlin would look totally ridiculous, sitting there in his robes and conical hat, holding his staff propped up beside him, yet somehow, despite it all, he managed to look positively regal. There were one or two titters in the audience, but most of them fell silent, uncommonly so, especially after the fever pitch they'd been whipped up to by Satan's sexy messenger.

"How, exactly, does one address a wizard?" Martens asked, tongue-in-cheek.

"By name, usually," Merlin replied.

"Well, then, Merlin, if I might be so familiar, I must say you're looking very spry for a man your age, which must be, what, about two thousand?"

"Thank you," Merlin said.

"You're quite welcome," said Martens with a chuckle.

"Now, your own solution to the problems of the Collapse, as I understand it, is to bring back magic to the world. You've heard the comments of our other guests," said Martens. "What is your reaction?"

"I think that you have been insufferably rude and boorish to them," Merlin said. "We certainly did not treat guests in such a manner in my time."

"Oh, dear me," said Martens with feigned contriteness. "It seems I've been put in my place."

"When the Prince of Darkness comes, you'll find your place, all right," Lucretia said, and the audience at once responded with jeers and catcalls.

"Now, now, let's try to keep some semblance of control here," Martens said. "We haven't yet heard from the greatest wizard of them all, and we may yet learn a thing or two."

"Perhaps the audience might," said Merlin, "but I have my doubts about you."

The audience appreciated this riposte, and Martens affected a wounded expression.

"Ohhh," said Martens, "low blow, low blow. Let's play fair now, shall we? I haven't said anything rude or boorish to you . . . yet. Now then, tell us, Merlin, how is it that you managed to survive for all this time? Do you possess the secret of eternal life?"

"No," said Merlin. "I was tricked by the enchantress, Morgan le Fay, a pupil of mine, and placed under a spell that kept me asleep within an oak for all these years. I was only recently set free."

"Ah, *cherchez la femme*," said Martens, with a knowing look. "So then I gather you've got quite a lot of catching up to do."

"I would agree with that," said Merlin. "Fortunately, I require little sleep, and have been watching television and reading a great deal."

"Yes, well, you've already had quite a nap, haven't you?" said Martens, with a grin at the tittering audience. "In any case, it's good to have you back, old chap. Lord knows, we need all the help we can get. So then, magic is the answer. What are you going to do? Say abracadabra and wave your wizard's staff and make all our problems disappear?''

"No, regrettably, I do not possess such power," Merlin said. "Nor would I presume to exercise it if I did. People must all work together to solve the problems of the Collapse. Magic is merely a useful tool that will help bring that about.''

"Ah, I see," said Martens with an expression of mock seriousness. "There's just one problem, though. Most of us aren't great wizards, like yourself. We're all just simple people, who don't know how to work magic. How do you propose to remedy that situation?''

"I intend to start a school," said Merlin, "and teach the thaumaturgic arts.''

"The thaumaturgic arts!" said Martens. "That's incredible! You mean we can all actually *learn* how to do magic?''

"The ability is inherent in most people," Merlin said, "although to varying degrees, of course.''

"Of course," said Martens. "And, one assumes, if people come to this school of yours, and pony up the appropriate tuition, you will be only too happy to assess the degree of their abilities and enroll them in your course. That's the bottom line here, isn't it, Merlin, or whatever your name really is? You're really just another con artist, and not a very clever one, at that. Surely, you don't expect anyone to swallow this nonsense? Do you take us all for fools?''

"No, not all of you, merely some of you," said Merlin.

"Why don't you show us some of this 'magic' you propose to teach?" said Martens. "My staff tells me you can levitate a coffee cup. Why don't you levitate that one there, on the table behind you?''

"Very well," said Merlin. He made a simple pass and the drinking cup provided for him obligingly rose up into the air.

"Amazing! Astonishing! *Stupendous*!" Martens said sarcastically. "Why with a little sleight-of-hand and stage illusion, we can change the world! We can all learn to do card tricks and produce pigeons from our sleeves and presto-chango, the world will be a better place! You call that magic? You must take me for an ass!"

"Indeed, I do," said Merlin, allowing the cup to settle back down onto the table behind his chair. "And I do not think that I shall be the only one."

Martens snapped back at once, launching into a tirade against thieves and con artists who sought to profit from other people's misery and gullibility, yet even as he did so, Merlin made a slight gesture with his hand and Martens's ears began to grow.

For a few moments, the audience didn't notice, and Martens himself apparently felt nothing. He was in full rave, pointing at Merlin and calling him a fraud and demanding that he confess his real name, suggesting that if he refused, it was probably because he had a police record. Meanwhile, his ears continued to grow steadily.

"Perfect!" I said as I watched the monitor in the green room. "Absolutely *perfect*!"

The audience inevitably noticed and there were gasps and exclamations of astonishment. Martens's ears were growing more and more rapidly, becoming longer and more pointed, reaching up above his head, turning gray and sprouting fur. He was condemned out of his own mouth. Merlin took him for an ass, indeed, and now he was turning into one.

He stopped, abruptly, momentarily disoriented, perhaps beginning to feel something strange. Then, still holding the microphone, he raised his hands up to his ears. "What the . . . *my ears*!"

He resembled the transformation of Pinnochio, with gray, tufted donkey ears sticking up almost a full foot above his head. He dropped the mike and spun around, facing the audience, but looking up toward the central booth, where the director, whatever reactions were taking place up there, instinctively kept on calling the shots. The monitor screen before me showed a close-up of Martens, his face white as a sheet, with sweat breaking out on his forehead as his eyes registered first complete incomprehension, and then panic.

*"My ears! What the hell's happening to my ears?"*

The audience was confused. Some, certain that this was some sort of special effect, broke into laughter. Others simply stared in disbelief, while others still cried out and recoiled in horror. And then Martens's nose began to grow.

*"What is this?"* he shouted. And then, forgetting himself completely, he screamed, *"What the fuck is this?"*

His teeth looked larger now, his jaw was elongating, and his hands, still clapped up to the sides of his head, were growing dark and misshapen, turning into hooves.

*"Jesus Christ!"* yelled Martens. *"What's happening to me? Help me! Somebody help me!"*

There was now no mistaking what was going on and pandemonium broke out in the audience. People jumped to their feet, some screaming, some running for the exits, others simply trying to get a better view. Merlin merely sat there, calmly, saying nothing, while the matron from Luton fled from the stage, presumably to seek security in the embraces of her alien benefactors, and the man with the miracle organic fuel merely chuckled with amusement. The Princess Isis stood on her feet, her arms raised to the heavens, chanting to the ancient gods, and Lucretia simply stared at Merlin with awe, then got out of her chair and dropped to her knees before him, grasping his hand and kissing it fervently.

Merlin gently took his hand away and leaned down to say something to her. She responded with some sort of reply, but their exchange was inaudible. He told me later that he asked her to stop it and get up, and her response was that his slightest wish was her command, and that she was his, body and soul, to do with as he pleased.

He did, in fact, take her up on that offer, though not quite in the way one might suppose. He recruited her to help out with the school, and in the process, helped her to deal with her severe psychological problems, stemming from horrendous abuse she'd suffered as a child at the hands of her parents, who were psychotic Satan worshippers. She is now a university administrator at one of the many Colleges of Sorcery that Merlin founded (for which reason her name has been altered in this narrative). However, I digress.

The spectacle of Billy Martens turning into an ass was truly the sort of dramatic demonstration that I'd had in mind. I watched, delighted beyond words, as he screamed, "*Help me! Help me! Hellllp meeee, hawwww, heee-hawww! Hee-haw!*"

His expensive suit had burst apart at the seams and he had stepped out of his shoes, his socks still on his hind legs, and he was trotting about, knocking things over as he kicked out with alarm and brayed hysterically. I couldn't resist. I had to see what was happening in the control room. I hurried up there and everyone was in such a state that no one prevented me from going in.

"*Stay on him!*" the director was shouting into his headset mike. "*Stay on him, Goddamn it!* Jesus, this is unbelievable! Camera Three . . . *Steve!* What the hell are you doing? *Focus*, for God's sake! Give me a wide shot! *Take Three!* Wait a minute, what's he doing? Merlin's getting up! He's going to do something, Two, get on him! *Take Two!*"

"Silence!" Merlin said, and he must have used that same power behind his words he'd earlier demonstrated on me, because the audience fell silent instantly, as one, and stared at him. "Take your seats," said Merlin.

"Give me a wide shot, Three!" said the director, his gaze glued to the monitors. "*Take Three!* Stand by on close-up, Two. *Take Two!*"

"Come here, Billy," Merlin said. "Be not afraid."

The ass obediently trotted over to him and gave him a pathetic little whinny.

"Medium shot, Camera One! *Take One!* Damn it, his mike's come off. Get the boom on him!"

Merlin put his hand on the donkey's head and said something inaudible, and slowly, Billy began to change back into his normal form. In a matter of moments, he was restored, except he still possessed the donkey ears. And he was completely naked.

"Oh, Jesus, *pan up, One, pan up!* Get off his bum, for God's sake! *Take Two!*"

Merlin's face appeared in close-up on the screen. "Let that be a lesson in humility to you, Mr. Martens," he said. Then, turning directly to the camera, he continued, "And let what happened here stand as proof of my assertions. I *am* Merlin Ambrosius, and I have come to bring back magic to the world. I have come to offer aid, and urge a return to the old knowledge, and the old ways of respect for the Earth and her resources. Let those who sincerely seek to help, and who wish to learn the thaumaturgic arts, seek me out. I shall determine if they possess the ability and the purity of heart and spirit to be accepted as my students. Fear not, the future holds a bright new world in store. I have spoken."

And, with that, he left the stage.

"Where is he *going*?" the director shouted. "Bloody hell, we've still got four minutes! One, get off Billy, for God's sake, he looks like an idiot! *Take Three!* Zoom in, I want to see the faces in the audience! Right, *take Two!* Ready One, *take One!* Stand by to roll credits . . . I know we're short, Goddamn it, but Billy's in shock or something, what the hell do you expect me to do?"

I quietly left the booth. No one had even noticed my presence. As for Billy Martens, he was left with his donkey's ears, as a guarantee against his failing to air the tape. When the program aired, unedited, Merlin promised him that he would restore his ears. Martens blanched, but he was too unnerved to protest. His assinine condition, Merlin reminded him, might easily return, and be rendered permanent. So the program aired, unedited.

And then all hell broke loose.

# CHAPTER
## 6

I had underestimated Merlin. I had thought that despite his uncanny powers, he would be out of his depth when it came to dealing with the media and the uproar that would result when he announced his presence to the world. In fact, it was *I* who was out of my depth. Merlin seemed to take it all comfortably in stride. I had also underestimated how people would react to him, and I had underestimated television's power to make people believe.

It had seemed to me, as I look back on it now, that our biggest obstacle would be overcoming people's disbelief. Today, when magic is commonly accepted as an everyday part of the world, and no more remarkable than the sun's rising in the morning, that might seem like an odd statement to make, and yet in those days, no one believed in magic, at least no one who was considered rational. If that seems strange, then it must be recalled that there was a time in history when people thought the world was flat, and a time when a man named Giordano Bruno was burned at the stake for having the temerity to suggest that there were other worlds than this.

Today, everyone knows a talent for precognition or some

other psychic faculty is merely evidence of a strong latent magical ability, or as it's more commonly referred to, thaumaturgic potential. There is now even a scale for measuring T.P. and the ability is so highly respected and so much in demand that children are routinely tested in elementary school for their potential to become adepts. So much has changed. Yet, I can still remember, as if it were only yesterday, how different things were then.

Had I been asked to predict what would happen after Merlin first appeared on television, I would have predicted widespread disbelief. I was convinced people would think the whole thing was a hoax, that special effects and trickery had been employed, and that we would have an uphill battle to convince the world Merlin was genuine. We did, in fact, have an uphill battle ahead of us, but it was not quite what I would have predicted.

People *believed* they saw Billy Martens turn into an ass, even before members of the studio audience testified they saw it happen and that no video trickery had been involved. People believed it even before the press got on the bandwagon and Merlin became the story of the century, and they believed it before Merlin performed any other demonstrations. They believed it, amazingly enough, simply because they had seen it on TV.

Perhaps I should not have been surprised. A great many people have always believed the most unlikely and questionable things, merely because they'd seen it on television or read about it in a newspaper or a magazine. Even during the Collapse, there was widespread belief in the existence of UFO's, space ships from some other world that came to our planet to kidnap people and conduct experiments upon them, mutilate cattle, and make large, mysterious circles in wheat fields. They were either causing the Collapse by sucking the world dry of its resources, or they were going to save us all with "stellar rays." Stories reporting strange disappearances in the Bermuda Triangle, people spontaneously bursting into flame, dead celebrities being sighted in the supermarket, and tribes of natives the size of Mexican chihuahuas discovered in the Amazon were all taken as gospel by an amazing number of seemingly rational human beings. Such was the power of the printed word, and it was a power that was magnified significantly through the medium of television.

Even today, unlikely as it seems, there are people who believe that actors appearing on their favorite programs are actually the characters they portray. Television *is* reality for many people, perhaps because what it purveys appeals directly to the senses. (Save for that sense in all too rare supply, common sense.) All of which is not to say that there weren't skeptics. There were, and plenty of them. But in the days immediately following the broadcast of the show, it seemed to me that they were hopelessly outnumbered.

In brief, what occurred after the taping of the show was this: Merlin and I quickly left the studio, as he judged the moment was not right for further demonstrations or discussions.

"This is not the time," he said. "We have whet their appetites. Now let that anticipation mount."

It did, and quickly. I learned later that Martens had fled the studio following the taping, wearing nothing but his overcoat, and with his head covered by a towel. There followed frantic phone calls from his home to his executive producer, demanding that no one else be given access to the tape. By that time, however, the news programs had already heard about what happened, and what they heard sounded so incredible, and at the same time so delightful, that they were all demanding to see copies of the tape. One of these copies eventually found its way into my possession, in much the same manner as the food found its way into my pantry. We had great fun viewing it at home.

There was apparently some friction between Martens and his executive producer, the latter feeling that since the program would be broadcast anyway, there was little point in withholding copies of the tape from the news media, who could provide a great deal of advance publicity and thereby boost the ratings of the show. However, on threat of losing his job, the producer relented and copies of the tape were never made available. There seemed to be some question as to exactly how many copies were made, which made Martens absolutely frantic, but with the exception of the one copy that strayed into my possession, he apparently managed to get his hands on all the others.

Members of the studio audience were customarily prohibited from bringing cameras and taking photographs during the taping of the program, but there were professional still photographers present, on the payroll of the show, and one of these enterprising individuals "leaked" a photograph of Martens with his donkey ears, which wound up appearing on the newscasts and in all the newspapers. Most treated the whole thing as a joke, believing it was some sort of publicity stunt, while others simply reported what they'd heard and showed the photo, without making any judgements or conclusions.

Martens himself said nothing and, despite a siege by reporters outside his London townhouse, never left his home until after the broadcast of the show, when his ears had returned to normal. By the time he finally emerged, he'd developed his own spin on the story and cheerfully admitted "allowing" himself to be turned into an ass, to display his sense of humor about himself, as well as help announce Merlin's arrival and demonstrate his powers in a visually dramatic way.

The whole thing had been a setup, in other words, choreographed by Martens. At least, that was his version. In reply to questions about the other members of the panel, and how he'd treated them, Martens simply stated that he wished to have them on as a contrast, comparing various pretenders to "the real thing." Thereafter, those other panelists were totally forgotten. By the time Martens made his statement to the press, however, there had already been considerable attention given to the story . . . and to us.

It began with our neighbors in the town of Loughborough, before the *Billy Martens Show* was aired and even before the advance publicity had spread. We arrived home to find a mob waiting for us, and I immediately became concerned about Jenny and the girls.

"*There they are!*" I heard several people shout as we approached, and I half expected to be rushed, but curiously, no one moved. They waited as we came up the street and then, like the Red Sea parting for Moses, made way for us as we came up to the house. They all became utterly still, and no one tried to stop us or ask questions. They merely stood aside as we went up the steps to the front door, where Merlin paused and turned to address them.

"I know why you've come," he said. "You have all heard incredible things about the strange old man staying with the Malorys, and you came to see if they were true. Indeed, they are."

He spoke to them for the better part of an hour, explaining who he was and how he came to be there, then answering their questions patiently, concluding with a request for their help in the great task that lay ahead. I did not stay to hear his entire speech, for I more or less knew what he was going to say and was anxious to get inside and see how Jenny and the girls were holding up. They were all perfectly fine, as it turned out, except that Jenny had grown weary from answering the phone all day.

There had been a flood of calls, jamming the local switchboard, resulting from word of mouth spread by our neighbors. I found Stewart there, with his sleeves rolled up, as well as several other neighbors of ours, giving yeoman service by answering the phone and keeping order among the waiting throng outside. The task, apparently, had not proved difficult at all.

"It's the strangest thing," said Stewart. "Jenny said they began arriving shortly after you and Merlin left this morning.

As the crowd grew, she became concerned and called me, but there have been no incidents whatsoever. They've all been very polite and orderly, conversing quietly among themselves, and they've bothered no one. They've been simply waiting, patiently. And they all seemed somehow happy and content.''

"It works," said Jenny with a smile.

"What works?" I asked.

"The warding spell," she said. "They must have felt it, even outside the house."

"I've felt it, too," said Stewart. "When I arrived the other day, I was frothing mad, you know, convinced some dotty, old relative of yours was getting the kids all worked up over a bunch of nonsense. Yet, from the moment I came into the house, I found it difficult to maintain my anger and was able to do so only with a concerted effort. This morning, the effect seemed to be much stronger. The moment I came in the door, I felt absolutely marvelous. It was like that sense of contentment you feel on a morning after it's just rained, and the air is clear and brisk, and the sun is shining, and you step outside, breathe deeply, and all feels right with the world.''

Stewart almost seemed to glow. I felt nothing different, myself, save for the contentment I've always felt being at home with my family. Jenny said that she felt nothing different, either, but Stewart and our other neighbors who'd come by to give Jenny some support were all brimming with the enthusiasm of newly enlightened converts. None of us had ever been particularly close before. In fact, having been away from home so often, I barely even knew most of them. Yet, they all suddenly seemed like members of the family.

"It's the most wonderful thing, Tom," Stewart said. "I feel positively imbued with hope! Everything's going to be different now, isn't it? The Collapse is going to end and the world will never be the same. And to think that in some small way, we're all going to be a part of it!''

Listening to Stewart's almost evangelical enthusiasm, I felt a peculiar sense of foreboding, despite the warding spell. Perhaps, because my own energies had been involved in casting it, I was not as affected by it as the others, but I felt an odd disquiet, a brief pang of anxiety that seemed to flare for a moment and was gone as quickly as it came. I had no idea what it was then, and I soon forgot about it, but the feeling was to return before too long.

I had already become accustomed to Merlin's charisma, what he would call his "aura," and I had observed the effect it had on others. Not all people were affected by it the same way, or to the same degree. I suppose, to some extent, it had to do with their own personalities and their degree of sensitivity. I discovered later it was something Merlin could project at will, though it was always there to be perceived by those disposed to notice it. He was capable of volitionally increasing its effect, though not without a cost to him in terms of energy, and I was to learn that, despite his enormous vitality, Merlin *could* grow tired. However, at the same time, it was all still very new to me, and I was not yet familiar with the ways of magic.

Knowing what lay ahead, Merlin conserved his energies as much as possible. He performed no demonstrations of his powers for the crowd gathered outside our home. He merely spoke to them, and they all went away convinced, full of the same sort of spirit Stewart and the others felt. Clearly, he had been projecting as he addressed them. As the crowd outside dispersed, he came in and sat down on the couch to fill his pipe.

"Ah, Stewart," he said. "I perceive that you've been making yourself useful."

"I'm only too happy to help in any way I can," said Stewart. "How did the taping go?"

As they spoke, I put my arm around my wife and whatever strange concern I'd felt earlier vanished. I was home, we were surrounded by friends, and a strange and wonderful new chapter had opened in our lives. Everything was going to be all right.

In the days ahead, our home became a hotbed of activity, especially after the Martens broadcast aired. Jenny and I enjoyed no privacy, save for late at night, after we'd retired to our bedroom, both exhausted. It was as if our home had been turned into the center of a political campaign. Word spread quickly, and we were soon getting calls from all the people who'd so rudely dismissed me before, as well as many others. Merlin was interviewed extensively, both on television and for the newspapers, and he performed more demonstrations of his powers, though nothing quite so dramatic as turning Billy Martens into what he really was, despite an astonishing number of requests for him to do precisely that. Not necessarily to Billy Martens, though there were a few of those, but to the interviewers themselves.

It was surprising how many people wanted to experience being an animal. And the choice of animals was quite surprising, too. One newspaper reporter wanted to become an eagle, briefly, so he could experience the joy of flight among the clouds. That was not so surprising, perhaps, but others were, to the point of being downright bizarre. One man wanted to become a pig, Lord only knows why. Another reporter wanted to be a giraffe. Still another wished to become a gorilla. And a very attractive young woman anchoring a popular late-night newscast wanted to become a python, with the special provision that the metamorphosis would not take place until morning. Merlin declined her request politely, though she was quite insistent.

In the broadcast for the BBC, for which the well-known interviewer Robin Winters brought a camera crew to our home and conducted over six hours of taping, Merlin demonstrated the possible applications of thaumaturgy by levitating Winters's car and taking him for a ride in it, with a camera unit along to record the event. He explained that a levitation spell, coupled with a spell of impulsion, was not a very difficult spell to execute for a trained adept, and with enough adepts trained to at least that level, the problems of public transportation resulting from the scarcity of petrol could be solved.

"Amazing!" Winters had exclaimed as the car floated around the block at approximately twenty-five miles per hour or so, with the cameraman and myself in the rear seat, and Merlin and Winters in the front. The exact speed was impossible to determine since, of course, with the wheels about two feet off the ground, the speedometer was useless. "What about buses and lorries? Would this work for them as well?"

"Certainly," Merlin replied. "It would merely require a bit more effort, as a greater mass would be involved. In principle, the same method could also apply to trains, though a more efficient method might be to have a team of adepts working together to generate the power for the trains to operate normally. Even aircraft could be operated in this manner, though levitating a passenger aircraft to the necessary altitude and maintaining it at that height would be extremely taxing on the adept, and the speeds would necessarily be significantly slower. Even with an advanced level of skill in thaumaturgy, it would be best for there to be at least two or three advanced adepts on board to pilot the aircraft, so they could relieve one another to prevent exhaustion. And they would, of course, require time to recuperate before another such flight could be performed."

"But this is absolutely astonishing!" exclaimed the normally reserved Winters, practically bouncing in his seat. "Here we are, moving along at a speed of approximately thirty miles an hour, floating smoothly two feet or so above the surface of the roadway, yet you are able to converse with me, and your hands are not even on the wheel!"

"What would be the point?" asked Merlin. "The wheels are not controlling the direction of this vehicle, my will is."

"Yes, precisely," Winters said. "One would think that such a feat would require an amazing amount of concentration, but you seem to be doing it with no apparent effort, as automatically as I would drive this car myself in the normal manner."

"To say that it requires no concentration would be quite misleading," Merlin said. "I imagine that when you first learned to operate this vehicle, you needed to think about it very consciously, is that not so?"

"Well, yes, of course," said Winters.

"It is much the same with thaumaturgy," Merlin said. "For the beginning student of the art, the least demanding of all thaumaturgic exercises seem as formidable as driving this car would be to a child. Even if the child were quite intelligent and capable of learning some of the rote tasks by observation, that child would still not have the proper knowledge or, more importantly, would not possess the proper skills or development to be a good driver. His legs would not be long enough to reach the pedals, for example, and he would not be tall enough to see above the wheel. He would not possess the necessary physical reactions to accomplish the task safely. So it is with thaumaturgy."

"In essence, then," said Winters, "what you're saying is that practice makes perfect."

"Not quite," Merlin replied. "That would be an oversimplification. True, with practice, one becomes more proficient. That is as true in thaumaturgy as in anything else. However, there is much more to it than that. To use an example from my day, a squire might serve a knight and practice diligently with his wooden sword and lance, but no matter how skilled he became with these implements, he would still be unable to enter a tournament until such time as his physical strength and dexterity had developed to the point where he could wield a real sword and lance, and at the same time control a horse, all while wearing heavy armor."

"So then you're saying it requires more than mere study, but a process of development," said Winters, "strengthening the powers of concentration and developing . . . what? One's will?"

"Yes, that is an excellent way of putting it," said Merlin. "Except that along with will, one other faculty must be developed, one which is normally atrophied or stunted in most people, and that is intuition."

"*Intuition*?" Winters said, frowning. "I'm not sure I follow."

"I will try to put it another way," said Merlin. "I have been doing much reading since I awoke in this time, and I have found, to my great interest, that some of your scholars have been stumbling toward a discovery of the very principle of which we speak. This interests me, and I have learned much of value in their writings, things I knew before on what we might call the intuitive level, but that I now understand on a more rational, logical level. They speak, for example, of right-brain consciousness and left-brain consciousness."

"You mean the theory of the bicameral mind?" said Winters, not to be left behind.

"It is much more than a theory," Merlin said. "It is a fact. The universe is composed of opposites, what some may call the masculine and feminine principles, or the yin and the yang, as the Oriental scholars say. When these two principles are complementary, the universe can be said to be in harmony. Yet, when they are not complementary, then what we have is discord. We may regard the human mind as a model of these principles. The mind is of two aspects. There is the logical, reasoning faculty, what we may call the masculine, or the left brain, and the intuitive faculty, the feminine, or the right brain. Each has its purpose, and they are meant to be complementary. In fact, they are. However, in most people, it is the left brain that is dominant, that which reasons logically and rationally, while the right brain, that which is intuitive and receptive, is largely passive, to the extent that it may be regarded as stunted in its development.

"Your technological society has encouraged the development of the mind's masculine, controlling, logical faculty," he continued, "while the feminine, receptive or intuitive side has fallen into disuse. I have heard the expression, 'It's a man's world,' and there is truth to that, only not in the literal sense most people mean. People have become crowded together in large cities, with dense populations, surrounded by the emanations of your technological achievements, cut off from the pastoral world. London is such a large and noisy city, with so many things constantly impinging on the senses, that the intuitive faculty becomes deafened. I find it disquieting to be in such surroundings, and while I do not allow myself to become intuitively deafened by them, I must take care to pay greater attention."

"You mean you have to concentrate more?" said Winters.

"No, I mean that I must pay attention," Merlin said. "Most people these days seem to be very inattentive. Undoubtedly, this is because there is so much to pay attention to. It becomes difficult to pay attention to everything, and remain in a constant state of alertness and receptivity. People learn to become logically receptive, rather than intuitively receptive, which is to say, they choose those things to which they will respond."

"How?" asked Winters.

"Well, say you are walking down a city street," said Merlin. "It's the middle of the day, and many people are about, walking in both directions all around you. You are aware of their presence, and yet, you do not really *see* them. You select those to whom you pay attention. You become aware that among the crowd, someone is walking toward you, and perhaps their attention is distracted, and you perceive that if you both continue in the same direction, you will collide. So you alter your course to avoid this collision. In a similar manner, you may notice objects in the street that are in your path, and make conscious choices to avoid them. But if there were any objects in the street not directly in your path, while you might notice them, you would choose not to pay particular attention to them, and in the same way, people walking around you might impinge on your awareness, but if I asked you later to describe some of them to me, you probably would not be able to.

"However," he went on, "imagine that same city street, only now it is late at night, and the street appears deserted. You are aware of how much crime there is in the city, and how dangerous the streets are at night, and now you suddenly notice everything around you in much greater detail. You have made a different choice about your level of awareness. You are paying more attention. At such times, your normally dormant intuitive faculty is stronger. Perhaps, as you are walking along, you experience a peculiar feeling that you are being followed. You turn to glance over your shoulder, and in fact, there *is* someone walking along behind you. We shall assume that this person has no threatening intentions, but the fact is that in your state of increased attention, you became receptive to his presence in an unconscious, intuitive way that you may not be able to explain."

"I see," said Winters. "That makes sense."

Merlin smiled. "Yes, it may not sound logical, but it makes sense."

"So in order to learn thaumaturgy," Winters said, "it becomes necessary to pay more attention and develop intuition."

"Exactly," Merlin said.

"But if you're constantly paying attention to everything that's happening around you, won't your mind tend to become overloaded?" Winters asked. "Must we all live in pastoral surroundings in order to develop our full, latent potential?"

"No," said Merlin, "we merely need to stop distracting ourselves and learn how to become less preoccupied with our own concerns. We need to learn how to relax into an attentive state, rather than drive ourselves purely with directed logic. You will observe that small children are infinitely more attentive than adults. I've heard it said that children have a 'limited attention span,' when in fact, quite the opposite is true. They are simply paying attention to a great many more things than adults are, and it would be more correct to say that they do not limit their attention span to any one thing at a time, as adults are accustomed to doing.''

"*Accustomed* to doing,'' Winters repeated, seizing on the word. "You mean we learn how to filter things out and, in fact, it is *we* who have the limited attention span.''

"Precisely,'' Merlin said. "It is not necessary for the mind to become overloaded with trivial information, as you put it. It is possible to pay more attention on a continual basis, without feeling the necessity to store that information and constantly make logical decisions based upon it. You ask a child to walk down that same crowded street with you, and the child will later be able to give a much more detailed description of the experience than you could, simply because the child was in a more attentive state, without feeling the pressing need to make logical decisions about everything he saw. The intuitive faculty does not respond well to conscious, logical commands. It responds to relaxed attention and a receptive state.''

"It sounds as if you're saying that all we need do to study magic is learn how to relax,'' said Winters.

"Regrettably, it is not quite that simple,'' Merlin said with a smile, "but it *is* one of the first things a prospective adept must learn to do. It is necessary to learn how to see with the eyes of a child, and exercise the will of an adult. However, that is the first step on the path to mastering the Craft.''

After we had settled down in the living room and Winters resumed taping, he asked me a few questions, which he would later edit together with some footage he had taken in the woods where I had first met Merlin. To his disappointment, nothing remained of the tree Merlin had been confined in except a stump. What Merlin had not magically "chopped up" and transported to my home as firewood had been cleared by loggers working under permit. Nevertheless, Winters stood dramatically in the center of the tree stump and taped the introduction to the program, speaking about how Merlin had "allegedly emerged." Hedging his bets, he was not committing himself on that score.

"Who *is* this man who calls himself Merlin Ambrosius, and has so captured the imaginations of people everywhere?" he asked rhetorically as he taped his opening remarks. "And what, precisely, is the nature of the mysterious powers he claims to possess? And who is Thomas Malory, the former soldier and London police officer who acts as his intermediary and advisor? Is it possible that we are actually witnessing a legend come to life, or have we, perhaps, been taken in by two charismatic charlatans? Is there, in fact, any substance to their story, which, if true, promises to change the world, or is this thing some sort of elaborate hoax? During the course of this program, we shall attempt to discover the answers to those and other tantalizing questions, in what bodes to be one of the most unusual and fascinating interviews ever broadcast. Join us tonight as we begin the first in a series of in-depth interviews with 'The Wizard of Camelot' . . . the man known as Merlin, the Magician."

That "Wizard of Camelot" tag was to stick like glue, and though Merlin eventually succeeded in getting people to refer to him as Professor Ambrosius, rather than "Merlin the Magician," he remained "The Wizard of Camelot" to the news media, who became so enamored of the title they simply couldn't let it go. The other thing that was extremely difficult for him to shake were the negative religious associations with sorcery, and he never entirely succeeded in doing that. To this day, there persists a belief among some people that magic is "the Devil's work," an expression of subservience to Satan, and it was to this subject that Winters turned next after he finished questioning me and resumed his interview with Merlin.

"Having established the mind-boggling veracity of your claims concerning magic," he began, "we come now to what is possibly the most controversial aspect of this interview, and that is the negative, dare we say evil, connotations of sorcery and witchcraft throughout history."

Merlin merely nodded, knowing what Winters was getting at, but waiting for him to frame the question.

Winters paused a moment, then continued. "What do you say to people who will regard necromancy as a sin, as an evil tool of Satan, the use of which may jeopardize the soul?"

"First, I wish to correct a misapprehension on your part," said Merlin. "If people remember nothing else about this interview, they should remember that thaumaturgy is *not* the same thing as necromancy."

"Oh? How does it differ?" Winters asked.

"In one vitally important respect. In the practice of necromancy, there is death involved. Thaumaturgy utilizes the forces of Nature and the energies of the adept. Necromancy utilizes the life force of another living being, which brings us to the question of Satanism. Let me be very clear on this point. I do *not* believe in Satan. I am not a Christian, and though I have no quarrel with Christians, a belief in Satan requires an underlying structure of Christian belief. The Christian tradition tells us that God represents all that is good, and that there is no evil in God. Yet, just as light would be meaningless without darkness as a contrast, so the concept of good would be meaningless without the concept of evil. Therefore, in the Christian tradition, Satan is the adversary of God, representing all that is evil."

"And you do not agree with that?" asked Winters.

"I agree that in the Christian tradition, God represents good and Satan represents evil," Merlin replied. "However, I am not an adherent of the Christian tradition, though I have studied it and found much in it to admire. Not being an adherent of the Christian tradition, I do not believe in Satan, for the concept of Satan did not exist until Christianity created it. This is not to say that evil did not exist prior to Christianity, of course, merely that it was the Christian tradition that gave birth to the concept of Satan as the embodiment of all that is evil.

"Now if you wish to say that the concepts of ultimate evil and Satan are essentially the same," he continued, "I shall not argue with you, for I think we can agree that evil, however you choose to think of it, is not to be desired. However, in order to be a Satanist, one must believe in and worship Satan, and to worship Satan, one must worship evil as opposed to good. It must be understood that Satanism is a perversion of Christianity, and it could not exist *without* Christianity, for it is a direct reaction to it. It is a willful rejection of the Christian God and a worship of His adversary. It is for this reason that Satanists invert the symbol of the Christian faith, the cross, as if to say, we are doing the opposite of you, we are turning your religion upside down. Nor do they confine themselves only to inverting Christian symbols. They also invert the pentacle, which is the symbol of the old, pre-Christian religion known as Wicca. For Satanists, it is a way of showing contempt for all beliefs except their own."

"Getting back to the subject of necromancy," Winters prompted him.

"I was just getting to it," Merlin said. "One of the gravest injustices of history was the association of the witch with something evil, with worship of the Devil. A witch does not worship death, a witch worships life. A witch does not destroy Nature, a witch reveres it. A witch does not worship evil, a witch shuns it, because those who pursue the Craft believe in following the threefold path, which is to say that whatever energy you direct outward, you receive the same in return, threefold. This would mean that if a witch were to cast some sort of evil spell, she would receive three times the evil in return, and this would obviously be self-destructive.''

''It sounds rather like the Golden Rule,'' said Winters. ''Do unto others as you would have others do unto you.''

''Precisely,'' Merlin said. ''A witch would never make a sacrifice of another living being, for that would violate everything the witch believes. Necromancy means, literally, the sorcery of death, and it is as much a perversion of thaumaturgy, the art practiced by the witch and by the wizard, as Satanism is a perversion of Christianity. One of the chief tenets of the Christian faith is that life is to be revered, and the witch believes that, also. To practice thaumaturgy is to seek power within oneself, in accordance with the principles of Nature. To practice necromancy is to steal power from another living being, and in the course of doing so, to rob that being of its life force. To practice necromancy, in other words, is to practice murder. I do not practice murder, nor do I condone it, nor shall I allow it to occur, if it is within my power to prevent it.''

These words, spoken with sincerity, were to return to haunt him, though at the time, I could never have suspected it. Whether Merlin suspected it or not, I cannot say, but I can assert that to the best of my knowledge, those words embodied his beliefs, and no one knew Merlin better than I.

''So then you repudiate any association between sorcery, or thaumaturgy, and Devil worship, or black magic,'' Winters said, ''but there does seem to be a connection between the two, though you draw the distinction that in thaumaturgy, it is the energy of the sorcerer in conjunction with natural forces that is employed, while in necromancy it is the energy of another living being that is used, with the results being fatal.''

''That is correct,'' said Merlin.

''But isn't it essentially the same thing?'' asked Winters. ''No, allow me to rephrase that,'' he added quickly. ''What I mean to say is, dramatic as the difference may be, from what you say, isn't the essential difference primarily one of approach? That is, isn't the power being employed essentially the same, only in the case of thaumaturgy, it is being used ethically, while in the case of necromancy, it is being used unethically? It sounds, and you must excuse me if I misunderstood, as if that is the only real difference.''

"I would say it is a very significant difference," Merlin said.

"In terms of the approach and of the outcome, yes, it most certainly is," said Winters, pressing his point, "but in terms of the actual *process* involved, that is to say, magic, it's really the same thing, isn't it?"

Merlin nodded. "I see what you are getting at," he said. "You are trying to suggest that there is no essential difference between thaumaturgy and necromancy, that both are magic, only in one case, it is magic used for good, while in the other it is used for evil. However, aside from that, magic is magic, is that what you wish me to say?"

"Well . . . I'm not attempting to put words in your mouth," said Winters, "I'm merely trying to clarify the matter in my own mind."

"Then allow me to help you," Merlin said. "You are correct in your basic assumption that magic is magic, and that considered in that way, and *only* in that way, the essential difference between thaumaturgy and necromancy is the intent of the adept. However, it is not as simple as that, though even if it were, the difference would still be quite significant. We may just as easily say that you have the power to grasp something with your hands with considerable strength. Now, you could employ that strength to catch someone about to fall from a cliff, for example, and thereby save a life, or you could use that same strength to strangle someone, thereby taking a life. The difference would be essentially in the way you chose to use your strength, and though the force itself would be the same, the difference would be most significant, wouldn't you say?"

Winters nodded. "Well, yes, of course, I see your point. Magic is a force, neither inherently good, nor inherently evil. It's the will of the adept that determines what direction it will take."

"Considered in such simple terms, yes," said Merlin, "but as I've said before, it is not that simple. For one thing, the spells one would employ in necromancy are very different from the ones employed in thaumaturgy, and you must realize that we are not speaking of sacrificing a chicken or a cat in some nonsensical and ill-motivated rite. We are speaking of the real thing. There once *were* necromancers, adepts who misused their powers, and they were very powerful adepts, indeed, though fortunately for the world, their time has passed."

"Perhaps," said Winters, "but the time for thaumaturgy had passed as well. Yet now, here you are, proposing to teach the art of thaumaturgy, and couldn't that mean that the time of the necromancer could come again as a result?"

"No, most definitely not," said Merlin. "No one will be able to perform necromancy as a result of anything they learn from me. Aside from that, it would be far more difficult to perform necromancy than to perform thaumaturgy, not only because of laws prohibiting the taking of life, but because the spells themselves would be much more complicated and demanding, not to mention dangerous. The power that can be obtained from a necromantic spell is considerable, but the power required to cast it is also considerable, and would prove extremely taxing to the adept. It could easily prove fatal. It is a most destructive art, and one which would require a master sorcerer, a mage."

"Someone, say, with the same level of ability as yourself?" asked Winters.

"Yes, I would say so, and it would be dangerous even for me to attempt it," Merlin said.

"So, then, speaking purely theoretically, of course, you could do it?"

"For me to even attempt a spell of necromancy, to even *consider* doing it, would be a violation of everything that I believe and hold sacred."

"Granted," Winters said, "but we were not speaking of whether you *would* do it or not, merely if you *could*, if you had the capability. It was purely a theoretical question."

"Then, speaking theoretically, yes, I suppose I could," said Merlin. "But I most certainly would not."

"Well, then, if you *could*, which is not to say you would, of course, then that would mean to imply that you knew the necessary spells."

There was nothing I could have done to prevent it. It took a clever interviewer such as Robin Winters to accomplish it, but Merlin had finally fallen victim to a media ambush. He realized it, of course, and I suppose he could have attempted to wriggle out of it, but he'd been taken off guard after hours of friendly chat and he was suddenly faced with an unenviable choice. He could deny he knew the spells, but then that would leave the lingering question of why he had admitted he had the skill and capability to do it. And Merlin, quick study that he was, had not yet learned the evasive reply of "No comment," which would have been just as damning, under the circumstances. For a moment, he said nothing, and his face remained in a completely neutral expression. Finally, he gave an answer.

"Yes," he said, matter-of-factly, "I know the spells."

"So then the time of the necromancer has *not* passed," Winters said significantly.

There were a few more questions, but I had little doubt as to how the actual broadcast of the interview would end. It would conclude precisely on that note. As the crew was wrapping up, Winters approached Merlin and held out his hand.

"Well, I think that was very good, indeed," he said with satisfaction. "Undoubtedly, one of the best interviews I've ever done," he added with classic understatement. It would

become his most famous interview, and perhaps the most cele-
brated interview of all time.

Merlin looked down at his outstretched hand, then took it.
"You are a very clever man, Mr. Winters. And a very devious
one."

"Well now, look, it was nothing personal . . ." Winters
began, but Merlin shook his head.

"No, Mr. Winters, I am certain it was not."

"I trust there won't be any hard feelings?" Winters said
uneasily.

"You mean you hope there won't be any personal repercussions," Merlin replied wryly. "You may rest easy on that score,
Mr. Winters. I promise to cast no spells at you in revenge. Not
even a little one. That would be unethical, as you put it."

"Well . . . I'm certainly relieved to hear that," said Winters
with a nervous chuckle. "You understand, questions of that
nature simply must be asked. I was merely doing my job as a
journalist. I'm glad to see you're being a good sport about it."

"A good sport," said Merlin. He smiled. "Interesting
expression. Good night, Mr. Winters. Have a safe journey
back to London."

I waited until they all left, then I gave vent to my frustration.
"God, I *knew* it!" I said. "I *knew* they'd be laying for you
and, sooner or later, one of them would trip you up. I just knew
it! Damn it, I should have seen it coming!" I went on in that
vain for a while, until Merlin finally stopped me.

"Never mind, Thomas," he said placatingly. "It was a
good lesson for me. I had underestimated our friend, Winters,
and allowed my guard to slip. Rest assured, it shall not happen
again. However, do not be concerned. No harm's been done."

"*No harms been done?*" I said. "Do you have any idea
how many people will *see* that program? Despite everything
you said during the interview, he left it on a note that had you
admitting you could do black magic! The media will have a
field day with that one! I can see the headlines now, 'Merlin

Admits to Necromancy!' 'Black Magic Possible, Says Sorcerer.' That sly bastard's done us irreparable harm!''

"Did he?" Merlin said. "I wonder. What was it he said as he was leaving, that I was a 'good sport'? Well, perhaps we should enjoy a bit of 'good sport' with Mr. Winters."

"Now wait a minute," I said apprehensively. "You said you wouldn't do anything. You promised."

"I beg to differ, Thomas," he replied. "I never said that I would not do *anything*. I merely promised that I would cast no spells at Mr. Winters. As I recall, I said nothing about his tape."

# CHAPTER
# 7

The Robin Winters interview is now considered a classic, and is always referred to in any book or documentary about Merlin as the single, most important event that brought him to the general public. Billy Martens was totally upstaged, despite the dramatic transformation he experienced. Though nothing quite so spectacular had taken place during the Winters interview, it was the demonstration of practical uses for thaumaturgy coupled with the sustained, in-depth discussion, broadcast over six successive nights during peak viewing hours, that left its mark on people's minds.

Winters timed it perfectly. Up to that point, there had been the spectacular appearance on the Martens show, followed by a great deal of news coverage, but the opportunity to do the first truly in-depth interview had been seized by Winters at a time when the public interest was at its highest. It seemed absolutely everyone had watched that program. The audience share was greater than at any other time in history, except for one broadcast back in the late twentieth century, some sort of popular American serial where someone named "J.R." was shot.

The general public has never been aware of it till now, but the fact is that Merlin had magically altered the videotape. I never did discover just how it was done, and whenever I asked him about it, he always smiled and replied, "With mirrors." (I assumed that was a joke. He was absorbing popular culture like a sponge, and from time to time, would come out with some surprising bit of contemporary humor, but for all I know, he might well have used some sort of mirror spell.)

At the conclusion of the interview, the camera had been on Merlin while Winters asked the questions, and later on, Winters was taped asking the questions again, so these shots could later be edited-in back at the studio. Somehow, Merlin altered the tape after all this was done. When the conclusion of the interview was broadcast, instead of the camera cutting back to Winters asking the leading question about necromancy, it stayed on Merlin and he continued to speak about the benefits magic had to offer society, and how, combined with judicious policies, it could bring us out of the Collapse.

The lesson was not lost on Robin Winters, nor on any of his colleagues in the media. They all knew about what happened, of course, through their own grapevine, but no one ever went public with it because, for one thing, they had no proof and, for another, I don't think any of them were eager to admit that Merlin could so dramatically manipulate the media. It frightened them. They handled him with kid gloves from that point on. Winters called the morning after the last segment of the program aired and I answered the phone.

"Well, I don't know how the old fox did it," he said, "but he's made a believer out of me. You may tell him that from now on, I'll be treading very softly around him."

"You want to tell him yourself?" I asked.

"No, I don't think so," he replied uneasily. "I'd rather you pass on the message. Frankly, he makes me very nervous. More than nervous. To be honest, he scares the hell out of me."

"I don't see why," I said. "He's not an evil man, Mr. Winters. He means well. He's only trying to help."

"Perhaps," said Winters. "But strictly between you and me, Malory, hasn't it occurred to you how dangerous he could be?"

"Dangerous?" I said.

"Yes. One man with all that power. . . . He can do just about anything he wants."

"He only wants to start a school," I said.

"For now," said Winters. "Or at least, that's what he says."

"Are you implying that he has some sort of hidden agenda?" I asked defensively.

"I don't know," said Winters. "Frankly, I don't know *what* to think about him. I don't know if he's some sort of incredibly gifted telekinetic, or if he really is a sorcerer, or for that matter, an alien from outer space. Whatever in hell he is, his powers are unquestionably genuine and quite unsettling. But if his intentions are purely philanthropic, as you claim, then why alter the tape? Why is he afraid to have the public know that he is capable of necromancy?"

"Oh, come on," I said, "you know very well what that was all about. You tried to pull a typical journalistic stunt to stir things up and create some controversy."

"All right, perhaps I did," admitted Winters, "but that doesn't alter the truth of what I said. The bottom line, Malory, is simply this: whoever he may be, and *whatever* he may be, he doesn't want people to know the true extent of his powers. One has to wonder why. So far, things have gone pretty much his way, but what happens when he receives some serious opposition?"

That nasty, nagging feeling of uneasiness had returned, and for the first time, I understood what it was. I had no idea how to answer Winters, for I had never really considered what would happen if someone set out to prevent Merlin from doing what he wanted. I had become so enthralled by him, so carried away with my own enthusiasm, that I could not imagine *why* anyone would want to stop him. Yet, after that brief conversation with Winters, I was awash in a flood of doubt and apprehension.

Merlin was, indeed, unique. He was a fairy tale come to life. But some fairy tales, I recalled, had certainly contained their share of violence and horror. Winters had been right. Merlin had enough power to do practically anything he wanted. Even given the most well-meaning motives, there were bound to be those who would regard such power as a threat. Merlin could easily become either a messiah or a monster. He didn't seem to care for either role, but the question was, would the world allow him any other choices?

Already, our lives had been turned completely upside down by Merlin's presence. We had no privacy at all. There was a constant flow of visitors, and the telephone rang incessantly. Fortunately, our home was protected by the warding spell, and by our astonishing familiar, who drew as much interest as Merlin did, himself.

Perhaps a week or so after the warding spell was cast, our household received a curious addition. I had no idea where Merlin found him, but one day he presented us with a Great Dane, a black hound unusually large even for that monstrous breed.

"His name is Victor," Merlin said to us, "and from now on, he shall be your familiar. Say hello, Victor."

I expected a loud bark and was absolutely flabbergasted when the huge beast cocked its massive head and said, "Hello. I'm very pleased to meet you."

"Oh, my God!" Jenny said, as I tried to pick my jaw up off the floor. "*It talks!*"

"*He* talks," Merlin corrected her. "And you will find him very well-disciplined, and quite good with the children. Victor's breed is very protective, and quite intelligent, as well."

He made the formal introductions, and Victor quite politely

offered his paw to each of us in turn. The girls couldn't have been more delighted, and Victor formed an immediate bond with them. He was soon giving them rides on his back, and he became very popular with all the local children, who were soon pestering their parents for a dog just like him. Needless to say, all our neighbors wanted Merlin to give them a familiar of their own, but Merlin politely declined all their requests and offers of compensation, by saying that if he were to create another one, everybody would want one, and it would only deplete his energy and take time away from the work he had to do. He did promise, however, that once the school was established, he would see what he could do about creating a few more such familiars, and perhaps teach his students to create them, as well. In this way, he gave many of the local townspeople an added incentive to help out with the school.

Today, thaumagenes can be purchased at any number of shops throughout the world, and the thaumagenetic engineer adept has raised the art of making magical beasts to new heights. Some are quite sophisticated, indeed, hybrids of various types of animals, and some even began as inanimate constructions. However, Victor the Great Dane was the first, and my family found not only security, but took great joy in his presence. Both my daughters are now grown, but Victor is with me still, and we are growing old together. He is no longer as fast or as strong as he once was—nor am I, for that matter— but he is an old and loyal friend and companion, who always beats me at chess.

With the security of Victor and the warding spell, we were spared the sort of lunatic behavior where people might have come tramping through our yard and peeking through our windows, or tried to break into our home to meet Merlin, or steal some memento, or do Lord knows what. For all I knew, some of our visitors had come with precisely such intentions, but the moment they came within the ward's sphere of influence— which was strongest in the house itself, but also extended across the yard and some distance out into the street—they became very peaceful and docile, and were always considerate and polite.

I had a hard time believing that the simple ritual we had participated in had been responsible for this invisible, protective aura around our home. Certainly, it seemed impossible that I could have had anything to do with it. However, while the ward, as the spell was called, was undoubtedly effective and may have eliminated any harmful intentions on the part of visitors, it did nothing to cut down on their numbers. And after the airing of the Winters interview, the situation grew much worse.

It got so that at almost any hour of the day or night, there was a crowd gathered in the street outside our home, waiting patiently, expectantly, for Merlin to show himself. It was positively eerie. They were always so quiet... waiting... watching... and whenever Merlin did come out, and he went out to speak with them frequently, they would all surge forward, although quietly, and without any attempt to overwhelm the efforts of our local constabulary to keep them in order.

Not all of our local police were professionals. There wasn't any money to pay for a fully staffed police department and the squad was heavily augumented by volunteers. There had been a great deal of concern about the large numbers of people arriving to see Merlin every day and considerable anxiety about how to control them. However, to the immense relief of our constabulary, this did not prove to be much of a problem.

"I've never seen anything like it," said Chief Thorpe, looking out at the crowd as he sat astride his horse one night. Like me, he had once been a cop serving with an urban strike force, and had survived more than his share of street riots. He watched as the crowd pressed in to hear Merlin speak, without any pushing or shoving or shouting. "I don't know how he does it, but I wish to hell I could learn the trick."

"Perhaps you can, Scott," I said. "Maybe you should ask him."

"No, not me," the chief replied. "I'm an old man, Tom, and I'm not up to learning any new tricks, no pun intended. I should imagine he'll want young people for his school. He'll teach his magic to the new generation. They're inheriting this mess, they'll need all the bloody help that they can get. Oh, and speaking of help, I had a call from New Scotland Yard this morning, asking me to pass a message on to you."

"Really? What's the message?"

"They'd like very much for you to come in and talk with them," said Thorpe.

"About Merlin?"

"Well, they didn't say, specifically, but that would be the obvious inference."

"Who was it who called?" I asked.

"Chief Inspector Carmody."

"The old man, himself?"

"None other. The message was, and I quote, 'Tell Malory I would appreciate seeing him as soon as possible. Say, nine o'clock tomorrow morning. Oh, and ask him to come alone, will you?' Unquote."

"Alone?" I said.

"Yes, he rather seemed to emphasize that part," said Thorpe. "There anything I can do?"

"Yes, thanks. Keep an eye on things for me while I'm gone," I said.

"You know, you don't really *have* to go," Thorpe said. "You've left the force, and I've neither a warrant nor a subpoena for you. I suppose you could refuse."

"I don't think that would be a very good idea," I said.

"No, neither do I," said Thorpe with a smile, "but I did think maybe I should mention it. Inform you of your rights and all that."

I grinned. "Thanks, Scott."

"Merely going through the motions," he replied. "I'll keep an eye out while you're gone, though with His Nibs around, I shouldn't think you'd have any cause to worry."

"Just the same, I'll be glad to know you're looking out for things," I said. "Thanks, Scott. I'll see you."

I never saw him alive again. The next morning, as I was visiting New Scotland Yard, Scott Thorpe was murdered.

I had met Chief Inspector Carmody before, in the course of my duties with the Loo, but we were hardly on a first name basis. He had been my superior, though not my immediate superior, that had been Captain Blassingame, the commander of the L.U.A.D. I fully expected Carmody not to remember me, but in fact, he did—or at least he acted as if he did—and he received me very cordially, despite the way I'd left the force. I had formally submitted my resignation, but not until after I'd walked off the job, which certainly wasn't cricket. If Carmody harbored any disapproval over that, he didn't show it.

He was not a young man. At the time, I believe he was in his early sixties, though one wouldn't know it to look at him. He did not look a day over fifty, and he was quite fit, tall and slender, with only a touch of gray around his temples. He was very much of the old school, which is to say, a proper gentleman, though every man and woman in the department knew how he could crack the whip.

I met him in his private office, but we were not alone. There were three other men present, two of whom I did not know, but I immediately recognized the Prime Minister, whose presence certainly took me back a bit.

"Come in, Mr. Malory," said the chief inspector. "You know the Prime Minister, of course."

"Well, I've never actually had the pleasure," I said. "It's an honor, Prime Minister."

"Nice to meet you, Mr. Malory," the Prime Minister said, shaking my hand. "Please, sit down."

I took the chair across from the chief inspector's desk, and the Prime Minister sat down behind the desk, in Carmody's chair. Carmody and the other two gentlemen remained standing. I felt like a suspect about to be given the third degree.

"This is Mr. Chambers," the Prime Minister said, indicating one of them. "Mr. Chambers is the director of our Security Service." Otherwise known as MI5, I thought. "And Major Fitzroy is our special liaison officer with the American intelligence community." This meant he was our ambassador, of sorts, to the CIA. It was going to be quite a meeting.

"This is about Merlin, of course," I said.

The Prime Minister smiled. "Consider this a sort of briefing," he said. "You happen to be in a unique position to provide us with some information concerning a rather unusual situation. Chief Inspector?"

Carmody cleared his throat. "I'll speak plainly, Malory," he said. "Cut to the chase, as it were. Now, just what in bloody hell is this all about?"

"Well, I'm not quite certain what you mean, sir," I said. "That is, with all due respect, I assume you *know* what it's all about. It's certainly been given quite a bit of coverage. Beyond that, I'm really not sure what I can tell you."

"The truth, for one thing," Chambers said. "Who, exactly, is this Merlin person? What's his real name and where did he come from? What's he after?"

I cleared my own throat. "Well, sir, your presumption seems to be that there's been some sort of deception involved, and I can assure you that is not the case. His real name is, in fact, Merlin Ambrosius, and he came from out of an oak tree in Sherwood Forest. As to what he's after, he's been very forthcoming about that. He wishes to start a school to train adepts in the art of thaumaturgy, and thereby bring magic back into the world."

"Do you take us all for fools, Malory?" said Major Fitzroy. "This isn't some chat show. We want some straight answers."

"I'm giving them to you to the best of my ability, Major," I replied. "And no, I most certainly do not take you for fools. I take you for skeptics, which is understandable, I suppose, considering the circumstances. However, I assure you that I'm telling you the truth. If you don't believe me, ask Billy Martens. Or Robin Winters, for that matter. Or any of the hundreds of people who have encountered Merlin for themselves."

"We've already spoken with both Martens and Winters," Carmody said. "And a number of other people have been questioned, as well."

That meant they had conducted an investigation, and I gathered they hadn't been very satisfied with its results.

"I will grant you that Martens seems to believe that Merlin is exactly who he says he is," said Carmody. "However, Mr. Winters seems to have some reservations on that point."

"Really?" I said. "What did he say?"

"He described what sounded like either a very sophisticated series of tricks or illusions," Carmody said, "or a dramatic display of a very highly developed telekinetic ability. He said he could not speak to the veracity of Merlin appearing from out of a tree, or of his being over two thousand years old, and you must admit that part, at the very least, is a bit difficult to credit."

I nodded. "I can certainly see where you would feel that way, sir. I felt the same way myself, at first. Nevertheless, I don't know what else to tell you."

"Do you know for a fact that he's two thousand years old?" said Chambers wryly. "I don't suppose you could prove it. Or can you?" he added with a smirk.

"I suppose that would depend on what you would consider proof, sir," I replied. "I haven't seen his birth certificate, if that's what you mean. I don't believe they had them in King Arthur's day."

"You find this amusing, Malory?" Fitzroy said.

"In an ironic sort of way, yes, sir. I do. I will tell you,

frankly, that I cannot prove his age. I will also tell you that nothing in British law requires me to do so, which I think you know as well as I. If you have some concerns about Merlin, why not address them to him directly?''

''Because for the moment, Malory, we are addressing them to you,'' Carmody said curtly. ''It is our presumption that you have come here at our request, to provide us with some information as a loyal citizen. We do not require lectures on the law, thank you very much. No one here is trespassing on your rights, nor are you being accused of anything at this point.''

''Are you planning to accuse me of something at a later point?'' I asked.

Carmody pursed his lips and gave me a disapproving look. No doubt, he was considering what he might have done had I not left the department.

''We are simply attempting to determine if some sort of fraud is being perpetrated,'' he replied. ''And if not, we would like to determine exactly what *is* being perpetrated.''

''To the best of my knowledge, Chief Inspector, nothing is being perpetrated, as you put it. Merlin hasn't broken any laws. I suppose, once he starts teaching, there may be some question about proper certification or whatever. I'll freely admit to ignorance on the requirements for that sort of thing. However, to date, he certainly hasn't done anything wrong. Unless, of course, you consider changing Billy Martens into an ass a form of assault. Although, he *did* change him back. Whether or not that was for the best, I'll leave you gentlemen to decide for yourselves.''

The Prime Minister tried, not altogether successfully, to repress a smile. Fitzroy and Chambers did not look very happy. I didn't think they had much of a sense of humor. Carmody simply regarded me thoughtfully.

''He's not being very cooperative, is he?'' Fitzroy said tersely, with a glance at Carmody.

"On the contrary, Major," I said. "I'm cooperating to the very best of my ability. You find it difficult to believe I'm telling you the truth. I can certainly understand that. It *is* difficult to believe. However, I would venture to suggest that if you met Merlin for yourselves, you would most likely have all your questions answered."

"Perhaps we should try another tack," the Prime Minister said. "Mr. Malory, you apparently believe that Merlin is exactly who he says he is, and that he can, in fact, accomplish what he says he can, is that correct?"

"Correct, Prime Minister. And, if I might add, I think that you believe that, too, at least to some degree. Otherwise, you wouldn't be here."

The Prime Minister smiled. "Quite so," he said. "Clearly, your friend, Mr. Ambrosius, is possessed of remarkable abilities. Astonishing abilities. The question is, precisely what is the *nature* of those abilities?"

I shrugged. "It's magic, sir."

"Well, so you claim, and you obviously seem to believe it. I am not questioning your sincerity. However, I do find a belief in magic difficult to support."

"I understand that, sir. Which is why I've suggested that you meet with Merlin yourself. I think then you'd be convinced beyond any shadow of a doubt."

"Quite possibly," the Prime Minister said. "Mr. Ambrosius certainly seems to possess extensive powers of persuasion. Perhaps that is why we are all a bit leery of confronting him directly. At least for the present."

"You think he's some sort of hypnotist?" I said. "Well, that thought also occurred to me, at first. But if he is, then he's hypnotized not only large crowds, but the entire television audience, as well. And somehow, he's managed to hypnotize inanimate cameras, too. How would you account for that?"

The Prime Minister nodded. "We don't know how to

account for it," he said. "That's the entire point. However, let us assume that what we are confronted with is not some paranormal, psychic talent, but actual sorcery, as it is depicted in the tales of the Brothers Grimm and Mr. Tolkien. That would leave us with some rather difficult decisions to make. And, frankly, at the moment, I'm at a loss to explain just what those decisions might be, and how we would go about making them. We thought, perhaps, you might help shed some more light on the situation."

"I'd be happy to help in any way I can, Prime Minister," I said. "But I can't force you to believe me. However, assume, for the moment, that everything I'm telling you is true. Just assume that, for the sake of the discussion."

"All right," the Prime Minister said. "Go on."

"What is there to be concerned about? Merlin is proposing to start a school to train adepts. He is not planning to charge any tuition, so there's no question of defrauding anyone. The entire venture is to be a nonprofit operation. We have already received donations, all voluntary and perfectly aboveboard and properly accounted for, and we've been offered the facilities of a public school in Loughborough that closed down about five years ago and has been standing vacant ever since. Part of the space will be used as dormitories for the students, and the local citizens have volunteered their labors to see to it that these dormitory rooms are properly refurbished to conform with health regulations and all that sort of thing.

"We are in the process of setting up a voluntary organization, and our accounts and files will be open for examination by the proper authorities at any time. True, we may be cutting through some bureaucratic red tape, but considering the circumstances, and that most of these bureaucracies have either collapsed or are in a hopeless state of limbo, we're doing the best we can to do everything properly. The whole thing is being run on the level of a cooperative. No one is taking any salaries, and no one is making any profit. However, society *will* profit as trained adepts provide a thaumaturgical support base for our collapsed technological infrastructure and bankrupt economy. So, I ask you, where's the harm?''

"That's just what we're attempting to find out," said Chambers. "Proceeding on the assumption that these paranormal abilities of Merlin's can be taught to others successfully, then we need to consider just what these trainees of his, for lack of a better term, will do with those abilities. We need to determine if this would pose any danger to society. Mr. Winters claims that Merlin was actually able to alter a videotape recording. Now, if this is true, it demonstrates a rather alarming and totally unprecedented paranormal talent. If he can actually psychically influence an electronic medium, then there's no telling what he might be able to do with, say, computer data, for example. That would make him a significant risk not only to our security, but to the security of any government or private corporation."

"Which would explain the CIA's interest, of course," I said. "I think I'm beginning to understand."

"We were hoping you would," said Fitzroy.

"I was going to add," I said, "that what I understand is that you gentlemen are being totally paranoid, no offense intended. Who gives a damn about classified computer files anymore, for God's sake? All the bloody computers are down at least half the time because there's no power. Corporations are going bankrupt everywhere and governments are hanging on by little more than their fingernails. People are starving and shooting each other in the streets! Everything's going to pieces and you're acting as if it's business as usual!"

I shook my head with disbelief. "This isn't about whether or not Merlin is genuine, or whether it's magic or some kind of psychic talent, it's about fear. You're afraid of him, afraid that he poses some kind of threat to you and to whatever remains of your precious power structure. Well, the fact is that without Merlin, whatever's left of the power structure is going to collapse completely, along with the rest of society. Can't you see that Merlin isn't the problem? He's the solution! He's not interested in raiding top secret files or taking over the government, what little of it there is left, all he wants to do is *teach*! If you're so concerned about him, then *I'm* not the one you should be talking to. You should be talking to *him*."

"All in good time, Mr. Malory," the Prime Minister replied. "However, I hope you'll understand why we asked you here today. And why we asked you to come alone. This is, to say the least, a highly unusual situation, and one which is being taken very seriously. Otherwise, as you quite correctly pointed out, I would not be here. There was no real reason for me to be present at this meeting, other than my own curiosity. I wanted to meet you face to face, and I personally wanted to hear what you had to say. These are difficult times, very trying times for all of us. We would all like to find some way out of this global disaster and, believe me, the finest minds in the world have been grappling with the problem. So far, no one has come up with a workable solution. We are in a downward spiral, and there seems to be no way to reverse it."

He held up his hand, forestalling my reply. "Please hear me out. This man whom you call Merlin suddenly appears out of nowhere, claiming to be a character out of mythology, and however incredible his claims may seem, bolstering them are some undeniably impressive and seemingly miraculous abilities. Now, I am not questioning your sincerity when you say you believe him to be exactly who he says he is, but then, as you yourself have said, you can understand our skepticism. You asked me, a moment ago, to assume that you were telling the truth, and that Merlin was exactly who he claims to be. Now, let me ask you, purely for the sake of discussion, as you put it, to assume that is not case. Given that assumption, where does that lead us?

"It leads us to suppose that this person, calling himself

Merlin, is either the cleverest illusionist that anyone has ever seen, or that he possesses astonishing paranormal abilities on a scale that no one has ever seen before. That, given all the evidence, happens to be the prevailing opinion among the experts."

"What experts?" I asked.

"That is not important for the sake of this discussion," the Prime Minister replied. "The fact is, we have a man with miraculous abilities and a great deal of charisma, as well as a considerable talent for self-promotion, whom no one has ever met or heard of before. No record of his existence can be found anywhere. He appears fully capable of doing things that are scientifically impossible. In a remarkably short time, he has captured the imagination of the public all over the world and his self-appointed task, if we are to take him at his word, is nothing short of messianic. Surely, you could see where this would be cause for some serious concern."

I sighed heavily. "I can't take issue with a single thing you've said, Prime Minister. I told you, I can fully understand the way you feel. You think there's some other explanation than the one I've given you, that Merlin isn't really Merlin, that he's some sort of gifted charlatan who happens to possess unprecedented psychic powers, such as telekinesis, and that one of those powers seems to be a hypnotic ability to charm people and make believers out of them. If that is your position, then I don't know what to say to you, because the obvious inference would be that he's used that ability on me, and my testimony, therefore, is unreliable. If that's what you really think, then inviting me to come here was absolutely pointless."

I may have said something else, I no longer remember clearly, because what happened next was so vividly shocking. I came to an abrupt halt at about that moment, because suddenly I couldn't see them any longer. In a flash, I was no longer in Carmody's office, but standing outside my own home.

At least, I *think* I was standing, but I don't have any memory of that sensation. All I know is that I seemed to have been somehow transported back to Loughborough, though I knew I wasn't physically there. I was seeing a vision, and the hallucination, if it can be called that, was so starkly real that I became totally disoriented for a time.

The street outside my home was a scene of pandemonium. I could hear screaming and shouting, and I saw people running in all directions, and there was a sudden pain in my shoulder that was immediately familiar, because I had been shot before.

"Malory? What the devil. . . . *Malory*!"

Just as abruptly, the vision faded and I was back in Carmody's office, slumped over in the chair.

"Malory!" Carmody was bending over me. "Are you all right? What's wrong?"

I shook my head and blinked several times, then after a moment, during which they stared at me with some concern, I got up and started for the door.

"Malory, wait!" Fitzroy grabbed me by the arm. "Where the hell do you think you're going?"

"I have to go," I said, shaking him off. "Merlin's just been shot."

I didn't know how I knew that it was Merlin who'd been shot, I simply knew. There had been nothing in that brief vision to clue me in. It seemed that it had only lasted perhaps a second or two; I had no way of telling what the duration of the experience had been. For all I know, it could have lasted several minutes, or merely a fraction of a second. However, I can still recall having the distinct sensation not of *being* shot, but of having *been* shot, and if I hadn't been wounded a number of times before, so that the feeling was all too unpleasantly familiar, I may well not have known what it was.

There is a great deal more knowledge about this sort of phenomenon today. It is known as "projection," and it most often occurs between people who have established some sort of bond, though it can also occur between perfect strangers. Before it was better understood, it was usually a spontaneous occurrence, meaning one that took place without any volitional intent on the part either of the projector or the receiver. These days, however, a trained adept can do it consciously, selecting not only the receiver and the method of projection, but exercising complete control over it, as well.

Most common, of course, is "astral projection," in which the image of the projector is manifested to the receiver, appearing quite solid and often capable of communicating. This is the method most frequently chosen by the trained adept wishing to project to someone. Less common is the sort of projection I received, in which there is a period of shared consciousness. This is known as "sensory projection," and unless it is being consciously directed by an adept, its duration is normally quite brief. Indeed, these days it occurs most frequently with warlocks, and most of the time, they are unaware of what they're doing.

As beginners, they are only starting to get their magical "sea legs," and often their intuitive abilities start to develop before they've learned how to exercise control over them. Consequently, the relatives and intimates of warlocks frequently find themselves suddenly plunged into a brief, sensory, shared consciousness, sometimes with rather amusing results. For example, I knew of one case of involuntary sensory projection involving a young female warlock that wound up causing her considerable embarrassment.

The term "warlock," incidentally, now commonly used to refer to adepts in training, was once used to describe a male witch. As with many slang expressions, its origin as a modern, non-gender-specific term to describe students of thaumaturgy is unclear. Merlin himself disliked it, explaining that its origins in Old English were with the word "*wærloga*," which meant "oathbreaker," and that the word "*witch*," derived from the Old English "*wicce*," which meant "to more proper and non-gender-specific to begin with. The negative connotations of those words can be directly traced to early Christianity, which was intolerant of pagan beliefs and customs. Thus, "*wicce*" became, in time, "wicked."

In any case, so much for linguistics. This young female warlock possessed a strong latent talent for projection and, unknown to her, her thaumaturgic training had triggered it, so that she became capable of unconsciously projecting at moments of peak sensory experience. In other words, she developed the subconscious ability to project while she was making love with her fiancé. Unfortunately for her, the receiver turned out to be her mother, with whom she had a very close bond, and the poor woman suddenly found herself experiencing the physical sensations of her daughter's lovemaking. Eventually, the whole thing was sorted out, but not without some awkwardness, and the mother was never again able to face her daughter's husband without blushing.

The point of the preceding digression is that while projection is a far more common thing today and much better understood, it wasn't so in those days, and I had never experienced anything like it before. My initial response was shock, then a brief period of disorientation, during which Carmody apparently thought I had fallen ill or something, and then resolve was galvanized as the realization sank in that Merlin had been shot. It did not even occur to me to question what had happened until I was on the train to Loughborough.

I felt riddled with anxiety, and I began to have doubts about my initial response. When it happened, it was almost instinctive. Something was wrong at home; Merlin had been shot; possibly my wife and daughters were in danger, and the knee-jerk reaction was to rush home as quickly as possible. However, on the train, I had some time to think, and having never experienced projection before, I had no frame of reference for it.

I began to question whether the whole thing had merely been a figment of my imagination, some sort of brief, paranoid delusion brought on by the questioning I had been subjected to, an emotional response to a perceived threat. I would almost get to the point where I had rationalized it all away as some kind of temporary aberration, and then I'd swing the other way, as I considered the fact that I'd never had such an experience prior to meeting Merlin and that it was undoubtedly his way of communicating with me at a moment of great stress. I kept vacillating back and forth, not knowing what the hell to think, so that by the time the train pulled in to the station (mercifully, without any breakdowns for a change), I was worked up into quite a state. I ran all the way home, and as I turned down our street, I knew with a sinking feeling that it had not been my imagination at all.

There was a paramedic van parked in front of our home, and I saw several members of our largely volunteer police force on horseback, keeping back a crowd of curious onlookers. Unless what had happened to me back in Carmody's office had been a precognitive experience, then a significant amount of time had elapsed. Why was the ambulance still there? Was Merlin in there, fighting for his life? Or, worse yet, was it one or more members of my family? With a mounting sense of dread, I rushed up, out of breath, and pushed my way through the crowd. One of the officers interposed his mount between me and my front door.

"Hold on, there . . . oh, Mr. Malory. It's you."

"What happened?" I managed to get out, between gasps for breath.

"There's been some trouble," he said. "Someone shot at Merlin."

"Is he all right?"

"I think so, but one of the bullets struck Chief Thorpe and killed him."

"Oh, no!" I said. "What about my family?"

"They're all right. They were all safely inside when the gunfire broke out."

"Thank God. Who did it?"

"No idea. We haven't established the gunman's identity yet. But he's dead. Carr got him. They've taken the body away."

I thanked him and hurried inside, where I found Merlin sitting on the couch, leaning back, his robe cut away from his shoulder. He was arguing with the doctor. Several police officers were present, both volunteer auxiliary and a couple of our permanent, full-time officers. Jenny came rushing up to me.

"Oh, Tom, it was awful!"

"Thank God you're all right," I said, hugging her to me. "Where are the girls?"

"In their room with Victor. They're quite upset, of course, but they're unharmed."

"Thomas! There you are, at last!" said Merlin. "Get this fool away from me!"

"Mr. Ambrosius, *please*," the doctor said. "If you won't allow me to treat your wound, there could be a danger of infection and further complications."

"The only complication I'm concerned about is *you*," said Merlin irately. He turned to me. "Look what this idiot did! He ruined my robe!"

The doctor turned to me in exasperation. "Will you please talk some sense into him?" he said. "The bullet's still lodged in there and he won't let me treat him."

"I'll give you a treatment," Merlin said, glaring at him.

"Take it easy," I told him. "You've been shot, for God's sake. The man's a doctor. He's only trying to help."

"I don't require any help," said Merlin.

"Look, you're being stubborn and unreasonable," the doctor told him. "That's bullet's not going to come out by itself."

"Is that so?" said Merlin. "Thomas, if you will kindly restrain this overly zealous samaritan, then perhaps he might learn something.'' He turned to the doctor. ''Observe.''

He took a deep breath and closed his eyes. His brow furrowed in concentration and, a moment later, the skin over the wound began to twitch, as if with a muscular spasm.

''Damn,'' the doctor said, starting forward. ''He's started bleeding again.''

''Wait,'' I said, holding him back. Some clotted blood exited the wound, followed by a fresh red flow that trickled down his chest, and then, as the area over the wound throbbed visibly, we saw the bullet emerge.

''Good Lord!'' exclaimed one of the officers. ''Will you *look* at that!''

''Well, I'll be . . .'' the doctor shook his head in amazement. ''I've never seen anything like that in all my life!''

As we watched, the blood flow ceased and the wound began to close before our very eyes.

''It's incredible!'' the doctor said. ''Human tissue can't possibly heal that fast!''

''Perhaps not through traditional forms of healing,'' I said. ''This is something else entirely.''

Merlin sighed heavily and opened his eyes. ''There. Satisfied?'' he said. He sounded weary and he looked extremely tired. Not surprising, considering he'd been shot, but clearly, expelling the bullet and healing his own wound had taken a lot out of him.

''They never covered anything like this in medical school,'' the doctor said. He started to bend down toward Merlin, then hesitated. ''Please. . . . May I? Do you mind?''

''Go ahead and look,'' said Merlin with an air of resignation.

The doctor drew closer and peered at the wound, which had closed completely, though the skin around it was still bloody and a bit raw. He probed, gently. ''Does that hurt?''

Merlin winced. "Yes, of course it hurts, you dolt! Are you finished, or do you now wish to perform an augury?"

The doctor straightened up and stared at him. "If you can teach me how to do that in that school of yours, I'll be first in line to sign up, and the medical establishment be damned."

"Indeed?" said Merlin. "Come see me again, then, and we shall discuss it. For the present, there are more pressing matters of concern." He turned to me and Jenny. "Thomas, I must humbly beg your forgiveness."

"For what?" I said.

"For exposing your family to danger," he replied. "It was inexcusable. I had foolishly failed to consider that your modern weapons can reach out from beyond the ward's protective influence. It was stupid of me, and I am aghast to think that one of them could have been struck down instead of me. Can you forgive me?"

"It wasn't your fault," I said.

"Oh, yes, it was," he insisted. "But for my presence here, this would not have happened. And that gallant man who was killed. . . ."

"Scott Thorpe," I said, with a guilty feeling, for in the past few moments, I had completely forgotten about him.

"Yes, Thorpe," said Merlin. "He bravely interposed himself between the assailant and myself, and took the mortal blow that had been meant for me. A most chivalrous and gallantly unselfish deed. And it cost him his life. Would that I could restore him as I have healed myself, but regrettably, that power is beyond me."

"He was a cop," I said. "And a damned good one. He knew the risks."

Merlin sighed. "I owe him my life. Did he have a family?"

"A wife," I said. "He had two sons, but they were both grown. One was with the army. He was killed in the riots at Coventry several years ago. The other is a police officer in London."

Merlin nodded. "Then at least I have not deprived young

children of a father. But I have deprived a wife of her husband."

"*You* haven't deprived anyone of anything," Jenny said. "There's no reason for you to feel responsible. You weren't the one who pulled the trigger."

"No," said Merlin grimly, "but if not for me, he would not have been there. I shall have to take steps to make certain such a thing does not happen again."

"You'd best leave that to us, sir," Lieutenant William Carr said. With the death of Thorpe, he was now in command of the force. "It's the sort of thing we're trained to do. I'll take that bullet now, if you don't mind."

"Why? What do you want with it?" asked Merlin.

"We'll send it to the ballistics lab in London, where they have a way of examining it that will enable them to match it to the weapon it was fired from."

"What use would that be?" Merlin asked. "The assailant has been slain."

"Well, there'll have to be a full report," said Carr, "especially since you've become so well-known. We'd better follow procedure all the way on this one. Go by the numbers, match the bullet to the gun, then try to use the gun to trace the perpetrator, because he wasn't carrying any identification. We have no idea who he was."

Merlin grunted. "It sounds quite pointless to me. I can tell you about the man who shot me and murdered Chief Thorpe."

"You *can*?" said Carr. "How?"

"I assume that to load this projectile in the weapon it was fired from, it was necessary for him to handle it. That means he will have impressed his energies upon it."

"What if he wore gloves?" I asked.

"If he wore gloves, that would weaken the impression, but it would still be there for me to detect," said Merlin.

"You mean the way psychics can hold an item of a missing person's clothing and deduce things from it?" Carr asked.

"The principle is the same," said Merlin. "As I have said before, there has been evidence of magic in your society all along. You have simply chosen to call it something else. I will be able to tell you something about the killer from the impressions on this bullet, but I could also work a divination spell, only that would require some time and I would need to be more fully rested. However, let us see what we can learn from this bullet for the present."

He picked it up and held it in his hand for a moment.

"Our man was very angry," he said. "More than angry, he was outraged. I appear to have been the focus of his outrage, which would explain, of course, why he tried to kill me. He was a Christian, but his faith was like a mania. He was consumed by it. The impression is extremely strong."

"A religious fanatic," Carr said.

I shushed him.

"This was not a man who attended church," Merlin continued. He frowned. "That seems peculiar. Why? Ah, I see. He believed that he had compromised his faith. He felt himself to be unworthy, a sinner. He was baptized in the Catholic faith, but he had strayed from it. I sense pain, and great feelings of guilt. He had killed before. Soldiers. British soldiers. He saw them as oppressors. He killed them with devices he constructed, devices that explode."

"Oh, bloody hell," said Carr. "A Provo."

Merlin opened his eyes. "A what?"

"He means the I.R.A.," I said. "Provisional Army of the Irish Republic. A terrorist, in other words, although they see themselves as freedom fighters. It's been going on for generations. To them, the Collapse is not a tragedy, it's an opportunity. There are fewer of them than there used to be, but they've been particularly active here doing the riots. But I don't understand why he'd go after you. You have nothing to do with the British government."

Merlin clutched the bullet in his fist.

"This man was torn," he said. "He felt he had to kill as a duty to his country, but that in killing, he had offended God. He spent long hours in private anger, attempting to atone for his sins. Killing me was to be a part of his atonement. He saw me as a servant of the Devil, and in killing me, he believed he was doing God's work.''

"A madman," Carr said.

"Yes," said Merlin. "He had been driven mad by his inner turmoil over what he had done in the past. Some innocent people had died as a result of his actions, and among them were small children. He could not justify that to himself. He was tormented. He was careless of his health and his appearance. He constantly smoked cigarettes and drank to excess. He felt he had been forced to steal to meet his needs, and he sought to place the blame for that on others, yet he could not escape his feelings of responsibility and guilt. His nose had been broken and had not healed properly. He had difficulty breathing through it. His teeth were bad, and were causing him considerable pain, but it was nothing to the pain his spirit felt. He believed that killing me would be a way of washing clean his other sins, and he was desperate to do so."

Merlin opened his hand and dropped the bullet on the coffee table. He sighed heavily. "Killing this man was only merciful," he said. "In a way, he was already dead."

Carr whistled softly through his teeth. "You could tell all that just from holding the bullet?"

"If you come back in the morning, perhaps I shall be able to tell you more," said Merlin. "But I fail to see the point in it." He took a deep breath. "I am weary. I shall ask your pardon, but I must rest now." He leaned back against the cushions and closed his eyes. A second later, he was fast asleep.

Carr glanced at me, then with a movement of his head, indicated that he would like to speak with me in private.

"He's really something, isn't he?" said Carr as we stood on the steps outside.

I nodded. "That's putting it mildly."

Carr took a deep breath and stared off into the distance for a moment. He shook his head. "I have to go see Anne Thorpe and break the news to her, though I suspect she's heard by now, poor woman. I can detail some more men to watch your place, but frankly, Tom, I'm in over my head. I haven't got enough people to deal with this sort of thing." He looked out at the crowd, which his officers had failed to disperse.

"I know," I said.

"I'll need to send for help from London."

I nodded again, waiting for him to get to his point. I had a feeling I knew what it was going to be.

"Look, Tom, I don't have to tell you how things are. You understand my position. I think this sort of thing is just the tip of the iceberg. Merlin's going to be a magnet for every lunatic and religious fanatic out there. Our resources are strained past the breaking point as it is. And you have your family to consider."

"Are you asking me to get rid of him, Bill?"

Carr sighed. "Look, Tom, I can't tell you how to live your life, and I wouldn't presume to do so. But you brought your family out here from London so they could be safe from just this sort of thing. And I'll be honest with you, I can't guarantee their protection."

"I think Merlin can," I said.

"For God's sake, Tom, he's just been shot! He can't even guarantee his own protection."

"He's never been exposed to modern firearms before," I said. "He was taken by surprise. He'll know what to expect now. He's probably the best thing that's happened to this town, Bill, and you know it. He's our one best hope to get out of this mess, and you want me to tell him to leave?"

"No, of course not. I couldn't ask you to do that, and I wouldn't. But I do think it would be in everyone's best interest not to have him in your home. Look, you've been offered the use of the old school out on the main road. It's situated on the outskirts of town, well away from any other buildings, and with a bit of work, it could be made quite livable. You're going to be converting some of the space to dormitories for the students, anyway. Why not simply move him in there? You're overburdened as it is. It has to be disrupting your family's home life. And, to be quite honest, while your neighbors are supportive, some of them are understandably concerned.''

I could not deny his logic. Everything he said made sense. He wasn't the only one in over his head. Ever since Merlin had started to receive publicity, there had been a tremendous influx of people arriving in Loughborough, and most of them headed straight for our home, as if on some sort of pilgrimage. Our local authorities and resources, such as they were, simply were not up to the task.

Many of our neighbors, as caught up in their enthusiasm over Merlin as was I, had volunteered their help and, for many of them, it had become an almost full-time job. We needed more organization. We needed *an* organization, something formally defined and structured, to deal with all the problems. Allan Stewart had already been pressing me on this matter, but I had kept putting him off, largely because I hadn't wanted to think about it. It was all getting to be too much for me, and I simply hadn't wanted to deal with it.

I was not being realistic. I had come to have a very proprietary feeling about Merlin. *I* had discovered him, therefore, he was ''mine.'' I had assumed the *de facto* role of his manager and I did not want to relinquish it. That was not only impractical, it was absurd. I certainly wasn't doing either of us any favors. Merlin had asked me to advise him, not control him, and subconsciously, I suppose, that was exactly what I had tried to do. I had even lashed out at the Prime Minister like some overprotective mother, and that was hardly productive to our cause. Carr's words to me, and what had happened to prompt them, were like a dash of cold water in my face.

''You're right, of course,'' I told him. ''The whole thing has gotten out of hand. I just hadn't wanted to admit it, I suppose.''

''Well, you've been at the center of it all,'' said Carr sympathetically. ''You've hardly had a chance to think about it very clearly. But something must be done. Merlin's abilities are unquestionably unique, but not even he can handle all this by himself. And you certainly can't do it alone, either. You need to get the government involved.''

A part of me realized that Carr was absolutely right, and another part of me rebelled at the idea, especially after my less than productive meeting at Carmody's office.

These days, with Merlin accepted as a sorcerer, the founding father of the Second Thaumaturgic Age, and an honored and respected educator, it may seem difficult for readers who have grown up with this reality to understand how he was regarded then. Among many people, there was a natural tendency toward belief, partly as a result of what they'd seen and heard on television and partly out of a basic *desire* to believe. Historically, at times of great stress, uncertainty, and hardship, there has always been a rise in spirituality. People need hope. They need to believe in something.

Those who met Merlin always came away from the experience convinced that he was genuine, and many other people were convinced as a result of the media coverage and their own predispositions. However, a significant number remained not only skeptical, but hostile, convinced by their own firmly held beliefs that magic could not possibly exist, no matter how it was defined, and Merlin took great pains to disassociate magic from its traditional, supernatural and mythological portrayals. In fact, he gradually started to avoid using the word ''magic,'' in favor of ''thaumaturgy,'' which was an astute and perceptive decision on his part.

''Thaumaturgy'' sounded more modern and scientific, much as the words ''psychic'' and ''paranormal'' sounded more plausible than ''medium'' and ''occult.'' And one of the chief difficulties we had in the beginning was the firm opposition of the scientific establishment, whose opinions were understandably given a great deal of weight, especially by the government. While I did realize we needed help, the last thing I wanted was to have the government involved.

I envisioned us becoming sidetracked as Merlin was co-opted and made the center of some sort of massive research effort, first to determine the validity of his claims and then, when that validity was demonstrated, to conduct a scientific study of them. I could certainly see the need for that, but even greater was the need for training adepts and spreading the knowledge of thaumaturgy if we were to find our way out of the Collapse. I did not think Merlin would have much patience with anyone trying to forestall his efforts in that regard. I couldn't see him acquiescing to the role of laboratory guinea pig.

I made a decision which, in retrospect, I still think was a good one, though it was to have unfavorable repercussions in the short term. I decided that to the extent the government wished to provide help, it would be gratefully accepted, but that I would resist any effort on their part in determining what we were to do. I would advise Merlin of my feelings, and the final decision would be his, but I had little doubt he would agree with me.

Carr's advice about the school, however, was quite sound. It would have to be more than just a school; it would have to become a residence for Merlin and a headquarters for an organization to support our efforts. If my home was not to be constantly besieged, and if my family was to have any peace at all, Merlin would have to leave. I hated the thought of telling him that, but as it turned out, he anticipated me. After he had rested, his first words to me echoed my own thoughts on the subject.

"I can stay no longer, Thomas," he said. "I have imposed upon you and your family long enough, and my continued presence here will not only make things more difficult for them, it will expose them to danger, as well. It's time I had a residence of my own."

# CHAPTER
# 8

For the next month or so, we were occupied with transforming the old, ivy-covered, red brick school building into the International Center for Thaumaturgical Studies. The name was decided upon by an *ad hoc* committee of Merlin, Allan and Elizabeth Stewart, Bill Carr, Warren and Linda Masterson, our neighbors from across the street, Roger and Roberta Truesdale, who had also been part of the parental delegation who came to see us, my wife Jenny and myself, and a few others. I no longer recall the names of everyone involved, as it was very much an impromptu sort of thing decided over lunch one day. Our group, at that point, was still very fluid and informal, with people regularly dropping in and out, depending on the demands of their own lives.

I had originally suggested calling it the Ambrosius School of Thaumaturgy, but Merlin modestly declined having his name formally associated with it. He pointed out that everyone would know he was the founder, anyway, and it would be just as well to simply call it the School of Thaumaturgy. Jenny suggested that College of Thaumaturgy had a nicer ring to it, and I think it was Stewart who suggested International College of Thaumaturgy, as we would hope, eventually, to draw students from all over the world. I don't recall exactly how we arrived at International Center for Thaumaturgical Studies, but after tossing some ideas back and forth, that was the name we finally settled on.

The initials I.C.T.S. sounded properly impressive and rather corporate, and Bill Carr jokingly suggested that they would look good on a sweatshirt. We kept the same name for our administrative group and, today, what began as a small band of friends and neighbors is now the vast organization known as I.T.C., the International Thaumaturgical Commission, which administrates the Bureaus of Thaumaturgy in every nation, as well as every College of Sorcerers at every university throughout the world. I have not been actively involved for many years now, and today I would not even come close to meeting the necessary qualifications, though I still proudly hold a position as an honorary member of the board.

The renovation was a fascinating project, with many members of the community pitching in, and as many came to watch the show as came to work. And what a show it was! Everywhere, people were bustling about, knocking down walls, installing plumbing and kitchen appliances, tiling floors and patching ceilings, rewiring electrical circuits and putting in new window glass, hammering and sawing. All around them, tools would be working at various tasks all by themselves, with no human hands to wield them, often working in conjunction with people who were initially quite unsettled by the process, but soon took to it with sheer delight.

Here a man would be steadying a board while a circular saw, unconnected to any source of power, made the cuts all by itself. And there someone would be holding a nail while a hammer floating in midair drove it in with no human hand to guide it. Buckets of paint and drywall compound would come floating in through open windows and set themselves down obligingly wherever they were needed. Paintbrushes, trowels, putty knives, and spreaders would flit about like humming-birds, doing the work all by themselves. Boards, boxes of nails, tubs of pipe joint compound, and spools of insulated cable seemed to develop sentience, responding to the spoken commands of the work force. It was like an animated cartoon come to life.

All this dramatic and delightful sorcery was directed by a wizard dressed in a plaid flannel shirt, lace-up work boots, and blue denim overalls, with a big, floppy, leather hat someone had given him. While Merlin did no actual physical work himself, the effort required to maintain so many spells at one time took its toll and left him exhausted. At the end of each day, he would eat a truly prodigious meal, enough to feed at least half a dozen starving lumberjacks, then fall into a deep sleep until the next morning, when he would do it all again.

At one such meal, I saw him devour six whole chickens, about ten generous servings of vegetables, at least twenty boiled potatoes, and five gallons of milk, all without so much as a belch. Then, in the morning, he would have a breakfast of about thirty scrambled eggs, several dozen sausages, an entire loaf of bread, a heaping mound of hash-browned potatoes, and enough tea and juice to float a battleship.

People came early and brought food, and a crowd would gather just to watch him eat. He didn't mind a bit. He said he enjoyed having company for breakfast, and held court throughout each meal, keeping up a steady stream of enter-taining conversation, usually with his mouth full, as he regaled the community with stories of King Arthur and his knights. The *true* stories, I should say, which were somewhat at variance with the legends and were highly in demand.

"What about Sir Lancelot, Professor?" someone in the crowd would ask.

Even then, we were calling him "Professor," the form of

address now most commonly associated with him. In later years, he was to receive a number of honorary doctorate degrees, and he eventually accepted the post of Dean of the College of Sorcerers at Cambridge, Massachusetts, yet hardly anyone ever called him Doctor. It was always Professor Ambrosius. In fact, it was a title he chose for himself. At one point, soon after we began working on the school, the question of his title came up in conversation over dinner one night. I don't recall who brought it up, but the question was should his title be Dean, or President, or Chancellor?

"What title is normally used for those who teach?" he'd asked.

And it was I who said, "Well, in universities, it's either Doctor, if they possess a doctoral degree, or it's Professor."

"Professor," he had said, as if trying it on for size. "Professor. One who professes knowledge. Yes, I like that. It has an honorable sound. Professor Ambrosius will suit me just fine."

From that point on, we all started calling him Professor, and everyone else simply picked it up. And he was right. It fit him perfectly.

"So you want to know about Lancelot?" he'd say, as he started cutting up his fourteenth sausage. "Very well, what is it you wish to know?"

"Is it true he was the best and bravest of all the Knights of the Round Table?"

"Ah. Well, to begin with, there never was any Round Table. It was rectangular, and made of oak, very crude and plain, much like an old picnic table, in fact, right down to the ants that crawled upon it. Ants on the table top, carrying off crumbs; hunting dogs beneath it, wolfing down the scraps that were thrown down to them or simply dropped by the inebriated knights. And there was none of this romantic nonsense I have seen on television, either."

With all the attention being paid to Merlin by the media, it was only natural, I suppose, for every film production ever made of the Arthurian myth to be dusted off and broadcast on the telly. He watched them all, and laughed himself silly.

"There was none of this sitting round the table, resplendent in their chain mail and baldrics and surcoats emblazoned with their crests, shields hung upon ornate chairs, swords placed on the table top before them, pointing inward. . . . Balderdash. It was nothing like that at all. What you had was a bunch of loud and unkempt, ill-mannered louts, sitting on benches at a long oak table, eating with their fingers, breaking wind and belching and throwing food at one another. And there was none of this dignified 'My Lord this and My Liege that' business. It was more like, 'Arthur, you bleeding old sod, more mead, damn your eyes!' All save Lancelot, who never uttered a single word throughout the meal, and meals were the only time they ever all sat down together at a table, regardless of its shape.

"Lance would sit hunched over his plate like a wild animal protecting its kill. Unlike the others, who would hack off a chunk of venison and place it on their plates—or somewhere in the general vicinity of their plates—tear at it with their fingers, wolf it down and grab some more, Lance would fill his plate but once, and he ate slowly, in a placid, bovine manner, his narrow eyes darting to the left and right to make certain none of the others took anything from his plate. No one ever did, of course, at least not after the first time, when Kay speared a chunk of bread off his plate and Lance beat him senseless with a leg of mutton.

"As to being the best and bravest," Merlin would continue, "I suppose that would depend on your perspective. If by being the best, you mean the handsomest and courtliest, then no, for Lancelot was neither. And if by being the bravest, you mean a man who had no fear, then no again, for Lance had fears that reduced him to a mewling infant, only not the sort of fears that you might think. He feared no man, that much is true, and he dearly loved a fight. None could match him for his prowess with a sword or lance, or mace or ax, and he could fell a horse with just one blow. I saw him do it once when a new horse nipped him on the shoulder as he led it. He turned around and smashed it with his fist so hard the animal went down to its knees. But he was terrified of spiders, and he was afraid of rats, and he had the most deathly, irrational fear of ducks—"

"*Ducks?*" said someone in the crowd with disbelief. "Why ducks?"

"We never knew," said Merlin with a frown. "But for the other knights, it was great sport to sneak up on Lance and start to quack, for he would leap and give a yell as if struck from behind with a hot poker. But it was dangerous sport, for if he caught the culprit, it was a busted head, for certain."

"You said he wasn't handsome, Professor," a young woman who was writing a piece for the *Times* said. "What did he look like?"

"Short and squat, with coarse, dark hair and dark eyes, the frame of a bull and the face of a wild boar. Terrible teeth."

"Well, if that was so, then what did Queen Guinevere see in him? Was it that she saw past his looks to his good heart?"

"I think that what she saw in him was located somewhat lower down."

This was received with great amusement all around.

"So then it's true, about their great love affair?"

"That part is true enough," said Merlin, "though it was not as poetic as it is frequently portrayed. They loved each other with a simple, pure and hearty, peasant sort of lust, and it was hardly the great secret commonly supposed. Everyone knew of it, for they were constantly exchanging torrid glances and could scarcely keep their hands off one another."

"And Arthur knew?"

"He later claimed he did, but knowing Arthur, I suspect perhaps he truly didn't know. At least, not until Modred threw it in his face in a way he could not possibly deny. I believe he didn't *wish* to know, and simply chose not to see what everyone around him saw quite clearly. He did, indeed, love Gwen, and he loved Lance like a brother, but love can be a very complicated thing. Arthur loved Gwen and she loved him. He loved Lance and Lance worshipped the very ground he walked on. But Gwen and Lance also loved each other, with a passion neither could deny. It was a passion, I think, that Arthur lacked. Not only toward Gwen, but toward anyone. His one consuming passion was a land united under one king, and there was scarcely room left in him for any other.

"Guinevere was a strong and lusty wench, not at all like the wistful and ethereal beauty of the legend. She was very young, and often lonely, and she had needs that Arthur apparently could not fulfill. Mind you, I could not tell you what went on in the privacy of their bedchamber, for I did not know and had no wish to know, but I believe that Arthur could only love a queen, while Lance could love a woman. Lance was a simple sort, and could only see and love her as she was, and as she wanted to be seen and loved. Arthur was a dreamer and a mystic. He saw her as an ideal, and treated her with a sort of worshipful reverence. To a woman, I suppose that may sound romantic, but I wonder if any woman can truly live with that from day to day and be content."

As he spoke, he seemed to go back to that time, and when he finished, he sat pensively, his meal momentarily forgotten as he stared off into the distance. The crowd gathered around him had fallen silent, and for a while, no one spoke. Then another question broke the spell.

"So then it really was their love that destroyed Camelot?"

Merlin shrugged. "Perhaps. There are many who seem to think so."

"What do *you* think, Professor?"

"What do *I* think? Oh, I do not think, I know. It was I who destroyed Camelot."

"*You?*" I said. "How? I mean, what did you have to do with it?"

"I had everything to do with it," Merlin replied. "It was I who taught Arthur and instilled in him the dream that he made into Camelot. And it was I who taught Arthur that honor and principle are everything, the only true ideals worth living for, and fighting for, and dying for. Those were and are important things, and in that I taught him well, but I forgot to teach him something equally important.

"I forgot to teach him that honor must be tempered by reason, and that principle must be administered with compassion. And there I failed him, for if Arthur had understood compassion, he would have felt it for his son, and loved him, instead of seeing him as a living reminder of his own human frailty. And if Arthur understood the reasoned principle, instead of the inflexible ideal, he would have pardoned Lance and Gwen, and been a better king for it. It was I who raised Arthur, and it was I who taught him and made him what he was. But I was a poor teacher, and I failed him."

He looked up and smiled wanly. "I shall endeavor to do better this time."

The powers that be were still uncertain what to make of Merlin, and so they kept their distance. However, they were very much aware of him and keenly interested in everything he did. We did, I should say, for they kept tabs on all of us. The government was only too happy to provide us with whatever assistance they could, despite the strain on their resources. An army unit was detailed to Loughborough as a security detachment and we were sent our own special liaison officer, a man named Bodkirk, whom Merlin immediately nicknamed "Bodkin," a jest most people missed completely, unless they had read their Shakespeare, for a bodkin was a dagger (as in Hamlet's famous speech) and with Bodkin around, joked Merlin, we all had to watch our backs. The jest turned out to be prophetic.

Stanley Bodkirk looked like a typical overworked bureaucrat, the sort of rumpled little man who would never stand out in a crowd. He was in his forties, lean and slight of stature, balding and nearsighted. He wore horn-rimmed glasses and had an anxious, nervous manner. He came with a staff of two young assistants, Jack Rosen and Linda Stern, who were promptly named Rosenkrantz and Guildenstern, and their duties seemed largely secretarial. In fact, they were both highly competent government agents and Stanley Bodkirk was a wolf in sheep's clothing. I never did find out exactly whom he worked for, but it's a safe bet that he was MI5. He was obviously sent to keep an eye on us, and he didn't miss a thing.

I don't think the government really regarded Merlin as a threat, but they certainly saw in him the potential of a threat. They simply would not accept that he was who he said he was, and that his magical powers were genuine. Genuinely magical, that is. The prevalent belief among them, at least in the beginning, was that he was merely an ordinary man—which is to say, not one who was two thousand years old—gifted with remarkable paranormal abilities. Telekinesis, which few people had seriously believed in prior to Merlin, became a catchall explanation for the things he was able to do. It did not quite cover what happened on the Billy Martens Show, of course, and I think that made them quite uncomfortable. Or perhaps they simply denied it really happened. Nevertheless, their degree of serious interest was certainly indicated by their actions.

I've often wondered what sort of discussions went on behind closed doors in London. I imagined some very serious and rather nervous people seated around a table, trying to account for Merlin in some logical, rational way, one that did not include the acceptance of the reality of magic. Doubtless, famous psychics of the past were mentioned, people capable of bending keys and whatnot, and scholars and writers were probably called in and questioned, as well as scientists who had not had any opportunity to examine Merlin's powers under laboratory conditions, though that did not prevent them from making conclusions about them. Perhaps they discussed the possibility that Merlin was an alien, or, like the eccentric lady from Luton, a human who'd had contact with aliens from some other world. It must have been very exasperating for them.

I do know for a fact, however, that there were those among them who believed the truth, for some of them later confessed as much to me, only the truth was so outlandish that they hesitated to admit what they really thought. It frightened them. And the idea of what Merlin might do frightened them, as well. He had attracted an enormous number of people to Loughborough, more than enough to strain the town's already limited resources, and that in itself could easily have caused trouble. Not that we were free from trouble, by any means, as the attempt on Merlin's life had clearly demonstrated.

The identity of the man who'd shot Merlin and killed Chief Thorpe had been discovered with the aid of Merlin himself, who performed a divination spell after he'd recovered. His name had been Clancy McDermott, and he had operated under a number of aliases, as well. He was known to Scotland Yard, and to the army. Merlin insisted that he had acted alone, and that the attempted assassination was not the result of any plot by the I.R.A. However, both the Army and New Scotland Yard were anxious to have Merlin use his powers to discover the identities and whereabouts of other members of the I.R.A., only Merlin had refused.

His refusal to cooperate had not gone down well. He insisted that he wanted to stay out of political matters. He was, he said, neither a soldier nor a policeman; he was a teacher. When they tried appealing to his moral character by saying that his cooperation would save lives, he wouldn't have any of it.

"I have no responsibility to make decisions concerning who is and who is not a criminal," he said. "That is a matter for the proper authorities. If a man commits a crime, then it is for the police to seek him out and bring him before your courts. I am not a policeman. I have far more important things to do. On one hand, the authorities question my abilities, and on the other, they seek to enlist them. You cannot have it both ways. If the government believes that thaumaturgy will be helpful to the police and to the military in the execution of their duties, then they have greater need of my teaching than my personal assistance in such matters.''

The logic of this argument was difficult to fault, but people in authority don't take kindly to those who won't submit to it. Merlin was determined to avoid any political involvement. He'd made that mistake once before and he was not anxious to repeat it. However, his refusal was misunderstood in almost every way imaginable. He was arrogant; he was unpatriotic; he was contemptuous of the government; he was afraid of the I.R.A.'s wrath; he was secretly sympathetic to the I.R.A.; he felt his own concerns were more important than those of the British people, etc., etc.

Initially the darling of the media, he now became their target, though they were cautious snipers. The memory of Billy Martens was still fresh in their minds, and they all knew about the mysterious, magical editing of the Robin Winters interview. So, rather than make outright accusations, they merely confined themselves to posing sly rhetorical questions, meant for their audience to answer. What did Merlin *really* want? Was there any truth to the rumors about a hidden agenda? What really went on behind closed doors at his ''exclusive retreat,'' and so forth. And when there was apparently no reaction from Merlin to these initial, range-finding shots, they became emboldened and started firing their first salvos.

It was generally thought that Merlin chose not to respond to these innuendos and allegations because he considered them unworthy of response. However, the fact is that he was not really aware of them. He had courted the media at first, because he needed what the media could provide, but once they had helped him start the ball rolling, he had no further use for them. All his energies had become directed toward the school.

We were inundated with applications, not only from all around the country, but from all over the world, and there was simply no way that we could accept more than a mere fraction of those applicants. Merlin had, indeed, reached "many people at one time," but as I had anticipated, he had vastly underestimated the power of the media. Things were threatening to get out of control.

It seemed, sometimes, as if I now saw my family less than when I had lived most of the time in London. I would snatch a quick breakfast and leave home early, usually before the girls were awake, and ride my bicycle to the school, where a daily madhouse of administrative activity awaited me. I would break for a midday meal around noon or so, lunching with my fellow staffers, and then back to work, often until ten or eleven at night. By the time I got home, the girls were both asleep and I was so exhausted that it was all I could do to enjoy a cup of tea with Jenny before we both retired for the night.

In the beginning, when most of the work was done out of our home, Jenny had helped out. However, now that things were underway at the school, she needed to remain home to take care of the girls. Victor was a great help in that, but no dog, however unique, could take a mother's place. I was putting in more hours than I had when I'd been a policeman, and I was frequently more tired, though I did not resent it, nor did Jenny. There was the feeling that we were doing something vitally important, something that would help a lot of people and change the entire world. Everyone involved with the school, and even many members of the community who had no direct involvement whatsoever, shared that feeling and it was a source of strength and energy and purpose. Something was happening in Loughborough, something very big, and we were all, in some way, a part of it.

Yet, at the same time, our sense of purpose and enthusiasm

blinded us to all the signs of trouble that were cropping up around us. The town could no longer support all the people who were arriving daily, and there was simply no room for them all. At first, the town was glad to have them, for they filled up the boarding houses and apartments and gave a much-needed boost to the economy. Not that many of them came with very much money, but times were lean and every little bit helped. However, as more people kept arriving, drawn to Merlin like a magnet draws iron filings, a certain amount of apprehension began to set in.

The resources of the town, already severely limited, became depleted and many of the new arrivals were willing to work for next to nothing in order to support themselves, often merely for a roof over their heads or a little food to eat, which cut a lot of the locals out of their meager sources of income and barter. Predictably, this brought about resentment against the new arrivals, particularly those who came with nothing and pitched tents or constructed ramshackle shelters wherever they could find free space. The crime rate began to rise alarmingly, and with only a handful of full-time, paid police officers and a few dozen volunteers, our local authorities were simply unequipped to deal with it.

It was a great help when the army arrived, but in time, even they became overburdened. Something had to be done. The demands for solutions fell on the narrow shoulders of Stanley Bodkirk, as the *de facto* government representative on the scene, and while Bodkirk freed us from the burden of having to worry about these things, his failure to keep us properly informed and our own ever-increasing involvement at the school kept us from realizing the full extent of these problems, until one day we woke up to find that we were totally besieged and that Bodkirk had assumed complete control.

By this time, Merlin had started teaching. The classes were full to capacity, so much so that it became necessary for us to break down some walls in order to create more space and

begin construction on additional, separate dormitory buildings on the site of the school's old playground and athletic
field. While the rest of us were still wrestling with the overwhelming organizational and management problems of "the
College," as we had started to refer to it, Merlin was in the
process of trying to hammer out a curriculum by trial and error.

We saw very little of him during this period, and a great
many people thought he was becoming distant. The truth was
that Merlin was working literally around the clock, cloistered
in his chambers, often going for days without any sleep at all,
performing the most important task of his life, which would
also become his most significant contribution to society. He
was in the process of structuring and defining his teaching
method, which was to usher in what is now called the Second
Thaumaturgic Age—the time in which magic would return.

Few people saw him during the times he wasn't teaching,
when he retired behind the closed doors of his private sanctum
in the east wing of the old school building.

In later years, when he went to America and taught in Cambridge, much was made of his "wizardly lifestyle" and the
outlandish choice of decor in both his offices and his mansion
on Beacon Hill. Writers loved to describe the antique furnish-
ings and the thousands of ancient, leatherbound books, the
deep Oriental carpets with their cabalistic motifs and the fantastic paintings, the "occult paraphernalia" coupled with
bizarre, kitsch decorations such as his famous cigar-store
Indian and stuffed owl, the dark and fantasylike ambience that
brought to mind a sorcerer's lair from some fairy tale. However, all that came about in part from Merlin's own idosyn-
cratic sense of humor and partly from his playful sense of
self-indulgence, which he was able to enjoy once he had laid
the groundwork for the revolution that was only just beginning
in the Loughborough days.

Most of the so-called "occult paraphernalia" in evidence at
both his office and his home consisted of gifts sent by

admirers, most of them people who'd had no direct contact
with him whatsoever, save for perhaps attending a lecture or
having read one of his books or seen him on a television program. The latter occurred with less frequency as time went on,
because Merlin quickly grew disenchanted with the medium
and its inability—or unwillingness—to cater to anything but
the lowest common denominator and the shortest attention
span. Eventually, he ceased to appear on television altogether,
but he continued to produce books, all of which became huge
international bestsellers and made him a rich man, though
most of the money was donated to his educational foundation.
These books gained him a new audience among the younger
generation, who were growing up with the reality of magic,
and he received an endless stream of gifts such as glass uni-
corns and bronze dragons, jeweled daggers and fantasy paintings, sculptures of himself and various mythological
creatures, silver and gold goblets in fantasy motifs, rings and
amulets, necklaces and charms, tarot decks and ceramic figu-
rines and on and on and on.

Rather than being driven to distraction by this cornucopia of
whimsical and fantastical bric-a-brac, Merlin cherished these
gifts as the honest outpourings of affection that they were and
the Beacon Hill mansion he eventually settled into was purchased primarily because it had the necessary space to house
this peculiar collection.

In the early days at Loughborough, however, Merlin lived in
a Spartan manner, in a small suite of rooms converted into an
office and living quarters on the top floor of the College. He
had one tiny office, with an outer office for his secretary, an
amazingly competent and industrious former school teacher
named Rebecca Wainwright, who at sixty possessed more
energy than most people a third her age, and one small study
and a bed-sitting room. The quarters were austere and plain,
with nothing in them to reveal the personality of their occu-
pant. He was there to work, and wanted no distractions.

His meals were brought in to him, and though he still ate prodigiously, he had cut down somewhat on the sheer quantity of food he consumed, and strange preferences began to emerge. One week, he ate nothing but hamburgers, then he abruptly switched to brown rice mixed with vegetables and sprinkled with soy sauce, then for a period of about two weeks, he ate nothing but deviled eggs and toast. The kitchen staff was at a loss to account for these peculiarities, and as the person who knew him best, I was pestered to find out the truth behind this bizarre diet. Did it have to do with magic? Was it part of some arcane ritual? Was it a special method of recharging his energies, or was it some sort of meditative process for the digestive system or what?

The answer was none of the above. Merlin simply was not in a frame of mind for giving much thought to what he ate. Usually, whenever he was asked what he wanted, he absently replied, "The same thing I had last time will be fine." He changed his preferences whenever he realized that the same dish was beginning to grow monotonous, and he was so preoccupied that this could take anywhere from a week to three weeks or so. However, he remained remarkably consistent about at least one thing. Somehow, he discovered peanut butter and banana sandwiches. He became hooked instantly, pronounced it a great energy food, and it became a staple in his diet. However, not even Merlin's immense magical demands on his body could burn up all those calories and he started gaining weight, so that before long he looked less like a wizard than like Father Christmas.

Once things got rolling, his typical day never varied. He would arise, assuming he had slept at all the night before, at five A.M., eat a "small" breakfast about the size of an average person's dinner, then begin interviewing prospective students at six. In the beginning, before classes formally started, this would take the entire day, but once he started teaching, prospective students had to make appointments to be interviewed between the hours of six and nine, and there was soon a very long waiting list. Promptly at nine-thirty, Merlin would begin teaching his first class. This process gradually underwent some change, as well.

At first, there was only one class, a sort of lecture hall-cum-laboratory session, which would last most of the day, with breaks for meals, and students would be added to it as they were accepted to the program. However, this soon proved to be unworkable. Students added to the class wound up behind those who had started earlier, and the class simply became too large and unwieldy. After about several weeks of this approach proved it to be unfeasible, the class was broken up among more traditional lines, as in universities, with shorter beginning, intermediate, and advanced sessions taking place throughout the day. (The terms ''intermediate'' and ''advanced'' are actually somewhat misleading in this case, for in no way could the intermediate and advanced classes of those beginning days compare with those of today, which demand a significantly greater level of accomplishment and knowledge on the part of the students.)

Merlin was a natural teacher, as I observed from attending some of his classes, though I was never to become an adept myself. Merlin's promise to me that we would each learn from the other was certainly fulfilled, but not in the way I had expected. I did learn a great deal from him, and he from me, but I never did learn much more than merely the rudimentary theories of magic. For one thing, almost all my time was spent performing my administrative duties, which were considerable, and helping to insulate Merlin from any concerns other than his teaching. For another, it turned out that I had no real aptitude for thaumaturgy. I made the discovery, or rather, it was revealed to me one night when Merlin and I were spending a quiet evening in his study, discussing matters pertaining to the College. At one point, I ruefully expressed my frustration over the fact that I was so busy with the administrative end of things that I had no time to attend the classes myself. All I'd been able to do was sit in on a few beginning classes, which were mostly theory and indoctrination. When, I asked, was my turn going to come?

"Thomas," Merlin said to me, in a warm and sympathetic tone, "I fear your turn may never come."

I blinked with surprise at the unexpectedness of this reply, then asked him why.

"Have you ever wondered how I decide who will be admitted to study at the College and who will not?" he asked.

"Well . . . no, as a matter of fact," I said, a bit surprised to find that I actually *hadn't* wondered about it. I had been extremely busy with my own work and if I'd thought about it at all, I must have assumed that Merlin had his own methods of selecting his students out of the vast numbers of applicants who came to seek admission.

"When they come to see me for their interviews," said Merlin, puffing on his ever-present pipe, "I spend some time talking with them, asking them questions about why they wish to study thaumaturgy and what they think they can contribute, asking some questions about who they are and where they come from, referring to their applications and generally making idle conversation designed to draw them out and leave them with the impression that their application was being given serious consideration. In fact, in most circumstances, I can tell within seconds whether or not they are suitable candidates for the program, before a single word is even spoken."

"How?" I asked, fascinated.

"By the strength of their aura," Merlin replied. "Those with strong, latent thaumaturgical potential have a significantly brighter aura than most people, and those whose potential has already been manifested in some manner, psychic experiences, for example, possess auras that are stronger still. It's something a trained adept can easily discern. If I encounter such an applicant, then the interview begins in earnest, but unless the presence of that aura indicates otherwise, I merely go through the motions, so that at least the applicant is not left with the impression of being summarily dismissed. People can live with having their hopes disappointed, but there is no reason to dash them to the ground.''

''As you are dashing mine right now,'' I said, rather petulantly, for I felt keenly disappointed.

''Thomas,'' he said, leaning forward in his chair to put his hand on my knee, ''you are my dearest and most trusted friend. And I would never lie to you, not even to spare your feelings, for such lies are often the cruelest of all. I have often said, in public, that everyone possesses thaumaturgical potential, at least to some degree. Unfortunately, that is not the truth.''

''You *lied*?'' I said. So high was the esteem in which I held him that it never occurred to me he might, for any reason, be duplicitous. I was frankly shocked.

''Yes, Thomas. I lied. The truth is that many people possess some degree of thaumaturgical potential, but by no means all or even most people. And of those who do possess potential, only a small percentage possess enough potential to become adepts. The others might be capable of learning a few relatively simple spells, but no more than that. For the present, I must select only the most naturally gifted of those who seek to study with me, because I must train them not only as adepts, but as teachers who can go out and spread the knowledge. And you, regrettably, have no thaumaturgical potential to speak of. Your daughters, on the other hand, do possess potential, which I suspect they inherited from Jenny.''

''It's hereditary?'' I asked with surprise.

''Oh, yes,'' said Merlin, nodding. ''Someone on Jenny's side of the family evidently possessed what you call 'paranormal abilities.' That is usually a good indicator of thaumaturgical potential.''

''Then . . . shouldn't Jenny be studying with you?'' I asked.

"Perhaps," said Merlin, "but I would not deprive your daughters of their mother at so young an age, and I could not spare you here for the sake of Jenny enrolling in the College. You are much too valuable to me."

"Well, I'm glad of that, at least. But I still don't understand why you felt you had to lie about it."

"Don't you?" he replied. "It was necessary in order to generate interest, and attract as many applicants as possible. Also, to give people hope. As it is, of all the students we've enrolled, only a handful possess any truly significant potential. As for the others, I fear they will be limited in what they will be able to accomplish, but we need them just the same, to help the momentum of our plan develop."

What he meant by referring to "our plan," of course, was merely what we had discussed from the beginning, the bringing back of magic to the world. Since I knew that, and obviously, so did Merlin, there was no need to elaborate. However, what we didn't know was that someone *else* was listening in on our conversation, and the innocent reference to "our plan" sounded like something entirely different, taken out of context. It must have sounded positively clandestine to Stanley Bodkirk, who had placed bugs not only in Merlin's private quarters at the College, but in all the offices, and in the homes of everybody in our group, as well.

# CHAPTER
# 9

The trouble began long before we became aware of it, and it came on several fronts. First, there was the media, which had initially regarded Merlin as a fascinating novelty, then as a serious news story, and finally as an object of unflattering speculation. To be sure, some of this was no more than natural progression, natural for the news media, at any rate. In order to keep the story alive and the public interested, they had to keep finding new angles of perspective, so they followed the formula approach, which was to build him up only so they could proceed to tear him down.

If that sounds cynical, then so be it, for a certain amount of cynicism is certainly justified when it concerns the press. However, to say they were motivated solely by sensationalism would be painting them with far too broad a brush. There were many people who genuinely feared Merlin in those days, and among them were influential members of the media. In the space of only a few months, Merlin had become, in many ways, a cult figure, and as such, there were those who regarded him with great suspicion. Merlin certainly did not help matters by magically altering the tape of his interview with Robin Winters.

I've always felt that was a bad mistake, and though Merlin had denied it, I felt his motives for doing it were purely vindictive. Winters had gotten cheeky with him, and Merlin wanted to pay him back. It was, perhaps, rather immature of him, but he did have that quality about him. Though he was a patient man, he was always quick to respond to any personal affront, and he often did so in a manner designed to embarrass or humiliate the offender. Robin Winters had been neither embarrassed nor humiliated. He was much too professional for that. However, he did not forget it. Merlin could have confronted the whole issue of necromancy head-on and defused it from the start, but by altering the videotape, he succeeded only in arousing the enmity and mistrust of one of the most powerful and influential men in broadcasting. Right up to the day he died, Winters continued to believe that Merlin was hiding his true colors.

Once things got rolling, Merlin confined his efforts to teaching at the College, and turned down all requests for interviews and appearances on television. He had given many such interviews in the beginning, and he had developed a rather jaundiced view of the media. Once he started teaching, he delegated the task of dealing with all such requests to me. Unfortunately, I served him very poorly in that capacity. Instead of handling such matters myself, I, in turn, delegated the task to Stanley Bodkirk, at his own request.

At the time, I did not suspect his true purpose, and it would never have entered my mind that he might have planted bugs and even several small, discreet surveillance cameras in the College. The concept was entirely unfamiliar to Merlin, of course, and while he might have been able to detect them, it never occurred to him to look. Consequently, we regarded our friend, "Bodkin," as nothing more than what he seemed—a government bureaucrat assigned as our liaison and supply officer. I can still recall the day I made that unfortunate decision, and I blame myself for what resulted from it.

Bodkirk maintained an office in a large trailer situated near the entrance to the College, and he also ate and slept there most of the time, except during his frequent trips to London. Those trips, I had always assumed, were to iron out some minor bureaucratic difficulty that may have arisen, or to see his family. He kept a framed photograph of them displayed prominently on his desk, and it depicted a rather plain-looking, dowdy woman with a small, chubby lad of about ten and a rather unattractive young girl of thirteen. However, this turned out to be a fiction he maintained as part of his cover. Bodkirk was unmarried, and he never had a family. Those trips he made to London were made for only one purpose, to brief his superiors on our activities.

I walked up the steps of the trailer and knocked on the metal frame door. From within, a voice asked me to come in. I entered into the outer office, where Rosencrantz and Guildenstern were housed. The trailer was a mobile home which had been modified for its intended purpose. What had been the living room had been turned into the outer office, with desks and phones and filing cabinets. The kitchen had been left essentially untouched, but the hallway leading from it gave access to a bathroom and a bedroom that had been turned into Bodkirk's private office, and the bedroom in the back was where he slept. There was another trailer set close by, outside the grounds near the prefabricated buildings that functioned as barracks for the army detachment, where Rosencrantz and Guildenstern were housed.

Linda Stern glanced up from her paperwork as I came in and smiled a mirthless smile. If this young woman possessed a personality, I remember thinking, I had yet to discover it.

"Good morning, Linda," I said. "Stanley wanted to see me?"

"He's in his office," she said flatly. "Would you care for some tea?"

"No, thanks, don't trouble yourself. I'll just go straight in."

I went through the kitchen and into Bodkirk's office. The door was open, but I knocked politely, just the same.

"Ah, Malory, come in," said Bodkirk, putting down the telephone. He sat behind his desk, which had two telephones on it, a computer, stacked trays for papers, notepads, pens, and a small pile of manila file folders. Everything was arranged very neatly, with anal retentive compulsiveness. There was also a television set placed on a shelf. Unknown to me, this television, which was often switched on to some news program or chat show when I came to see him, was also a monitor for the surveillance cameras he had placed inside the College. And there were additional monitors, as well as a listening post, in the other trailer.

"You wanted to see me, Stan?" I said.

"Sit down, Malory."

I'd started off calling him Mr. Bodkirk, then it had gradually progressed to Stanley, and finally to Stan, but no amount of attempted familiarity on my part would succeed in getting him to call me anything but "Malory." He never seemed to relax in my presence. Perhaps, he did not know how. I took a chair across the desk from him.

"I wanted to discuss a few matters with you," he said, taking off his glasses and wiping them with his handkerchief. I'd learned from experience that this meant he was going to ask for something he wasn't sure I would grant.

"Go right ahead."

"It's about this press thing," he said. "As you know, there's been a tremendous amount of curiosity about what's happening here, and Merlin's teaching methods and all that sort of thing."

"I know," I said. "I get calls about it all the time. It's maddening."

"Yes, well, we're constantly having to turn reporters from the gates, and they act surly and resentful when we're forced to do that." Bodkirk always used the word "we" when he actually meant himself. It wasn't a conceit, merely a little conversational trick meant to include the listener, to convey the impression that we were all on the same team, all in this together. "I frankly don't think that's helping us very much in terms of favorable publicity."

"What would you suggest?"

"Well, I know Merlin's far too busy to trouble with this sort of thing, and Lord knows, you're overworked yourself. Aside from that, public relations is not really your strong suit. It takes a certain kind of personality, if you know what I mean. Someone who's personable and glib, but at the same time someone who's something of a shark, always anticipating what the press might do, and able to always land on his feet and so on."

"Yes, I know," I said. "You don't really have to tell me I don't possess the right temperament for the job, Stan. I know that. My experience is in the military and in law enforcement. I have certain organizational skills, but I'm not really a publicity man."

"Quite," said Bodkirk, with a tight, humorless smile. "Neither, for that matter, am I. What I wanted to suggest was that we find someone who is, someone who'd be capable of handling that sort of thing for us. You know, deal with the press on a daily basis, coddle them along, provide releases, perhaps conduct an occasional tour when they wouldn't be disturbing anything, generally smooth things over, if you get my drift."

"What about Allan Stewart?"

"I'd thought of him," said Bodkirk, "but with all due respect to Stewart, he's not really our man. He's sharp enough, and quite presentable and articulate, but he's not really a flack, if you know what I mean. Besides, he's got enough work of his own as it is. I was thinking we could bring somebody in, someone who'd have no other responsibilities and could deal with the press more or less on a full-time basis."

"That might be ideal," I said, "but you realize we don't have the budget to pay someone like that. We're understaffed as it is, and as you know better than anyone, we're very dependent on government support right now. You think they'd spring for something like this?"

Bodkirk pursed his lips. "I've been thinking about it, and I think I can get them to go for it, on the theory it would help free me and my staff from the task, and keep down the criticism that we're all being very clandestine here. We could get someone who'd provide regular press releases, which we could write and he would punch up, as necessary, and conduct regular press briefings and all that sort of thing. You and I have to meet regularly, anyway, discuss requisitions and logistical problems and so forth. We could simply have you provide me with regular statements for the press, in sketchy outline form, at least, and then I could work things out with our press liaison, sort of guide him along, and pass on any pertinent questions to you during our regular meetings. It would save time, I think, and help us put a better face on things. It would also allow us to get on with our work without constant distractions. That is, of course, if you approve?"

"I think it's an excellent idea, Stan," I said, eager to see the burden lifted from my shoulders. "Frankly, I'd just as soon have someone else deal with the whole thing. It's been a terrible nuisance."

Bodkirk nodded. "Yes, I know what you mean. I'm sick to death of it, myself. We'll get someone who's more experienced at dealing with the press to handle it for us. I'll get on it right away."

After discussing a few more inconsequential matters, I left, thinking he was doing me a great favor, when in fact, what he'd done was take control of everything the press would hear about Merlin and the College. At the same time, he put himself in a position to decide which questions we would hear and reply to. Little by little, through Merlin's being too busy and my being too naive, Bodkirk was insinuating himself into a position of greater control over us.

Nor was that the only problem facing us.

Merlin had incurred the antagonism of organized religion. And thanks to Stanley Bodkirk, we did not find out just how far things had gone until it was too late to do anything about it. We were not completely cut off from the outside world, of course. We had access to the newspapers and to radio and television, though the power blackouts were getting more and more frequent, and lasting longer as the nation, and the world, continued its inevitable slide. There were times now when the power would be out for days on end, and such things as batteries and even candles were growing more and more expensive. Radio broadcasting truly came into its own during this period, because the television industry was practically on its last legs.

The newspapers were coming out with far less frequency now, due to the shortage of paper and the constant power outages. The avalanche of the Collapse was gaining more momentum every day. There were now only two newspapers still in operation, the *Times* and the *Mirror*, which had dropped the word "Daily" from its banner because, at best, they were able to produce only one edition each week. The *Times* suffered the same problems. Circulation had fallen off drastically. In order to stay in operation, they had to keep raising the price, and each time they raised the price, sales suffered. They were driving themselves out of business, and there was nothing they could do about it.

Everywhere, things kept getting worse. The trains to London hardly ran at all and with the reserve supplies of petrol almost totally depleted, bicycles and horses were now the chief modes of transportation. The government had first claim on any horses, for use by the police and military, and essential personnel were driven round in carriages. It was as if we were returning to the Victorian times of Sherlock Holmes. Unfortunately, there weren't enough horses to go around, so an emergency measure had been passed in Parliament, allowing the police and military to impound horses, which caused a great deal of resentment in the outlying areas, where people lost not only their sole means of transportation, but often their livelihood, as well.

Food deliveries to the cities were becoming scarce, and there were drastic shortages of every available commodity. Street riots had increased, and soldiers and police were often attacked. There were frequent fires, so many that the fire department couldn't keep up with them all, and entire city blocks burned to the ground.

As things grew increasingly more desperate, people sought an outlet for their anger and frustration. Some took it out on the police, some took it out on soldiers, some on members of the government. Three members of parliament were assassinated in one month, despite increased security precautions. And before long, people found another target for their rage.

Unknown to us, because Bodkirk hadn't said anything about it, a delegation of clergy had come to the College asking to see Merlin. I never did find out exactly what they wanted, but Bodkirk took it upon himself to refuse them admittance. The first I learned of it was when I heard about it on the radio. It coincided with the Pope's announcement that practicing sorcery, or thaumaturgy, was a sin, and that any Catholic who was found to engage in such practice would be excommunicated.

I was stunned when I heard the news. My first reaction was one of shock, and then anger. How could the Pope, residing in Rome, take a position on the issue when he hadn't even met Merlin, or communicated with him in any way? Then, as a follow-up to the story, the newscaster announced that Merlin had refused to meet with an interdenominational delegation of clergy, snubbing them at the gates of the college by not allowing them to enter. Reactions from the man in the street, as well as from religious leaders and members of the government, were quite predictable. I immediately rushed over to the College to confront Bodkirk.

"*Why wasn't I told of this?*" I shouted at him. He'd answered the door in his pajamas. It was late and I had roused him from bed. I pushed in past him and turned on him furiously. "I just heard on the radio about the Pope's position concerning thaumaturgy. That's bad enough, but by taking it upon yourself to turn away a delegation of the clergy, you only made it worse! What in God's name were you thinking of? Why wasn't I told that they were here? What the hell gives you the right to make those kind of decisions for us?"

"Are you finished?" he asked calmly.

"I'm waiting for an explanation!"

"Frankly, I don't owe you any," he replied, "but I'll give you one just the same, because this entire charade has gone on long enough."

"What charade? What are you talking about?"

"The reason I don't have to account to you for any of my actions is because I'm in charge here."

"You're *what*?"

"My job here was to keep an eye on Merlin, and the rest of you, contain the situation as much as possible, and report back to my superiors. I was to make every effort to minimize any contact between Merlin and the media, or any other outsiders, and observe everything that went on here and make regular reports concerning his activities and, in particular, the effectiveness of his teaching."

"Good God," I said. "You're a bloody spy!"

"I prefer the term 'intelligence operative,' but have it as you wish. In any case, you have little to complain about. There are people starving out there, while you've lacked for nothing. Your family has been well taken care of, and you have a comfortable roof over your head, and more than enough to eat.

Moreover, there is no reason why any of that should change, so long as you remain cooperative.''

All the wind had gone out of my sails. I was too shocked to speak. And then it sunk in that he was actually threatening me.

"What are you saying?"

"I should think it's simple enough," he replied. "The government is very interested in Merlin. They are taking him very seriously, indeed, and to a large degree, you have me to thank for that. I was able to convince them that he is, indeed, the real thing, though I had my doubts at first. They want to know how he is able to do the things he does, and if, indeed, it is a skill that may be learned. And apparently it is, though I never would have believed it if I hadn't seen it for myself. I've been watching those classes of his with great interest, and the tapes of those sessions have caused a sensation back in London.''

"*Tapes?*" I said. "What tapes?" And then it hit me. "My God. You've got the place wired for surveillance!''

"Of course I have," he said. "That's my job, isn't it? I've known everything that's gone on in the College from day one, even before I arrived. We had people in the work force that renovated the building. It was a simple matter to install some small surveillance cameras and bugs without anyone being the wiser.''

"You son of a bitch," I said.

He raised his eyebrows and gave me a curious look. "I'm a bit surprised at your attitude, Malory," he said. "Put yourself in my shoes and ask yourself if you wouldn't have done exactly the same thing. Bloody hell, man, you were a police officer, and a soldier before that. I should think you'd understand. We're living in a state of anarchy and things have gone from bad to worse, so much so that the government's decided to declare martial law, something they've resisted doing all this time, but now they simply have no other choice. What Merlin knows is of vital importance to national security, and as such, it's not the sort of knowledge that one man may be allowed to control all by himself. In a way, it's like allowing a private individual access to an atomic bomb. Thaumaturgy is much too important, and much too potentially dangerous for one man to control."

"I see," I said. "So the government's stepping in to take over, is that it?"

"That's the way it has to be, Malory. There's no alternative. Surely you can see that."

"Yes, I believe I can see the whole thing now," I said. "Why bother going to all the trouble of setting up some kind of top-security installation to house Merlin when we've already done it for you? All you had to do was infiltrate some agents into the work force so they could plant their cameras and bugs and then move in some troops to secure the area. Very neat. Very neat, indeed. Now all you have to do is drop the pretense and move in, so you can get rid of the rest of us and bring in your own people."

"It doesn't necessarily have to be that way," he said, "so long as you're willing to cooperate. You're Merlin's friend, and you have his trust. He listens to you. You've checked out; you're a capable man, and we can use you. There's no reason for anything to change, so far as you're concerned. All you have to do is work with me. You'll not only be doing your country a great service, but you'll be able to take good care of your family, as well. The nation that controls thaumaturgy will control the world, Malory, and anyone involved in this project is going to do very well for himself, indeed. Never mind what the Pope says, he's long since ceased to have any significant influence. Never mind what anybody says. What we've got here, right under our noses, is the most important discovery since atomic energy. And we are the ones sitting in the catbird seat, Malory. You and I."

"It sounds as if you've got everything worked out," I said. "You've neglected only one thing. Merlin, himself. He may have some very different ideas about how thaumaturgy should be controlled."

"Then you'll explain it to him," Bodkirk said. He opened a cupboard in the kitchen and took out two glasses, then poured us each some Scotch whiskey. "As I said, he trusts you. All you have to do is make him see reason."

He handed me a glass and I took a sip. "Single malt," I said appreciatively. "Very nice. You're not exactly suffering, either, I see."

"Nothing but the best," said Bodkirk, smiling a genuine smile for the first time since I'd known him. I found I much preferred his mirthless little grimace, instead. "There's no need to worry about Merlin. He'll be well taken care of. He's an important asset, Malory, a vital asset. His every need, his slightest whim, will all be seen to. It's not as if he's going to be held prisoner, you know."

"No, just confined here at the school, under constant surveillance, with the army protecting the gates and the perimeter, and the government dictating his every move. Somehow, I don't think he's going to go for that."

"Then it will be up to you to convince him that it's all for his own good," said Bodkirk. "Look, I can understand your feeling a certain amount of resentment right now. You feel that you've been dealt with in an underhanded manner. Well, all right, perhaps you have, but look at the wider picture. National security is at stake. Merlin's knowledge and his ability to teach it is absolutely vital to the future of this country. We can't afford to have anything happen to him. There's been one attempt on his life already, and what's being done is being done primarily for his own protection. No one is going to interfere with him in any way, nor prevent him from teaching thaumaturgy. In fact, that's precisely what we want him to do, only we're going to make certain he'll be teaching the right people."

"The right people? What do you mean?"

"Now that he's demonstrated that thaumaturgy can, in fact, be taught successfully, we want to make certain he's not teaching the wrong people, that's all. All applicants are going to be carefully screened and investigated, and once they've passed that preliminary process, they will be admitted, pending Merlin's approval of their qualifications, of course. And the same goes for the students currently in the program. After all, we want to make sure that the knowledge of thaumaturgy doesn't go falling into the wrong hands, don't we?''

''And by 'wrong hands,' you mean anyone who's not deemed a loyal British subject, I presume.''

''Well, yes, of course. With knowledge of this sort comes great responsibility. And after all, we don't want to go giving it all away, do we?''

''There's only one problem with that,'' I said. ''It isn't yours to give or keep.''

Bodkirk's eyes narrowed. ''Look here, old chap, the government's gone to considerable expense, at a time when we can ill afford it, to support your little endeavor here. Is it unreasonable for us to expect a return on our investment?''

''You're not talking about a return on your investment,'' I replied. ''You're talking about exclusive control. Merlin would never agree to that and, what's more, I'm not going to try to convince him. You want thaumaturgy to be completely under government control. That was never our plan.''

''Ah, yes, the plan,'' said Bodkirk significantly. ''Just what, exactly, is this so-called plan?''

''To give magic back to the world,'' I said. ''Make the knowledge available to everyone, not just one nation.''

''I'm not talking about the rhetoric you feed the media,'' Bodkirk said wryly. ''I'm talking about the hidden agenda, the secret plan you two have been discussing in private.''

I stared at him. ''Hidden agenda? What do you mean? I have no idea what you're talking about.''

''Come on, Malory, I've got you and Merlin on tape talking about it. There's no point in playing the innocent with me. I know better.''

"You're crazy," I said. "The only plan we've ever had in mind was this one, starting a school to train adepts. I don't know what sort of paranoid fantasy you've developed, but there is no 'secret plan.' If you've had us under surveillance all this time, you should certainly be aware of that."

Bodkirk gave me a hard stare and pursed his lips. "So then you're not going to cooperate?"

"I can't tell you about a hidden agenda that doesn't exist!" I said. "I don't know what you've got on tape, but whatever it is, you've clearly misinterpreted it. As for my cooperation, I'm not going to cooperate with any effort to limit Merlin's freedom, or place him under government control. This is not a totalitarian state, Bodkirk. And if you try to dictate terms to Merlin, I think you'll find you've bitten off a great deal more than you can chew."

"I would sincerely advise you to think this over, Malory," he said. "You have a family to consider."

"Are you threatening me, Bodkirk?"

"I'm merely telling you that we need Merlin," he replied. "We do not necessarily need you."

I met his gaze and he didn't flinch. "I think we understand each other perfectly," I said. I got up. "Thanks for the drink."

"Malory . . . I'd think about this if I were you. Sleep on it. Talk it over with your wife. Your decision affects her future as much as yours."

"You really are a bastard, aren't you, Stanley?" I said.

"I'm a realist, Malory."

"You're a fool if you think you can get away with this. Merlin won't stand for it."

"He'll have no choice."

I laughed. "Are you serious? Do you really think you can compel Merlin to do anything he doesn't wish to do? Do you honestly believe you can fight *magic*, Stanley?"

"I'm not interested in fighting anything," he said. "You've got the wrong idea. I want to see Merlin succeed as much as you do. I want to see him protected, and I want to see his knowledge protected, as well. Imagine what magic in the wrong hands could do. We can't afford to have egalitarian notions about this sort of thing, Malory. There's simply too much at stake. If Merlin's too naive to understand that, he'll have to be made to understand it, and I was hoping I could count on you for that."

"Well, you can count me out."

"I'm very sorry to hear that."

"Not half as sorry as you'll be when Merlin finds out what you're up to."

"Well, we'll cross that bridge when we come to it, won't we?"

"You're liable to find the bridge burning beneath you," I said.

I left the trailer and stood outside in the darkness for a moment, seething with anger, then I started up the drive toward the main College building. Merlin, as usual, was burning the midnight oil. I could see the light on in his room. I half expected to be stopped before I reached the building, but I wasn't. Bodkirk had to know that I'd go directly to Merlin and report our conversation. Apparently, he didn't care. I wasn't certain what to make of that. It worried me.

I went inside the building and climbed the stairs to the top floor. Merlin was in his study, seated at his desk, when I came in. He looked up, started to smile, then saw the expression on my face.

"What is it, Thomas?"

"I've just had a talk with Bodkirk. We've got trouble." I started searching the room.

"What sort of trouble? What are you looking for?"

"A bug," I said.

He frowned. "A *bug*?"

"A listening device," I said. "Bodkirk's bugged this place. He's planted hidden cameras and microphones throughout the building. He can hear every word we're saying."

"Indeed?" said Merlin, scowling.

I wasn't getting anywhere. I had no idea how many bugs he may have planted, but wherever he'd stuck them, they were carefully hidden. Perhaps they were in the walls.

"The hell with it," I said. "Let him listen. I don't care. He knows what I'm going to tell you, anyway."

"And what is that?"

"The government's taking over. Bodkirk's no bureaucrat, he's an intelligence agent, sent by the government to spy on us. The reason they've been so helpful is that it's given them a chance to observe you and find out if magic really can be taught. Now that they're convinced, they're going to take over the operation of the school, 'for your protection,' and they're going to make all the decisions about whom you're going to teach and how. Whoever controls thaumaturgy is going to control the world, as Bodkirk put it, and the government wants to make certain magic doesn't go falling into the wrong hands. Anyone's hands but theirs, in other words."

"I see," said Merlin. "Sit down, Thomas, please, and stop your pacing about. Would you like a cup of tea?"

"*A cup of tea?*" I said with astonishment. "Did you hear what I just said?"

"I heard every word," said Merlin. "As, I imagine, did our friend Bodkin. Listening devices. How very interesting. And cameras as well, you say?"

"That's what he said. All the tapes were forwarded to London. To MI5, I should imagine, which is the Security Service."

"It appears that they've gone to a great deal of trouble needlessly," said Merlin. "If they had wanted to know what I was doing here, all they had to do was ask. I would have been pleased to invite them here to observe my classes, if they'd wished."

"You don't understand," I said. "They intend to keep you here, and find out everything you know. They've been investigating all the students, and everyone they don't consider to be a loyal British subject will be sent packing. Maybe all of them, for all I know, now that they've served their purpose. They want you to teach only people they approve of, people they can control. We haven't built a school here, we've played right into their hands and built a prison for you. That's the real reason the army is here, to turn this place into a top-security installation. They've already taken charge. I just found out a delegation of clergy came to see you, and Bodkirk turned them away. You know how I found out? I heard it on the radio. It's being reported that you snubbed them, probably as a reaction to the Pope's statement."

"The Pope?" said Merlin.

I told him the position that the Roman Catholic church had officially taken regarding sorcery, and told him that he could now expect to be denounced from every pulpit, which in fact, had already begun, though I hadn't known about it at the time. He took this all in calmly, merely nodding as I spoke. At last, I ran out of steam and simply sat there, fuming.

"What are you going to do?" I asked.

"Just what I've been doing," he replied. "I shall continue to teach my classes."

"That's *it*?"

"And I will get rid of these bug listening devices," he added. "And the cameras, as well. If they have been recording my classes, then it's possible someone may try to learn from the recordings, and that could prove hazardous. Thaumaturgy should not be attempted without proper supervision. And it was also rather rude of Mr. Bodkirk to place them in my private quarters. I don't care for that at all."

"But what about the rest of it?" I asked.

"You mean the government keeping me prisoner here and dictating terms to me?" He shrugged. "I'm afraid that won't do at all. You can tell Mr. Bodkirk that."

"I've already told him," I said. "And he's already heard," I added wryly.

"Well, then that's all settled, then."

"*Nothing is settled!*" I shouted, jumping up out of my chair, no longer able to contain myself. "For God's sake, don't you understand what I'm telling you? *They intend to hold you prisoner here! They're taking control!*"

"Thomas, sit down and calm yourself," said Merlin. He continued to gaze at me steadily until I acquiesced to his wishes and sat back down, with a helpless, frustrated feeling. "That's better," he said. "Now, pray remain silent for a moment."

He sat still behind his desk, his hands clasped before him, then his eyes suddenly flashed with a searingly bright, blue glow and twin beams of force lanced out from them, like lasers, only they were not continuous. It was a brief burst, and the beams that left his eyes were no more than two feet long. They flew out into the center of the room, where they started to curve and go round and round in circles, like two bright, glowing snakes chasing one another, going faster and faster until they formed a sphere of glowing blue energy like Saint Elmo's fire that hovered and pulsated above the floor, as if with a life of its own. I stared, open-mouthed, as the ball expanded and contracted, as if it were a heart beating, then suddenly exploded, completely without sound, into dozens of tiny lightning bolts of energy that flew about the room like dragonflies.

A number of them zoomed past within inches of my face as I sat there, astonished, and they kept darting all around the room, like miniature heat-seeking missiles, until one of them flew into the telephone receiver, and another penetrated the desk. Several others entered the wall in various places, and went behind the bookshelves, while others still zoomed out the door and down the hall like a flock of angry hornets.

From the outside, the darkened building must have looked like a mad scientist's laboratory as the tiny bolts of energy whizzed through it, illuminating the windows with a

stroboscopic effect as they sought Bodkirk's hidden surveillance cameras and microphones. It must have lasted no more
than a minute, then it was over, and every one of Bodkirk's
monitors flashed a burst of static, then went dark. Each one of
his concealed microphones gave off a high-pitched whining
sound and melted.

"Now then," said Merlin, "we can speak without fear of
being overheard."

However, I was too stunned to speak. It was a display of
power such as I had never seen from him before. And he had
done it calmly, effortlessly, and instantly.

"I am not surprised at this development," he said. "If
anything, I am surprised it did not happen sooner."

"You mean you *expected* something like this?" I said, still
overwhelmed from the spectacle I had just witnessed.

"Sooner or later, I knew that there would be a conflict between those in power and myself," said Merlin. "Magic has a
most seductive lure, especially to those who would misuse it,
which is one of the reasons I have been so careful in my
selection of my students. I had a feeling it would come to this
before too long, and I am not completely unprepared." He
gestured toward one of his bookshelves. "Examine the titles
of those volumes there, on the third shelf."

I looked, and saw, with some surprise, that the entire shelf,
and part of the next one down, was filled with books concerning modern weapons, especially those used by the military and
the police.

"I realized, when I was shot, that I was woefully ignorant
about the weapons of this time," said Merlin, "so I took the
trouble to obtain some books in town that would fill this gap in
my education. I was very much impressed. We have come a
long, long way from the weapons of my time, indeed. The
destructive capability of a modern army is really quite astonishing. However, I already knew that. What I did not know
was how these weapons worked. I am not invulnerable, of

course, and it would take considerably less than an army to defeat me. One lone assassin almost succeeded in taking my life. However, now that I am much better informed, I can take certain precautions. Besides, the government doesn't really want me dead. At least, not yet. I have something they want, and unless they perceive me as a serious threat to their power, they will not seek to kill me.''

At that moment, the telephone rang and Merlin punched the call up on the speaker. ''Very clever, Merlin,'' Bodkirk said.

''Mr. Bodkirk,'' Merlin replied with a smile. ''You're working late tonight.''

''Very funny. I saw that fireworks display in there. All my monitors are dead. I imagine Malory's given you quite an earful.''

''As you knew he would,'' said Merlin.

''It saved me the trouble of having to confront you personally,'' Bodkirk said.

''Why, Bodkin, you wouldn't be afraid of me, would you?''

''The name's Bodkirk. And no, I'm not afraid of you, but let's just say I have a healthy respect for your capabilities. I was hoping I could persuade Malory to be reasonable and convince you of the necessity of what we're doing, but unfortunately, it didn't turn out that way. So now it's up to me. You know how things stand, though Malory's exaggerated matters somewhat. For one thing, no one's keeping your prisoner. We're simply concerned about your safety.''

''I'm touched,'' said Merlin.

''When it comes right down to it,'' said Bodkirk, ''we both really want the same thing. You want to teach magic. We want you to teach magic. We have no conflict there.''

''I'm pleased to hear it.''

''All we want to do is make certain that your students pass the necessary security clearances,'' said Bodkirk. ''In the wrong hands, magic could be a powerful weapon. I'm sure you appreciate that yourself. All we want to do is exercise greater responsibility over whom you teach and who has access to you. That's purely for your own protection, as well as ours."

"I appreciate your concern," said Merlin. "However, I believe that I am best qualified to decide whom I shall teach, and how. And while I am grateful for the government's concern for my safety, I am quite capable of protecting myself."

"You mean like the time you were shot?" said Bodkirk.

"I was taken by surprise."

"And it can easily happen again," said Bodkirk. "You're much too valuable to lose. We simply can't afford to take that chance. I'm afraid I'll have to insist on your cooperation."

"And if I refuse?"

"Then that will place me in a rather awkward position," Bodkirk replied. "If you refuse, I shall have to compel you to cooperate. I'm hoping it won't come to that, but if it does, rest assured that I have the ability to get the job done. It's nothing personal, you understand, but I've got my orders."

"I've never questioned your abilities, Mr. Bodkirk," Merlin said. "You've always impressed me as a very capable young man. And rest assured that whatever happens, I shall not take it personally. I appreciate your position. In return, I hope you can appreciate mine. Good night."

He punched a button on the speakerphone, severing the connection.

"What happens now?" I said.

"That is entirely up to our friend, Bodkin," Merlin said. "A dagger at our backs, indeed. I think it's time we summoned the students for a meeting."

# CHAPTER
# 10

The showdown between Merlin and the British government, in the person of one Stanley Bodkirk, might have become a famous incident were it not vastly overshadowed by an even greater event destined to go down in history as The Great London Riot of '82.

It all began the morning following my meeting with Bodkirk and my subsequent discussion with Merlin. The previous night, the students all came from their dormitory rooms and gathered in the meeting hall, where Merlin told them what the situation was. Not surprisingly, they were all angered and dismayed at the prospect of being forced to leave the school.

Anyone who has ever studied with a gifted teacher knows how important that teacher can become to the student, and what loyalty he can command. Merlin was certainly no exception. His students all idolized him, and would have done anything for him. Many of them had led very difficult lives up to that point, and at the College, they found not only a purpose, but a nurturing home.

Now they realized that they were being used, not by Merlin, of course, but by government officials who had regarded them

184

as nothing more than guinea pigs. They had been spied on and investigated, and once their hard work had demonstrated that thaumaturgy was not a freak ability and could, indeed, be taught, their role was at an end. The College would become nothing more than a classified research installation with participants handpicked by the government and they would get their walking papers. From the oldest, an American man of thirty-two who had worked his passage to England aboard ship just on the chance that he might be accepted, to the youngest, an Irish girl of seventeen who was thought mad because she adamantly claimed she could leave her body and visit other places in her dreams, they were outraged and furious. And not one of them would even think of complying with the government's demands.

They were a disparate group, most of them British, but some from as far away as the United States and Australia, and given the difficulties of travel during the Collapse, many of them had gone to a great deal of trouble and taken significant risks to come to Loughborough and apply, with no guarantee that they would be accepted. Indeed, the vast majority of applicants were disappointed in their hopes. All sorts of people came seeking to study with Merlin, from all walks of life. Male and female, young and old, rich and poor, rational and irrational. Merlin attracted the predictable lunatics and eccentrics, but he also received many tempting offers from those who were well off, offers to help subsidize the school or build additional wings and such. However, he would not be influenced by what he looked upon as nothing more than bribes.

He selected his students based solely on his own criteria, and he didn't care where they came from or what sort of lives they'd led. He looked primarily for evidence of the natural talent that would enable them to become adepts, and he sought people who were honest and sincere, with a desire to help others and to believe in something greater than themselves. He had started teaching with an initial group of thirty-five, which by the time of our trouble with Bodkirk had grown to about two hundred, chosen from thousands of applicants.

Most of them were young and had already demonstrated various paranormal abilities. Others, in whom the talent was latent, blossomed into a newfound self-awareness through their work with Merlin. All of them, without exception, were extremely bright and possessed strong personalities, as one of the main requirements of an adept was a strong will. Among that group, a few have not survived, but the rest all hold important positions in the thaumaturgic hierarchy today. Six are board members of the I.T.C., a dozen or so are directors and bureau chiefs of various Bureaus of Thaumaturgy throughout the world, and the rest are all high-ranking adepts, five of them having reached the level of mage, which means they have attained the same level as their teacher. It was a very gifted and a very special group, indeed, and their efforts, guided by Merlin, were about to show the world what magic could really do.

Merlin explained that nothing could be done until Bodkirk made the first move, because under no circumstances must they initiate any conflict. There was no way of knowing how long we'd have to wait, but Bodkirk wasted no time at all. Promptly at sunrise, we heard a bullhorn hailing us from outside. We all crowded up to the windows and saw the troops surrounding the building, and Bodkirk standing there with a bullhorn.

"*Attention! Attention! This is Stanley Bodkirk. All personnel must vacate the building immediately! I repeat, all personnel must vacate the building immediately!*"

The only people in the building at the time were Merlin, myself, and the resident students. The other members of our group, the administrative and support wing, were not due to arrive for several hours yet. It was barely dawn, and Bodkirk was obviously hoping to get the job done quickly and efficiently, before anyone else in the community knew what was going on.

*"This is your last chance! We don't want to see anyone hurt. All personnel must vacate the building at once!"*

No one moved to comply with Bodkirk's demand, but there was a great deal of movement in the meeting hall. The chairs and desks had all been cleared away and now the students all gathered into one large circle, with several concentric rings, as if they were all preparing to start some sort of folk dance. However, this would be a very different sort of dance. A *danse macabre.*

They all joined hands and began to move around slowly in a clockwise direction, chanting to gather their energy. It started slowly, then as their voices found a rhythm, it gathered strength. They were able to hear it outside. The words were ancient Celtic. Translated into modern English, Merlin told me later, the invocation would have sounded simple, like a nursery rhyme chanted by a group of children, but in old Celtic, a language no one outside understood, it sounded positively ominous, particularly given the dirgelike chanting of the students. Almost two hundred of them, circles within circles, all moving together and sounding like a chorus of Gregorian monks.

I looked out through the window and saw many of the soldiers exchanging apprehensive glances. They held their weapons nervously and fidgeted. It had to be unnerving. Hell, I found it unnerving myself!

*"Merlin!"* It was Bodkirk's amplified voice again. *"Don't do anything foolish! You don't want any of those people hurt! Send them out! Send them out now! This is your last chance!"*

The chanting grew louder and louder as the apprentices picked up their pace. I soon felt a heat rising in the room, more heat than could possibly be accounted for by the movement of all those bodies. The air inside the meeting hall seemed thick, and I felt drops of perspiration beading on my forehead.

Suddenly, the windows shattered as a volley of gas and smoke grenades came bursting through into the meeting hall. The students did not stop their circling and chanting. Through the stinging smoke, I watched as Merlin calmly levitated each cannister and floated them all out the window en masse, dropping them on the surprised soldiers. It caused a brief disarray among them, but they recovered quickly, donning masks, and fired another volley, only this time Merlin was ready for them. The smoke and gas cannisters all stopped short of the windows and hung motionless in midair for a moment, then curved back toward the soldiers and landed among them once again.

I grinned. I could imagine Bodkirk's fury. It served the bastard right. Then I saw the soldiers forming for a charge.

"He's going to send them in!" I said.

"Never fear, they won't get far," said Merlin. He glanced back toward his circling students. The air above them seemed to shimmer. He smiled.

The soldiers charged. Merlin closed his eyes. From below, I could hear the sounds of doors slamming open, followed by the running footsteps of the soldiers.

"Wind," said Merlin.

Above the heads of the circling students, the thickened, misty air took on a conelike form, like an inverted funnel, circling with them. I could see blue sparks of energy crackling within it. I felt a strong breeze in the room, a breeze that did not come through the shattered windows, but from the direction of that swirling cone.

"*Wind!*" said Merlin, raising his arms.

I could hear the soldiers running up the stairs.

There was a crackling discharge of energy and I could now see the funnel glowing with a bright blue light as wind blew through the room with rapidly increasing force, sounding like a gale on the seacoast. I had to grab onto the windowsill to steady myself. Then Merlin brought his arms down, just as I saw the first of the soldiers come up out of the stairway and start running toward us down the hall.

The funnel cone elongated and curved sharply, then shot out a long and swirling tendril toward the door. The soldiers running down the corridor were struck with hurricane-force wind that blew several of them right off their feet and sent them sliding backwards into those behind them. The sorcerous tornado drove them back, pushed them down the stairwells, smashing them into one another and forcing them to drop their weapons and shield their faces. They could make no headway against it. It forced them back and literally blew them all right out of the building.

"It does a teacher's heart good to see his pupils do so well," said Merlin with a smile.

"What if they open fire?" I said.

"I don't think he will dare," said Merlin. "He is a small man, drunk with his authority, and he does not really understand the power he is dealing with. I think he has taken too much upon himself. He is acting foolishly. Still, foolish men often make serious mistakes. It would be best to be prepared."

The wind kept pushing the soldiers back farther from the building, knocking them off their feet as they struggled against it. Some of them simply broke and ran, but that didn't make them cowards. They were up against something no soldier had ever faced before. It was more than a hurricane-force wind, it was a wind they could actually *see*, a sparking, glowing, directed storm of energy that forced them back relentlessly, and many of them panicked.

The wind pushed them back almost to the gates, then streamed back and curved around the building, swirling around it faster and faster until it formed a pulsating, glowing, blue wall around us. It looked as if the entire building were sheathed inside a shimmering cloud of Saint Elmo's fire that sparkled with electrical discharges. We were inside a thaumaturgic force field.

"How long can you keep this up?" I asked him.

"Not very long," Merlin replied. He glanced toward his students. "I am shaping and directing the spell, but their energy is the source. However, they are inexperienced, and they will soon grow tired. If Bodkirk has not become sufficiently discouraged by then, I shall have to deal with him personally.''

But Bodkirk had apparently had enough. At least, for the present. Either that, or he could not induce the soldiers to try again. There was no further attempt to rush the building or to force us out, not even after the energy of the spell had abated and the students all lay on the floor of the meeting hall, exhausted, yet exhilarated, filled with a newfound sense of power and purpose. Even in their weary repose, they talked excitedly among themselves, and laughed and hugged and rolled on the floor like children.

I looked out the window toward where the remaining troops had gathered just beyond the gates. They seemed to be milling around and arguing among themselves. There was no semblance of order at all. I could see no sign of Bodkirk.

"What happens now?" I asked.

"That depends on Bodkirk," Merlin said. "And on what orders he receives from his superiors. I doubt he will be anxious to report to them right now, because he's made a mess of things.''

"He's not the only one," I said. "The fools in London are responsible for this. They need this school, and they need you, but they're so paranoid and obsessed with having complete control that they can't see things clearly.''

Merlin sat down on the floor and leaned back against the wall. "I told you this would be a difficult task, Thomas. I expected resistance. New ideas or, as in this case, an old idea that merely seems new because it was forgotten, are often difficult for people to accept. And despite all we've managed to accomplish, we have barely even begun. This is only my first school. There shall have to be many others, in every country of the world, before the task can truly be complete. If I have to go through this sort of thing each time. . . ." He shook his head. "I am not a young man anymore.''

"That's right, at two thousand, you're not exactly a spring chicken," I said.

Merlin chuckled. Then his expression became serious. "So far, we have been fortunate. It could have been much worse. And it may yet become so, before the day is out."

"No," I said. "It doesn't have to·be that way! Not if we do it right!"

He glanced up at me. "What do you mean?"

"I mean we should do what I intended all along. We should use the media properly, and give them a *really* dramatic demonstration of what magic can accomplish! If they'd been here to see this. . . ." I stopped short. "God, I'm an idiot!"

I ran toward the door.

"Where are you going?" Merlin called out behind me.

"To do what I should have done in the first place!"

I ran upstairs to Merlin's office. Why it hadn't occurred to me to call the media about this before, I couldn't fathom, unless it was because I'd developed such an aversion for them over the past few months. Once Merlin started teaching, I was the one who had to deal with them all the time, until Bodkirk conveniently stepped in to take that burden from my shoulders, for his own purposes, and I was so glad to be rid of it that I had simply forgotten all about them.

I had also forgotten the cardinal rule of dealing with them. You could be used by the media, or you could use them. . . . so long as you gave them what they wanted. Merlin had purposely downplayed his powers, because he was concerned about frightening people. He had wanted to bring the public along slowly, play the charming old sorcerer, the new-age mystic, giving them demonstrations, but nothing too dramatic, nothing that would give any real indication of just how powerful his magic could be.

Except for his first television appearance, he'd shied away from giving anything but purely practical demonstrations.

That seemed a logical course to take, and I had supported it, but maybe we had missed the point. Perhaps frightening people was *exactly* what Merlin should have done. As a famous American president once said, "Speak softly, but carry a big stick." It was time, I felt, not only to show them that big stick, but give them a hearty whack with it. That conjured wind had sent experienced soldiers running. If Merlin were to do something like that before the news cameras. . . .

I burst into his office and lunged for the phone. It was dead. I realized that Bodkirk must have cut the lines. I tried the lights. Nothing. He'd cut the power, too. I slammed my fist against the wall in frustration and returned to tell Merlin what I had discovered. He was not surprised at all. In fact, he smiled.

"So," he said, "our friend Bodkin appears to be preparing for a siege."

"A siege?" I said. "You think he intends to *starve* us out?"

"Or prevent us from communicating with the outside, and cause us enough discomfort that we will give in to his demands," said Merlin. "His thinking may be sound enough, only not for someone dealing with a mage, as he will soon learn."

"I'm worried about Jenny and the others," I said. "He could decide to use them to bring pressure against us."

"Jenny and the girls will be safe enough at home," he replied. "The warding spell will protect them. And there's Victor, don't forget. If anyone tries to harm them, Victor will tear their throats out. But the others will be vulnerable. We had best send word to them."

"How?"

"Raise the window," Merlin said. "I would not want our messenger injured by the broken glass."

"Messenger? What messenger?" I said as I lifted the window and some of the shattered glass fell tinkling to the floor.

"Be quiet a moment," said Merlin. He stared out the window for a short while, and then a large crow came flopping through and landed on his shoulder. Merlin glanced at me and raised his eyebrows. "Air mail," he said. "I'll need some paper and a pen."

I brought him what he needed and he wrote a short note to Jenny, telling her to remain in the house and instructing her to contact the others. Then he folded up the paper and held it out to the crow. The bird took it in its beak and flew back out the window.

"That's amazing," I said. "Can you do that with all animals?"

"Some are more cooperative than others," he replied. "I have never been able to get very far with pigs, for instance. They resent people too much. And eagles can be somewhat temperamental. But I've always done well with cats and dogs, and bears, and some species of insects. I instructed the crow to wait and bring back a reply."

"You did? I didn't hear you say anything."

He tapped his forehead. "Words are not always necessary. Animals are very sensitive."

"You never cease to surprise me. I wish I could learn how to do that," I said.

"It requires a certain gift, more than merely being an adept," said Merlin. "It takes many years of patient effort. Aside from the necessary talent, you need to observe animals carefully, and learn to understand them. Many people have the gift, more than you might think, but they do not trouble to develop it. They take satisfaction in the fact that animals seem to respond to them, but they never work to form a closer bond. And then, the modern world does not facilitate such study. It moves too quickly, and patience and a deep reverence for nature and her creatures have ceased to be considered virtues."

"That's really what this is all about, isn't it?" I said as I watched the students resting on the floor, exhausted from their efforts. A lot of them were fast asleep. The rest were whisper-

ing quietly, so as not to disturb the others. "It's a battle between the modern world and an older, simpler time."

"I prefer to think that it is not a choice between two such
extremes," Merlin replied. "We cannot go back to the past,
and there is much about the past that is best left in the past.
However, we can move on into the future with an appreciation
for the lessons of the past, something humanity has never
profited from greatly."

"There's an old saying, those who do not remember the
mistakes of the past are doomed to repeat them," I said.

"True," said Merlin. "Consider our present situation. This
school, for instance, could just as easily be a castle fortress,
with men at arms inside, led by a warlord, and outside is a
besieging army, led by another warlord."

"It's a bit difficult to picture Bodkirk as a warlord," I said
with a grin.

"Nevertheless, in a very real sense, that is his role," said
Merlin. "And the root of our conflict is no different than the
struggle between Uther Pendragon and Gorlois of Cornwall. It
is a question of power. I possess it, Bodkirk and his superiors
wish to seize and control it. And so here we two warlords sit,
at loggerheads, while the common people starve and suffer.
Things have not changed so very much, after all."

"It's all so bloody stupid," I said.

Merlin shrugged. "You'll hear no argument from me. If
there was some way we could compromise, I would, but their
position does not allow for it. They would isolate me here, and
study me, and have me train only those whom they approve
of." He glanced toward his students. "Now that they have
served their purpose, they would be discarded and replaced by
others of Bodkirk's ilk. No, Thomas, I cannot allow that. It
was never what I had in mind. And I owe them more than
that."

"Then *fight* the bastards," I said. "Power is the only thing
they really understand. *Show* them!"

Merlin sighed. "I am sorely tempted to do just that. But don't you see, that would only prove them right. If I did that, then all those who have been saying I am dangerous, and that magic is dangerous, would have their claims vindicated."

"Perhaps," I said, "but then again, maybe that doesn't matter anymore. Perhaps there never was a way around that. The point is that a lot of people would support you, because they're fed up with the way things are. They're desperate. And a lot of them are dying. The old world order has fallen apart. We need a new one. And we won't bring it about with halfway measures."

"And if we fail?" said Merlin.

I glanced at him sharply. It was the first time I'd ever seen him exhibit any doubt. And it was the last time, as well. After that day, it was a different Merlin who emerged, a Merlin who had resolved upon a new, stronger course of action, and never once looked back.

"If we fail, then the world fails," I said. "We have everything to gain, and nothing left to lose."

"*Merlin!*" It was Bodkirk on his bullhorn again. "*Merlin, can you hear me?*"

Merlin took a deep breath, but said nothing. He had a distant look in his eyes. I answered for him.

"What do you want, Bodkirk?" I shouted out the window.

"*Malory?*"

"I said, what do you want?"

"*You know damn well what I want! I want you and the rest of those people out of there! Merlin stays. Tell him if he refuses to cooperate, I'll be forced to take drastic measures. I didn't want to see anybody hurt, but he's left me with no other choice now. This is a matter of national security. If the building is not cleared immediately, the troops will open fire. I will do whatever is necessary to shut this place down. You understand me? Whatever is necessary!*"

I glanced at Merlin. "You still think there's another way to deal with people like that?"

"No," said Merlin softly, "I fear not."

He got to his feet and turned toward his students, who were all awake now and watching him to see what he would do. He took a deep breath and exhaled heavily.

"We are about to pass the point of no return," he said to them. "If any of you have any doubts about following me, come what may, then now is the time to speak. I shall not hold it against you. If you choose to remain, then you will share in the consequences of my actions. If you leave now, you leave with a clear conscience, and I will think none the worse of you for it."

There was a long silence. No one spoke.

"*Merlin!*" Bodkirk shouted through his bullhorn.

"What happened this morning will be nothing compared to what will happen now," said Merlin. "If any of you have any reservations, this is your final chance."

"*Merlin! Damn you, answer me!*"

Not one of them stepped forward. Someone in the group said, "We're all with you, Professor! Give 'em hell!"

They started to applaud, but Merlin silenced them at once.

"Cease!" he shouted. "I will not have applause for what I am about to do."

"*Merlin! Merlin, I'll have your answer now or we will open fire in ten seconds!*"

Merlin stepped up to the window. "*Here is my answer!*" he shouted, and his eyes flashed with a bright, blue, incandescent glow as a beam of thaumaturgic force lanced out from them and struck Bodkirk where he stood, about fifty yards away. He screamed as his body was wreathed in blue flame and an instant later, there was nothing left of him but a scorched spot where he had stood and a few rising tendrils of smoke.

There was a stunned silence. I swallowed hard and said, "Jesus."

"Was that what you wanted, Thomas?" Merlin said tersely.

I took a deep breath. "I suppose there was no other choice," I said.

"Oh, yes, there was," said Merlin grimly. "But not quite so effective. Observe."

The soldiers were giving up. They'd had enough. Without Bodkirk there to give them their orders, they decided they weren't going up against anything like what they had just seen. Silently, they filed out through the gates and retreated to their barracks, across the road.

Merlin faced his students. "The responsibility for what I have just done is mine and mine alone. If any of you wish to leave, it should be safe now. It has been my privilege to instruct you."

He turned and walked out of the hall. Not a single student left.

The crow returned shortly with a note from Jenny. Not finding Merlin present, it delivered the note to me. I took it from its beak and, somewhat lamely, thanked it. It gave a raucous cry and flew back out the window. I opened the note and learned why we had no telephone service and no power. The power was out everywhere and all the telephone lines were dead. Jenny was at home, with the Stewarts and the others, listening to the radio. I hurried to my office on the first floor and switched on the small battery-powered radio I kept there.

"—continue to broadcast so long as our auxiliary generators can keep operating, which our chief engineer tells me will be only about another hour or two, at best. I repeat, remain indoors if at all humanly possible. Keep away from your windows. Lock your doors. Use your emergency supplies sparingly, because there is no way of telling how long this may continue. The fighting is apparently worst in the East End, but rioting has broken out all over the city, and in many of the outlying areas, as well. Looting is rampant. There are fires all over the city, most of them apparently burning out of control. The power is out all over

London, and the telephone switchboards are inoperative. Tony Sanders has just arrived in the studio, he's been out there, Tony, are you all right? You look terrible!''

"I feel terrible, Brian. It's awful out there, it's an absolute horror! Please, ladies and gentlemen, whatever you do, *keep off the streets!* Stay inside! The whole city has gone mad. It began, as near as we can tell, shortly after two o'clock this morning, with a skirmish between police and a gang of looters in the warehouse district, by the Thames, in what was apparently an organized attempt to break in and steal emergency food rations. The looters were well armed and a firefight ensued, which was shortly joined by a squad of L.U.A.D. commandos called in to assist the officers on the scene, who were both outnumbered and outgunned. As near as we can tell, the fighting was spontaneously joined by local residents, many of them armed as well, and it quickly escalated into a full-scale street riot, at which point the army was called in. However, that act proved to be tossing fuel onto the fire, for it resulted in people firing on the soldiers from concealment in nearby buildings, and the rioting spread from there.''

"How intense is the fighting right now, Tony?''

"There's no way to measure it, Brian, but it is very intense, indeed, on the East End, and sporadic fighting is taking place throughout the city. Looters are everywhere. People seem to have gone stark raving mad. I understand there is also rioting in Aldershot and Farnham, and we've had reports of fighting in Ashford, Brentwood, Watford, St. Albans, Letchworth, no way to substantiate many of these reports, I hasten to add, but it seems to be breaking out all over. Again, I repeat, we cannot confirm most of these reports, but we can confirm that the fighting in Greater London is very bad, indeed. What happened early this morning seems to have set off a chain reaction that is now running out of control, and there is literally no way of telling how long it may last or what the outcome may be. The government has declared martial law, but the authorities seem totally unable to deal with the scope of the situation. It's as if everywhere, throughout the city and beyond, people have finally reached the breaking point and we are in a state of total anarchy. This is a disaster, a tragedy of unprecedented proportions, ladies and gentlemen, and if you are within the sound of my voice, I urge you to barricade yourselves inside your homes and pray."

I picked up the radio and rushed upstairs to Merlin's quarters. It had finally happened, what we had feared most in my days with the army and later with the police department, a total breakdown of society. We had all been teetering on the edge of this for years and we had gone over the brink at last. Compared to this, our own crisis was insignificant.

Merlin stood at the window of his office, staring out toward the gate, toward the spot where Bodkirk had died. I had not switched off the radio when I rushed upstairs, and he turned at the sound. I said nothing, merely stood there, holding it. He looked at me, and I set the radio down on his desk. He stared at it, listening impassively as the two announcers continued their reports.

"Where are the students?" he asked, after a few moments.

"Still in the meeting hall," I said. "At least, they were when I left them."

He nodded. "Send word to Jenny. We are leaving for London at once."

"How?" I asked.

"Simple," Merlin replied. "We are going to drive."

I can't imagine what the soldiers must have thought when they looked out the windows of their barracks and saw the two of us approaching with a flag of truce, consisting of my handkerchief tied to the end of a ruler. A number of them came out, carrying their weapons, but holding them nervously. Their senior officer, a major, stepped forward, his sidearm holstered. He gazed at us uncertainly.

"I am Major Waters," he said flatly, and volunteered nothing further.

I'd never had any direct dealings with the soldiers before, so I introduced myself and Merlin.

"I regret the necessity for what happened earlier," said Merlin, "but there is a far more serious situation facing us now. You are aware of what is happening in London?"

Waters nodded. "We've been in radio communication," he said. "We have been ordered back to the city, to assist in putting down the rioting. The men are packing up their gear right now. I have no further orders concerning you and your people at present. And I have as yet made no report concerning this morning's events. Things are a bit hectic back at headquarters right now."

Merlin nodded. "We are going with you."

Waters raised his eyebrows. "To London? I'm afraid I can't allow that, sir. My initial orders concerning your group were—"

"Look, Major," I said, "we can stand here arguing all day while London burns, or we can go there and do something about it."

"We are going, in any event," said Merlin. "I would prefer to do it with your cooperation, but I do not require it. I could easily compel you."

Waters blinked. "I have little doubt of that," he said. "Very well. However, we do not have room for all your people."

"That won't be necessary," Merlin said. "Our party will consist of Thomas and myself, and six others. Have you room enough for them?"

"We can manage that," said Waters. "We will be leaving in less than five minutes, however."

"We'll be ready," I said.

"Sir . . ." said Waters, hesitantly addressing Merlin.

"Yes?"

"Do you think you can really stop it?"

"Yes, Major, I believe I can," said Merlin.

"Right. Let's go, then."

Merlin selected six of his most gifted students to accompany him to London. Young and unsure of themselves then, all their names are quite well-known today. Andrei Zorin was then an earnest young man of nineteen, from the city of Kiev, in the Ukraine. However, even then, his psychic abilities were well-developed and he had come to England to apply for the College with assistance from his government. Today, he sits on the board of directors of the I.T.C. and holds the rank of mage, one of only five people to attain the highest level in the discipline of thaumaturgy.

Another was Huang Wu Chen, a quiet and reserved young man of twenty, originally from the Himalayan ranges of Tibet, who had been living in Paris when he heard about Merlin. Today, he is better known by his magename, Tao Tzu, which means "Son of the Way," and he resides once more in his native country, in an isolated monastery on a mountaintop where he teaches students of his own. His True Light College of Sorcery is one of the most rigorous and demanding schools in existence, and has produced some of the finest adepts in the world.

Yoshi Kunitsugu, from Japan, is better known today by the magename of Yohaku, which means "blank space" or "white space" in his native language, and is a reference to the Japanese calligraphic art form known as *Sho*, in which the space that is left blank upon a canvas is just as important as that which is filled with ink. Empty space is not nothing in the art of Japan. It represents the realm of infinite possibilities. Like Tao Tzu and Zorin, he too attained the rank of mage. At the time, he was merely a boy, and he treated Merlin with the reverence of a Zen student toward his master.

Stefan St. John, of Manchester, was the only other man, except for Al'Hassan (who did not study with Merlin until he started teaching in America), who ever attained the rank of mage. He chose Gandalf as his magename, taken from a classic work of fantasy by Tolkien, and he, too, sat on the board of the I.T.C. until his recent death at the age of seventy-one. He was thirty at the time, one of the oldest students at the College.

Pierre Chagal, at twenty-eight, was also one of the older students, from Cherbourg. He eventually founded the College of Sorcerers at the Sorbonne and is currently the chairman of the board of the I.T.C., with the rank of twelfth-level adept. And the final member of our party was Ian Duncan, a twenty-two-year-old from London, particularly concerned about his family when he learned about the rioting. They lived in the East End.

We joined Major Waters in his convoy of army transports, along with a partially filled fuel tanker, which was all the reserve Waters and his men possessed. It would be enough to get us all to London, and it was placed in the center of the convoy, for protection.

I had sent word to Jenny with one of the other students, who would all remain behind at the College. All of them had been anxious to go, but Merlin did not wish to put any more of them at risk than absolutely necessary, and there was not enough room for them, in any case. The thought crossed my mind, as it had in my days with the Loo, that I might never see my family again. I'd been involved in some bad ones before, but never anything as bad as this. I was filled with apprehension.

We passed through Loughborough, and it was still early, but the town was strangely silent. I imagined everyone sitting in their homes, glued to their portable radios, listening to news of the rioting. Would it spread to Loughborough? Many of the transients who had arrived in recent months, attracted by Merlin's presence, had since moved on, but there were still crude shanties standing on the outskirts of the town, on both sides of the road, and as we passed, I was assailed by the smell of unsanitary latrines and rags and other refuse burning in iron barrels. What would these people do when they found the soldiers gone? I felt a tightness in my stomach. It wouldn't take much to entice them to join in a raid on the town. They had practically nothing, save the clothes on their backs and a few personal possessions, so there was little left for them to lose. Would Carr's largely volunteer police force be enough to stop them? Or would they remain peaceful, thinking Merlin was still in town? In the covered transports, no one could see us, and so no one had any reason to suspect that Merlin was leaving with the soldiers. Perhaps that would be enough to keep them all in line. I certainly hoped so.

As we drove along the cracked and buckled pavement of roads that could no longer be maintained, past rusting cars that had been pushed off to the sides of the road and abandoned because their owners could no longer purchase fuel for them, Merlin outlined his plan to the others. It would prove taxing on him, and on them, as well. They were gifted, but they were not experienced adepts. They'd had only a few months of training, and the days when adepts would become board-certified were still a long way off. Hardly any of their training had consisted of learning spells. The most difficult part of becoming an adept was developing the mental powers of concentration and learning how to tap the intuitive, subconscious potential of the mind. However, Merlin had selected these individuals because they were already well ahead of all the others in that respect. Still, he had to give them a crash course along the way in the spells that they would use and there would be no chance for them to practice.

When it came right down to it, they would go in cold, and it would be all or nothing. I had wished for the chance to study thaumaturgy myself, but been denied it for lack of natural ability. Now, I did not envy them one bit. Nor did I envy Major Waters, who had taken it upon himself to disregard his orders and divide his men, so that each of the students, in addition to Merlin and myself, would be accompanied by an armed security detachment. If we failed, Waters would face the gravest penalties. But then again, he reasoned, if we failed, being charged with mutiny or disobedience to orders would be the least of his concerns.

# CHAPTER
# 11

The responsibilities were divided up *en route*. Zorin, Chen, and Kunitsugu and the men who would go with them were given the task of restoring power to the city. They would cast the spells Merlin had taught them to get the generating plants operative again and make sure work parties were sent out to repair any power lines that had been damaged. It was a formidable task, and the most advanced students were given that responsibility.

St. John would be dispatched with his party of soldiers to the studios of the BBC, to get them on the air and to start broadcasting as soon as possible. Chagal would handle the radio end of the broadcasting operation. Duncan's job would be to act as liaison with the military and the police. Waters would go with him, along with another detachment of men. That left the toughest job to Merlin.

It would be up to Merlin to stop the violence in the streets, and I would go along with another detachment of soldiers to watch his back, because it would take all his concentration and energy to bring such a massive undertaking about. The various army detachments would all have officers or noncommissioned officers in command, save for the group that went with me, because with Merlin's safety at stake, I insisted on being placed in charge. Waters was hesitant about placing some of his men under the command of a civilian, until he found out what my background was, and then his reservations disappeared. By the time we reached the outskirts of the city, everyone knew what he would have to do.

We heard the rioting before we saw it. The sharp, crackling bursts of automatic weapons fire filled the air. It sounded as if we were driving straight into a war zone and, to all intents and purposes, we were. We stopped the convoy and reshuffled the passengers quickly, so that each group could take transports and depart for its objective. We made sure that all the tanks were full, then abandoned the fuel tanker, even though it still contained some precious fuel. It would be too cumbersome, and much too risky to bring along.

We had brought my radio, and a small, battery-powered, portable TV. These would be vital in helping us to gauge the success or failure of our efforts. I also had my old 9-mm semiautomatic, with two spare clips, and I had procured a drum-magazine, short-barreled riot shotgun from Waters. I desperately hoped I wouldn't have to use them.

We were heading for a roughly central location in the city, Trafalgar Square. As we drove quickly through the streets, we had to slow down on a number of occasions because of fighting up ahead of us. Several times, groups of people came running out toward us as we passed, hurling rocks and bottles, anything that came to hand. Our driver simply took to leaning on his horn and plowing straight on through.

On Oxford Street, we had to smash through a barricade that had been erected in the middle of the road, just a pile of broken furniture and junk that had been thrown up. At least a dozen times or more, bullets fired at us penetrated the flimsy canvas covering around us and we decided it would be more prudent to lay down in the lorry bed and hope that no stray rounds would find a mark.

It was bedlam. Entire city blocks were in flames, bodies lay helter-skelter in the street, and there was a noise in the air unlike any I had ever heard before. It wasn't the sound of gunfire multiplied many times, like a massive fireworks display, or the sound of sirens, or the popping, hissing, crackling, and groaning of many buildings burning, it was the sound of *people*, people driven past all limits of endurance, so that they were reduced to beasts. The air seemed filled with one long, vast, ululating howl, rising and falling, rising and falling, and it was a chilling thing to hear. It made the hairs on the back of my neck bristle and my skin feel clammy. The scent of fear was in the air, fear and madness. Almost the entire populace of London had turned into a mindless mob.

Something struck the side of the transport and a moment later, the canvas covering burst into flame. Someone had tossed a Molotov cocktail at us. The soldiers quickly stripped off the burning canvas as we careened through the streets, tossing it behind us. One of them was nicked in the scalp by a passing bullet and he fell down beside me.

"Are you all right?" I shouted.

He brought his hand up to his head. "I think it only grazed me, sir. I'll be okay."

"Stay down, for God's sake."

The sky was black with smoke and the streets were a litter of debris. People were running everywhere, some brandishing weapons, others carrying looted items, still others fighting among themselves. It was overwhelming.

"How the hell are you going to stop this?" I asked Merlin.

He said nothing. He sat with his eyes closed, withdrawn deep into himself, either thinking or summoning up his energy, I couldn't tell. It was as if he hadn't heard me.

"It's like the end of the world," the wounded soldier said.

"Or maybe the beginning," I replied.

He looked up at me and moistened his lips nervously. "I hope so," he said. "You were a sergeant-major in the army, sir?"

"That's right."

"You must've seen your share of action, then."

"More than my share," I replied.

"Ever anything as bad as this?"

I hesitated before replying, but I owed the lad the truth. "No," I said. "Never like this."

We pulled into Trafalgar Square and drove around to the north side, coming to a stop before the National Gallery. The soldiers piled out first, deploying around the entrance and covering us, in case someone opened fire, but the square appeared deserted. The Nelson Column had been spray-painted with graffiti and someone had knocked the head off the statue of Charles I. We ran out and broke down the doors of the Gallery. All the monuments were vandalized in one way or another. In years past, every New Year's Eve, Trafalgar Square was the scene of celebration. Now, it was a scene of desolation, of a city in its death throes.

We made our way up to the roof. Some of the men stayed below, to guard the entrance. Merlin had remained silent all this time. Now he stood upon the rooftop, dressed in his conical hat and robe, which Jenny had repaired for him, and carrying his staff. It was a surreal sight. A figure out of the past, a storybook wizard, standing on a rooftop looking out over a modern city, a city that was in flames, and plunged into a state of total anarchy. Irrationally, I suddenly wished that I had brought along a camera, to capture this moment.

The soldier who'd been wounded was one of several who had come up on the roof with us. One of the others had bandaged his head with gauze from a first-aid kit. The bandage was bloody, but he looked none the worse for wear. "What happens now?" he asked me softly, his gaze on Merlin.

"Magic," I replied. "Magic happens."

Merlin raised his staff and started chanting.

"What's he saying?" asked the soldier.

"I don't know. I don't speak ancient Celtic."

"He's casting a spell, isn't he?"

I nodded.

The soldier shook his head. "It's like something out of a movie."

"Quiet," I said. "Just watch. And cross your fingers."

Overhead, dark clouds began to gather. They appeared from out of nowhere, gradually fading into existence, and drifted in, converging from all directions. The wind picked up. It smelled like rain.

Thunder rolled. The wind grew stronger, and stronger still. Sheet lightning flashed behind the clouds, lighting up the sky. It grew dark, even though it was still the afternoon. The wind was blowing even harder now. Merlin's long hair streamed out behind him. His robe billowed in the wind.

He stood, with arms outstretched, his staff held high, crying out his chant into the wind. There were dark clouds all over the city now, low clouds, ominous and threatening, spreading out in all directions. They were like a vortex, swirling around and around, like a whirlpool in the sky, spreading wider and wider until it seemed to cover everything. Thunder rolled and lightning flashed. Then Merlin held his staff out in both hands, pointed at the sky, and a jagged beam of force burst out from its tip and shot up into the sky, striking the clouds and causing bright blue sparks of energy to spread through them, like cracks appearing in a sheet of ice.

A devastatingly loud clap of thunder broke out like a sonic boom and a jagged bolt of lightning lanced down from the sky and struck the Nelson Column, causing it to crumble. Then it began to hail.

At first, the hail came down in small, stinging pellets, falling hard and fast, then gradually, the size of the hail grew greater, until chunks of ice the size of golf balls were raining down on the city. We retreated from this furious onslaught, back into the stairwell, but Merlin remained standing on the edge of the roof, apparently unaffected, as the hail fell so fast and thick that it obscured almost everything from view. Some of the pieces were the size of a man's fist.

"How in hell can anyone stay outside in that?" the young soldier said, staring at Merlin with astonishment.

I laughed. "That's just the point!" I said. "They *can't*!"

It was brilliant. I had no idea what Merlin had intended, but now I saw the beauty of it. No one would be able to stand beneath such a relentless, hammering hail for long. It would drive everyone to seek shelter. I fumbled for the little radio and switched it on.

"—all over the city, falling so fast and furiously that everyone has cleared the streets," said the announcer. "It's like a miracle, only I'm told that it's no miracle, nor even an act of nature, but of magic! Here in the studio with me is Pierre Chagal, a student of Merlin Ambrosius, the Wizard of Camelot, and we have him to thank for being able to get back on the air again. Mr. Chagal comes to us with startling news. I'll turn the microphone over to him. Mr. Chagal. . . ."

"Thank you. This morning, as soon as we heard news of the rioting, a group of thaumaturgy students from the International Center for Thaumaturgical Studies accompanied Professor Ambrosius to London, along with a military escort. Even as I speak, some of those students, acting under the direction of Professor Merlin Ambrosius, are in the process of employing their knowledge of thaumaturgy to restore power to the city. Radio broadcasting has now been resumed, and television broadcasting should resume shortly, if it has not done so already. We are also working in cooperation with the military and the police to help restore order to the city. The hail presently falling on the city is the result of a storm conjured by Professor Ambrosius himself, with an aim to disrupting the violence in the streets. There is no cause for alarm. The hail will continue until the streets are completely cleared and there are no further reports of rioting or looting. It is recommended, however, that people remain indoors, if possible, or if not, seek shelter, for the hailstorm will be followed by a driving rain that will continue until the fires are all under control.

"This will, in all likelihood, take days of hard, unabated rainfall. However, telephone operation should be resuming shortly, and we shall be working in close cooperation with the authorities to set up a crisis center. The number will be made available as soon as possible, but we urge people not to call unless faced with a serious emergency. Professor Ambrosius has requested that all citizens of London and the outlying areas work together in a spirit of goodwill and cooperation to overcome this crisis. Violence is not the answer. We at the International Center for Thaumaturgical Studies pledge our full support to the people of London and all of Great Britain in a mutual effort to bring about the end of the Collapse, once and for all, and to once more restore the country, and hopefully the world, to a more stable footing. If we all pull together, we can *all* make magic."

A similar announcement followed shortly thereafter on the BBC television network, with Stefan St. John looking very competent and self-assured on camera, and sounding very professional, indeed. The announcements were repeated, and St. John and Chagal were both interviewed extensively on the air, and later, crews were sent to interview Kunitsugu, Zorin, and the others and show how their use of thaumaturgy had restored power to a blacked-out city. It was a media tour de force, and by the end of the day, Merlin and his students were all heroes.

After the hail had ceased and the rain began, the spell-gathered storm followed its course and Merlin made his first public appearance on TV. His words were also broadcast over the radio simultaneously. In a canny move, he appeared with the Prime Minister, as well as the commissioner of New Scotland Yard and General Boyd-Roberts, representing the police and the military respectively. He appeared modest, but determined and full of self-confidence. He required no further coaching from me when it came to dealing with the media. He had learned his lessons well.

No reference was ever made to any government plan to take over the operation of the College or to exercise any direct control over Merlin and his pupils. The Prime Minister hailed him as a great humanitarian, thanked him for his efforts, and pledged the government's full support in furthering "thaumaturgic education and establishing a thaumaturgical support base for a new source of energy and a new and brighter tomorrow."

Everyone was eager to get on the bandwagon and claim some affiliation with Merlin and the College. At some point, someone even proposed Merlin for the Nobel peace prize, which was actually awarded to him several years later. No one ever mentioned the death of Stanley Bodkirk, and the incident was not even reported until several years had passed and some disgruntled, down-on-his-luck soldier who had been there sold the story to the tabloids. That was the beginning of the rumors and innuendos that spread through the succeeding years concerning Merlin's alleged use of "necromancy" to eliminate anyone who stood in his way. Nor did Merlin help the situation any by admitting that he had used magic to kill Bodkirk.

Those of us who were close to him had tried to isolate him from reporters anxious to pursue the story, and we pleaded with him to at least issue a statement of "No comment," but Merlin would have none of it. Though we all insisted it was self-defense and in defense of the students who were in the College building at the time, for Bodkirk had announced, in no uncertain terms, that he would order the troops to open fire in ten seconds, Merlin never shied from taking full responsibility for Bodkirk's death. He admitted it, and he did not apologize for it, which only made things worse. He has always remained, as a result, a figure of controversy.

The truth was that Merlin did, indeed, hold life to be sacred, and he did not condone the taking of it. Yet he had done so purposely, and in many ways, I shared in the responsibility, for it was I who urged him to fight back and do something so demonstrative of his power that it would frighten the opposition into submission.

I had not actually told him to kill anyone, but that is merely rationalizing. In all honesty, I must admit that I would have done the same thing myself. And I have done so. I killed people when I was a soldier, and I killed people when I was a police commando, as I had killed poor James Whitby, acting as the instrument of his suicide. My conscience does not disturb me, for I believed that what I had done was necessary, and I continue to believe it. But Merlin was always deeply disturbed by Bodkirk's death, which he considered to be murder, as he remained disturbed by the part he had played in helping Arthur kill Gorlois, over two thousand years ago. Merlin always was a very complicated man, capable of gentleness and compassion, yet at the same time, he could be utterly ruthless and implacable. But he had a conscience, and Bodkirk's death weighed heavily upon it.

The end of The Great London Riot marked a turning point in history. It was the beginning of the end of the Collapse. For one day, mass insanity had reigned in London, and but for Merlin, it could have marked the day that plunged the nation into a Dark Age from which there may have been no recovery. There were similar incidents in other nations of the world, but they did not have Merlin to bring an end to them. At least, not right away. Like a wire drawn tighter and tighter until, finally, it snaps, so it is with human nature, and with that curious amalgam of flesh and concrete, blood and steel, the modern city. Hardship piles upon hardship, and people suffer patiently, until at last all patience is exhausted and an entire city under-goes a nervous breakdown. At such times, psychosis can be catching. It is a very virulent disease.

When New York city "went critical," as the Americans say, bodies piled up by the thousands and the devastation was perhaps as great as might have occurred in the blast of an atomic bomb. In Tokyo, when the city reached its break-ing point, mass suicides resulted. Paris burned, so much so that it took years before the City of Light could be fully reconstructed. But what made London different was that the end of The Great London Riot brought hope not only to every British subject, but to people all throughout the world. The eyes of the entire world were on Great Britain, and specifically London, and Merlin and his fledgling stu-dents worked around the clock to usher in the Second Thaumaturgic Age.

In time, as their education was completed, those students went out to start schools of their own. Merlin and I traveled extensively to pave the way for the establishment of programs of thaumaturgical studies at every major university throughout the world. Within a year of The Great London Riot, the first Bureau of Thaumaturgy was formed, with Merlin as its direc-tor initially, until Stefan St. John took over the post approx-imately five years later. By the time Bureaus of Thaumaturgy had also been established in Washington, D.C., Moscow, Paris, Tokyo, Peking, Berlin, Montreal, and Tel Aviv, the International Center for Thaumaturgical Studies had become the I.T.C. and moved its headquarters to Geneva. The con-verted public school building in Loughborough, where it all began, is now The Ambrosius Museum.

But that day in London, when we finally had a chance to take a break and sleep for a few precious hours before we began the long, hard task of bringing order back to the city and dealing with endless logistical problems and bureaucratic frustrations, Merlin and I collapsed into the beds provided for us, utterly exhausted.

Ahead of us remained an arduous task, and later a reception at Buckingham Palace and the awarding of the O.B.E.'s, and more media coverage, and more work, and more frustrations, but in the few moments during which we could still keep our eyes open, there was a sense of accomplishment that would never quite be matched by anything that happened afterward.

"You did it," I said, leaning back against the headboard wearily. It was late and we were both spent. Merlin in particular. He looked completely drained. "You really did it."

"No, Thomas, *we* did it," Merlin said.

I shook my head. "It was your magic that pulled it off. Hell, what did I do?"

He looked at me and smiled. "You took a wild and crazy old man you met in the forest and brought him home to share what little you had, despite your hardship. And magical things began to happen, just like in a fairy tale."

I smiled and shrugged. "Hell, anyone would have done the same."

"Oh, I doubt that very much," he said. "Most people would have taken one look at my long hair and wild beard, the robe with its magical symbols and the staff and the conical wizard's cap. . . ."

He glanced toward the chair where he had hung his clothes. There they were, the robe emblazoned with its symbols, the conical hat and staff, and there he was, stretched out on the bed in a white T-shirt and pair of boxer shorts. On the floor beside the chair where he had hung his clothes stood a pair of lace-up army boots, with white athletic socks tucked into them.

"I always detested that damned cap," he said. "And I always thought the bloody robe was a bit much."

I raised my eyebrows. "Why did you wear them, then?"

"They were a gift from Arthur," he said sourly. "The uniform he had decreed for his royal court magician. I protested, but he merely gave me one of his imperious looks and said, 'I am king and I have spoken.' I told him, 'I *made* you king, you bloody idiot!' But he folded his arms across his chest, turned away, and said, 'I did not hear that.' He was impossible when he got like that and there was simply no talking to him. So I said the hell with it and wore the stupid costume. But at least now, at last, I shall be free of it.''

"Well, now, I don't know about that,'' I said. "It's become part of your image. And as you, yourself, once pointed out to me, image is important. You may be stuck with that outfit for a while longer, I'm afraid. People will expect it.''

He sighed with resignation. "Yes, I suppose you're right. But promise me one thing, Thomas. When all of this is over, whenever that may be, you'll take me shopping for some normal clothes.''

"I'll take you to the best tailor on Savile Row,'' I said with a grin. "And he'll probably be delighted to give you an entire wardrobe for nothing, just so he can say he's Merlin's tailor. You'll be able to have a whole closetful of handmade suits.''

"I would like a pair of blue jeans,'' Merlin said. "And some flannel shirts. The plaid ones. And perhaps one of those black leather jackets, like the young people wear.''

"I can see you going to Buckingham Palace dressed like that,'' I said with a chuckle.

"It would not be appropriate?''

"No, I shouldn't think so.''

He sighed. "It seems I still have much to learn about the modern world. I shall have to depend on you to teach me, Thomas.''

I smiled and looked up at the ceiling. "You can count on me, old friend,'' I said, recalling the words he'd said to me shortly after we first met. He said that each of us would teach the other. I had thought he meant that he would teach me magic. Well, I never did learn any magic, but I learned more from him than from anyone that I had ever met. I turned toward him and said, "Good night, Professor.''

But he was already fast asleep.